PRICKSONGS & DESCANTS

Robert Coover lives with his wife in Providence, Rhode Island, where he teaches at Brown University. His books most recently published by Heinemann include: *Whatever Happened to Gloomy Gus of the Chicago Bears?*, *Gerald's Party* and *Spanking the Maid*. He has also written *The Origin of the Brunists*, which won him the William Faulkner award for a first novel, *The Public Burning*, about Julius and Ethel Rosenberg and *A Political Fable*.

He has recently been elected to the American Academy and Institute of Arts and Letters. He is the winner of the 1987 Rea Prize for the Short Story, the largest literary prize of its kind in the United States.

D0994928

Robert Coover

PRICKSONGS & DESCANTS

Minerva

A Minerva Paperback

PRICKSONGS & DESCANTS

First published in Great Britain 1971
by Jonathan Cape Ltd
This Minerva edition published 1989
Reprinted 1991
by Mandarin Paperbacks
Michelin House, 81 Fulham Road, London SW3 6RB

Minerva is an imprint of the Octopus Publishing Group

Copyright © Robert Coover 1969

Some of the stories in this volume originally appeared in the
New American Review, the *Quarterly Review of Literature*,
Evergreen Review, *Playboy*, *Esquire*, *Cavilier* and *Olympia*.

British Library Cataloguing in Publication Data

Coover, Robert, *1932–*
    Pricksongs & descants.
    I. Title
    823'.54[F]
    ISBN 0 7493 9008 5

Printed in Great Britain
by Cox and Wyman Ltd, Reading

CONTENTS

For You, QBSP

He thrusts, she heaves
— JOHN CLELAND, FANNY HILL

They therefore set me this problem of the equality of appearance and numbers.
— PAUL VALERY, 'VARIATIONS ON THE ECLOGUES'

The Door: *A Prologue of Sorts*

This was the hard truth: to be Jack become the Giant, his own mansions routed by the child he was. Yes, he'd spilled his beans and climbed his own green stalk and tipped old Humpty over, only to learn, now much later, that that was probably the way the Old Man, in his wisdom, had wanted it.

He swung, chanting to himself to keep his stroke steady, and he dropped those tall hard trees, but he was all too aware of what he was really doing, of what was happening up there, or about to, and how the Ogre in him wouldn't drop away and leave her free. And, look, he was picking on the young trees today, too, he caught himself at that, my God. Was it envy, was that all it was? Feeling sorry, old man, that all that joy and terror is over for you, never to rise again? Hell, now.

But, no, it wasn't jealousy, she was his own blood, after all. And just a child.

He swung, a sinew snapped, the tree leaned, crackled, toppled with a great wheeze and crash. He decided to chop it up into foot-length logs.

And, listen, he wished her the joy, yes, he did, both of them for that matter, if not all the world. He had told her about it, he'd wanted her to love life and that was part of it, a good part of it. Those frantic trips up and down his beanstem had taught him that much. But he liked to hear her laugh and watch her wonder with a smile, and, well, he hadn't said much about the terror.

He saw the tree had held a nest. Its pale speckled eggs lay

scattered, all broken but one. He stared at the unbroken egg. He removed his hat, wiped the sweat from the back of his neck. But what could he do about it? Nothing.

And so he was afraid. For her. For himself. Because he'd given her her view of the world, in fragments of course, not really thinking it all out, she listening, he telling, and because of her gaiety and his love, his cowardly lonely love, he'd left out the terror. He'd smelled the blood, all right, but he'd called it essence. And when she encountered it, found herself alone and besieged: what then? He'd be part of it, that's what, feared and hated. And he'd thought the old Giant had lived in heaven, the poor bastard!

He swung furiously at the felled tree, his whole body vibrating from the shock of the blows, enraged at life that it should so resist. People-agony. Love. Hanging on. A goddamn mess.

There was his old mother up there, suffering continuance, preferring rot to obliteration, possessed like them all by a mad will, mindless and intransigent. Did he resent her? yes, he did. There they all went, birthing hopelessly sentient creatures into the inexplicable emptiness, giving carelessly of their bellies, teats, and strength, then sinking away into addled uselessness, humming the old songs, the old lies, and smiling toothless infuriating smiles. God! he leaned into the tree with all his strength.

And worse: that she *could* fear, his daughter, that she *could* hate. He'd willingly die to save her from death, live with all the terror if he could but free her from it. But, no, he thought, remembering the world's dead and all their forgotten itches, you can't get out of it that easy, old buddy, only kings could sleep and rise again, and all the kings were gone.

He paused in his chopping. Yes, a knock, he'd heard it. Perhaps today then. Perhaps very soon. He leaned his axe against the felled tree, turned anxiously towards the cottage. He remembered the old formula: fill the belly full of stones.

But wait. Sooner or later, it must happen, mustn't it? Sooner or later, she'd know everything, know he'd lied. He'd pretended to her that there were no monsters, no wolves or witches, but yes, goddamn it, there were, there were. And in fact one of them got ahold of him right now, made him grab up his axe, dig ceremonially at his crotch, and return to his labours, and with a weird perverse insistence, made him laugh . . .

so bless me I'm ruminatin on the old times when virtue was its own so-called reward and acquired a well-bejewelled stud in the bargain propped up there in the stale limp sheets once the scene of so much blood and beauty like I say propped up and dyin away there in my old four-poster which on gamier days might seem a handsome well-lathed challenge to an old doxy but which this bad day threatens to throw up walls between the posts and box me in God help and I'm wonderin where's my goodies? will I make it to the end? where's the durned kid? and to while the awful time workin up a little tuneful reminiscence or two not so much of the old obscenities suffered but rather of the old wild dreams of what in some other kinda world I mighta had yes me with my wishful way of neckin ducks and kissin toads and lizards

oh I know why she's late you warn her and it does no good I know who's got her giddy ear with his old death-cunt-and-prick songs haven't I heard them all my God and smelt his hot breath in the singin? yes I know him can see him now lickin his hairy black chops and composin his polyphonies outa dread and appetite whisperin his eclogues sprung from disaster croonin his sacral entertainments yes I know him well and I tell her but Granny she says Granny you don't understand the times are different there's a whole new —

don't understand! whose nose does she think she's twistin the little cow? bit of new fuzz on her pubes and juice in the little bubbies and off she prances into that world of hers that ain't got forests nor prodigies a dippy smile on her face and her skirts up around her ears well well I'll give her a mystery today I will if I'm not too late already and so what if I am? shoot! let her go tippytoin through the flux and tedium and trip on her dropped drawers a few times and see if she don't come runnin back to old Granny God preserve me whistlin a different tune! don't understand! hah! for ain't I the old Beauty who married the Beast?

yes knew all the old legends I did and gave my heart to them who wouldn't that heard them? ain't there somethin wrong with Beauty Papa? my sisters would ask ain't she a little odd chasin about after toads and crows and stinky old creatures? but I had a dream and Papa maybe was uneasy about it but he was nothin if not orthodox and so had to respect it and even blessed my marriage when I found me a Beast

only my Beast never became a prince

but Granny it's a new generation! hah! child I give you generations without number transient as clouds and fertile as fieldmice! don't speak to me of the revelations of rebirthers and genitomancers! sing me no lumpen ballads of deodorized earths cleansed of the stink of enigma and revulsion! for I have mated with the monster my love and listened to him lap clean his lolly after

and the basket of goodies? is that you on the path my dear? hurry! for my need is great and my wisdom overflows and your own time is hard by

for listen I have suffered a lifetime of his doggy stink until I truly felt I couldn't live without it and child his snore would wake the dead though now I cannot sleep for the silence yes and I have pawed in stewpots with him and have paused to watch him drop a public turd or two on sidewalks and seashores in populous parks and private parlours and granddaughter I have been split with the pain and terrible haste of his thick quick cock and then still itchin and bleedin have gazed on as he leapt other bitches at random and I have watched my own beauty decline my love and still no Prince no Prince and yet you doubt that I understand? and loved him my child loved the damned Beast after all

yes yes I hear you knockin come in! hurry! bring me goodies! for I have veils to lift and tales to tell ...

Something had changed. She stood motionless at the cottage door. Suspended. She felt abandoned, orphaned. Yet discovered. The bees hummed relentlessly among the flowers alongside the path. The sun beat down on the white weatherboards with an incessant, almost urgent, calm. What was it – ? Aha! To begin with: the door was open!

Yes, she had been coming here for years and years, forever it seemed, and many times each year, always for the same reason, if that's what it was, a reason, and always – she hesitated: some dim memory – ? no, no – always the door had been closed.

Well, and so what? She stepped back from the door, and a kind of relief swept over her, and a kind of anxiety. It was curious. That door. Yet, otherwise, things seemed about the same: the cottage itself, white in the sun; the garden, well cared for and in neat little rows, and over there the small shed where the garden tools were kept; the old well with the bucket drawn up under the small parasol-like roof, the bucket itself dry and cracked, surely useless, but much as it had always been; finally, down a short distance from the cottage, the woods, where even now could be heard the familiar chuck-chuck-chuck of the lumberman's axe, measured, deliberate, solemn, muffled but clearly audible. It was simply that the door was open.

But wait! She frowned, clutched her basket to her side, glanced around. The sun, like just the sun: wasn't it somehow hotter today, brighter, didn't it seem stuck up there, brought to a strange deadly standstill? And the cottage, didn't the cottage have a harder edge, the vines a subtler grip on the weatherboards, and wasn't the air somehow full of spiders? She trembled. The old well seemed suddenly to hide some other well, the garden to speak of a stranger unimagined garden. And even the friendly rhythmic chucking of the lumberman's axe: wasn't it somehow too close by today, perversely insistent in its constancy?

Old stories welled in her like a summation of an old woman's witless terrors, fierce sinuous images with flashing teeth and terrible eyes, phantoms springing from the sun's night-tunnels to devour her childhood – in fright, she reached impulsively for the doorknob, glittering brassily in the sun's glare. She hesitated. Beyond the door? The knob was warm in her grip, and she had a new awareness of breath and motion. She stared at the aperture and knew: not her. No. That much was obvious, an age had passed, that much the door ajar had told her.

She listened to the lumberman's steady axe-stroke. The woods. Yes, an encounter, she smiled to recall it, to remember his deference, surprised by it then, but no longer. An encounter and an emergence. And so: she had known all along. And knowing she'd known somehow eased her anguish. She smiled faintly at the mockery of the basket she clutched. Well, it would be a big production, that was already apparent. An elaborate game, embellished with masks and poetry, a marshalling of legendary doves and herbs. And why not? She could well avail herself of his curiously obsequious appetite while it lasted. Even as the sun suddenly snapped its bonds and jerked westward, propelling her over the threshold, she realized that though this was a comedy from which, once entered, you never returned, it nevertheless possessed its own astonishments and conjurings, its towers and closets, and even more pathways, more gardens, and more doors.

Inside, she felt the immediate oppression of the scene behind drop off her shoulders like a red cloak. All that remained of it was the sullen beat of the lumberman's axe, and she was able to still even that finally, by closing the door firmly behind her and putting the latch.

The Magic Poker

I wander the island, inventing it. I make a sun for it, and trees — pines and birch and dogwood and firs — and cause the water to lap the pebbles of its abandoned shores. This, and more: I deposit shadows and dampness, spin webs, and scatter ruins. Yes: ruins. A mansion and guest cabins and boat houses and docks. Terraces, too, and bath houses and even an observation tower. All gutted and window-busted and autographed and shat upon. I impose a hot mid-day silence, a profound and heavy stillness. But anything can happen.

o   o   o

This small and secretive bay, here just below what was once the caretaker's cabin and not far from the main boat house, probably once possessed its own system of docks, built out to protect boats from the big rocks along the shore. At least the refuse — the long bony planks of grey lumber heaped up at one end of the bay — would suggest that. But aside from the planks, the bay is now only a bay, shallow, floored with rocks and cans and bottles. Schools of silver fish, thin as fingernails, fog the bottom, and dragonflies dart and hover over its placid surface. The harsh snarl of the boat motor — for indeed a boat has been approaching, coming in off the lake into this small bay — breaks off abruptly, as the boat carves a long gentle arc through the bay, and slides, scraping bottom, towards a shallow pebbly corner. There are two girls in the boat.

o   o   o

Bedded deep in the grass, near the path up to the first guest cabin, lies a wrought-iron poker. It is long and slender with an intricately worked handle, and it is orange with rust. It lies shadowed, not by trees, but by the grass that has grown up wildly around it. I put it there.

o   o   o

The caretaker's son, left behind when the island was deserted, crouches naked in the brambly fringe of the forest overlooking the bay. He watches, scratching himself, as the boat scrapes to a stop and the girls stand – then he scampers through the trees and bushes to the guest cabin.

o   o   o

The girl standing forward – fashionbook-trim in tight gold pants, ruffled blouse, silk neckscarf – hesitates, makes one false start, then jumps from the boat, her sandaled heel catching the water's edge. She utters a short irritable cry, hops up on a rock, stumbles, lands finally in dry weeds on the other side. She turns her heel up and frowns down over her shoulder at it. Tiny muscles in front of her ears tense and ripple. She brushes anxiously at a thick black fly in front of her face, and asks peevishly: 'What do I do *now*, Karen?'

o   o   o

I arrange the guest cabin. I rot the porch and tatter the screen door and infest the walls. I tear out the light switches, gut the mattresses, smash the windows, and shit on the bathroom floor. I rust the pipes, kick in the papered walls, unhinge doors. Really, there's nothing to it. In fact, it's a pleasure.

o   o   o

Once, earlier in this age, a family with great wealth purchased this entire island, here up on the border, and built on it all these houses, these cabins and the mansion up there on the promontory, and the boat house, docks, bath houses, observation tower. They tamed the island some, seeded lawn grass, contrived their own sewage system with indoor appurtenances, generated electricity for the rooms inside and for the japanese lanterns and postlamps without, and they came up here from time to time in the summers. They used to maintain a caretaker on the island year round, housed him in the cabin by the boat house, but then the patriarch of the family died, and the rest had other things to do. They stopped coming to the island and forgot about caretaking.

o   o   o

The one in gold pants watches as the girl still in the boat switches the motor into neutral and upends it, picks up a yellowish-grey rope from the bottom, and tosses it ashore to her. She reaches for it straight-armed, then shies from it, letting it fall to the ground. She takes it up with two fingers and a thumb and holds it out in front of her. The other girl, Karen (she wears a light yellow dress with a beige cardigan over it), pushes a toolkit under a seat, gazes thoughtfully about the boat, then jumps out. Her canvas shoes splash in the water's edge, but she pays no notice. She takes the rope from the girl in gold pants, loops it around a birch near the shore, smiles warmly, and then, with a nod, leads the way up the path.

o   o   o

At the main house, the mansion, there is a kind of veranda or terrace, a balcony of sorts, high out on the promontory, offering a spectacular view of the lake with its wide interconnecting expanses of blue and its many islands. Poised there now, gazing thoughtfully out on that view, is a tall slender man, dressed in slacks, white turtleneck shirt, and navy-blue jacket, smoking a pipe, leaning against the stone parapet. Has he heard a boat come to the island? He is unsure. The sound of the motor seemed to diminish, to grow more distant, before it stopped. Yet, on water, especially around islands, one can never trust what he hears.

o   o   o

Also this, then: the mansion with its many rooms, its debris, its fireplaces and wasps' nests, its musty basement, its grand hexagonal loggia and bright red doors. Though the two girls will not come here for a while — first, they have the guest cabin to explore, the poker to find — I have been busy. In the loggia, I have placed a green piano. I have pulled out its wires, chipped and yellowed its ivory keys, and cracked its green paint. I am nothing if not thorough, a real stickler for detail. I have dismembered the piano's pedals and dropped an old boot in its body (this, too, I've designed: it is horizontal and harp-shaped). The broken wires hang like rusted hairs.

o   o   o

The caretaker's son watches for their approach through a shattered window of the guest cabin. He is stout and hairy, muscular, dark, with short bowed legs and a rounded spiny back. The hair on his head is long, and a thin young beard sprouts on his chin and upper lip. His genitals hang thick and heavy and his buttocks are shaggy. His small eyes dart to and fro: where are they?

o   o   o

In the bay, the sun's light has been constant and oppressive; along the path, it is mottled and varied. Even in this variety, though, there is a kind of monotony, a determined patterning that wants a good wind. Through these patterns move the two girls, Karen long-striding with soft steps and expectant smile, the other girl hurrying behind, halting, hurrying again, slapping her arms, her legs, the back of her neck, cursing plaintively. Each time she passes between two trees, the girl in pants stops, claws the space with her hands, runs through, but spiderwebs keep diving and tangling into her hair just the same.

o   o   o

Between two trees on the path, a large spider – black with a red heart on its abdomen – weaves an intricate web. The girl stops short, terrified. Nimbly, the shiny black creature works, as though spelling out some terrible message for her alone. How did Karen pass through here without brushing into it? The girl takes a step backward, holding her hands to her face. Which way around? To the left it is dark, to the right sunny: she chooses the sunny side and there, not far from the path, comes upon a wrought-iron poker, long and slender with an intricately worked handle. She bends low, her golden haunches gleaming over the grass: how beautiful it is! On a strange impulse, she kisses it – POOF! before her stands a tall slender man, handsome, dressed in dark slacks, white turtleneck shirt, and jacket, smoking a pipe. He smiles down at her. 'Thank you,' he says, and takes her hand.

o   o   o

Karen is some distance in front, almost out of sight, when the other girl discovers, bedded in the grass, a wrought-iron poker. Orange with rust, it is long and slender with an elaborate handle. She crouches to examine it, her haunches curving golden above the blue-green grass, her long black hair drifting lightly down over her small shoulders and wafting in front of her fineboned face. 'Oh!' she says softly. 'How strange! How beautiful!' Squeamishly, she touches it, grips it, picks it up, turns it over. Not so rusty on the underside — but bugs! *millions* of them! She drops the thing, shudders, stands, wipes her hand several times on her pants, shudders again. A few steps away, she pauses, glances back, then around at everything about her, concentrating, memorizing the place probably. She hurries on up the path and sees her sister already at the first guest cabin.

o   o   o

The girl in gold pants? yes. The other one, Karen? also. In fact, they are sisters. I have brought two sisters to this invented island, and shall, in time, send them home again. I have dressed them and may well choose to undress them. I have given one three marriages, the other none at all, nor is that the end of my beneficence and cruelty. It might even be argued that I have invented their common parents. No, I have not. We have options that may, I admit, seem strangely limited to some . . .

o   o   o

She crouches, haunches flexing golden above the bluegreen grass, and kisses the strange poker, kisses its handle and its long rusted shaft. Nothing. Only a harsh unpleasant taste. I am a fool, she thinks, a silly romantic fool. Yet why else has she been diverted to this small meadow? She kisses the tip — POOF! 'Thank you,' he says, smiling down at her. He bows to kiss her cheek and take her hand.

o   o   o

The guest cabin is built of rough-hewn logs, hardly the fruit of necessity, given the funds at hand, but probably it was thought fashionable; proof of traffic with other cultures is adequately provided by its gabled roof and log columns. It is here, on the shaded porch, where Karen is standing, waiting for her sister. Karen waves when she sees her, ducking down there along the path; then she turns and enters the cabin through the broken front door.

o   o   o

He knows that one. He's been there before. He crouches inside the door, his hairy body tense. She enters, staring straight at him. He grunts. She smiles, backing away. 'Karen!' His small eyes dart to the doorway, and he shrinks back into the shadows.

o   o   o

She kisses the rusted iron poker, kisses its ornate handle, its long rusted shaft, kisses the tip. Nothing happens. Only a rotten taste in her mouth. Something is wrong. 'Karen!'

o   o   o

'Karen!' the girl in pants calls from outside the guest cabin. 'Karen, I just found the most beautiful thing!' The second step of the porch is rotted away. She hops over it onto the porch, drags open the tattered screen door. 'Karen, I – *oh, good God!* look what they've *done* to this house! Just *look!*' Karen, about to enter the kitchen, turns back, smiling, as her sister surveys the room: 'The walls all smashed in, even the plugs in the wall and the light switches pulled out! Think of it, Karen! They even had electricity! Out here on this island, so far from everything civilized! And, see, what beautiful paper they had on the walls! And now just look at it! It's so – oh! what a dreadful beautiful beastly thing all at once!'

o   o   o

But where is the caretaker's son? I don't know. He was here, shrinking into the shadows, when Karen's sister entered. Yet, though she catalogues the room's disrepair, there is no mention of the caretaker's son. This is awkward. Didn't I invent him myself, along with the girls and the man in the turtleneck shirt? Didn't I round his back and stunt his legs and cause the hair to hang between his buttocks? I don't know. The girls, yes, and the tall man in the shirt – to be sure, he's one of the first of my inventions. But the caretaker's son? To tell the truth, I sometimes wonder if it was not he who invented me ...

o   o   o

The caretaker's son, genitals hanging hard and heavy, eyes aglitter, shrinks back into the shadows as the girl approaches, and then goes bounding silently into the empty rooms. Behind an unhinged door, he peeks stealthily at the declaiming girl in gold pants, then slips, almost instinctively, into the bathroom to hide. It was here, after all, where first they met.

o   o   o

Karen passes quietly through the house, as though familiar with it. In the kitchen, she picks up a chipped blue teakettle, peers inside. All rust. She thumps it, the sound is dull. She sets it on a bench in the sunlight. On all sides, there are broken things: rubble really. Windows gape, shards of glass in the edges pointing out the middle spaces. The mattresses on the floors have been slashed with knives. What little there is of wood is warped. The girl in the tight gold pants and silk neckscarf moves, chattering, in and out of rooms. She opens a white door, steps into a bathroom, steps quickly out again. 'Judas God!' she gasps, clearly horrified. Karen turns, eyebrows raised in concern. 'Don't go in there, Karen! *Don't go in there!*' She clutches one hand to her ruffled blouse. 'About a hundred million people have gone to the *bath*room in there!' Exiting the bathroom behind her, a lone fly swims lazily past her elbow into the close warm air of the kitchen. It circles over a cracked table – the table bearing newspapers, shreds of wallpaper, tin cans, a stiff black washcloth – then settles on a counter near a rusted pipeless sink. It chafes its rear legs, walks past the blue teakettle's shadow into a band of pure sunlight stretched out along the counter, and sits there.

o   o   o

The tall man stands, one foot up on the stone parapet, gazing out on the blue sunlit lake, drawing meditatively on his pipe. He has been deeply moved by the desolation of the island. And yet, it is only the desolation of artifact, is it not, the ruin of man's civilized arrogance, nature reclaiming her own. Even the wilful mutilations: a kind of instinctive response to the futile artifices of imposed order, after all. But such reasoning does not appease him. Leaning against his raised knee, staring out upon the vast wilderness, hoping indeed he has heard a boat come here, he puffs vigorously on his pipe and affirms reason, man, order. Are we merely blind brutes loosed in a system of mindless energy, impotent, misdirected, and insolent? 'No,' he says aloud, 'we are not.'

o   o   o

She peeks into the bathroom; yes, he is in there, crouching obscurely, shaggily, but eyes aglitter, behind the stool. She hears his urgent grunt and smiles. 'Oh, Karen!' cries the other girl from the rear of the house. 'It's so very sad!' Hastily, Karen steps out into the hall-way, eases the bathroom door shut, her heart pounding.

o   o   o

'Oh, Karen, it's so very sad!' That's the girl in the gold pants again, of course. Now she is gazing out a window. At: high weeds and grass crowding young birches, red rattan chair with the seat smashed out, backdrop of grey-trunked pines. She is thinking of her three wrecked marriages, her affairs, and her desolation of spirit. The broken rattan chair somehow communicates to her a sensation of real physical pain. Where have all the Princes gone? she wonders. 'I mean, it's not the ones who stole the things, you know, the scaven-gers. I've seen people in Paris and Mexico and Algiers, lots of places, scooping rotten oranges and fishheads out of the heaped-up gutters and eating them, and I didn't blame them, I didn't dislike them, I felt sorry for them. I even felt sorry for them if they were just doing it to be stealing something, to get something for nothing, even if they weren't hungry or anything. But it isn't the people who look for things they want or need or even don't need and take them, it's the people who just destroy, destroy because — God! because they just want to destroy! Lust! That's all, Karen! See? Somebody just went around these rooms driving his fist in the walls because he had to hurt, it didn't matter who or what, or maybe he kicked them with his feet, and bashed the windows and ripped the curtains and then went to the bathroom on it all! Oh my God! Why? Why would any-body want to do that?' The window in front of Karen (she has long since turned her back) is, but for one panel, still whole. In the ex-cepted panel, the rupture in the glass is now spanned by a spiderweb more intricate than a butterfly's wing, than a system of stars, its silver paths seeming to imitate or perhaps merely to extend the deli-cate tracery of the fractured glass still surrounding the hole. It is a new web, for nothing has entered it yet to alter its original construction. Karen's hand reaches toward it, but then withdraws. 'Karen, let's get out of here!'

o   o   o

The girls have gone. The caretaker's son bounds about the guest cabin, holding himself with one hand, smashing walls and busting windows with the other, grunting happily as he goes. He leaps up onto the kitchen counter, watches the two girls from the window, as they wind their way up to the main mansion, then squats joyfully over the blue teakettle, depositing ... a love letter, so to speak.

o   o   o

A love letter! Wait a minute, this is getting out of hand! What happened to that poker, I was doing much better with the poker, I had something going there, archetypal and even maybe beautiful, a blend of eros and wisdom, sex and sensibility, music and myth. But what am I going to do with shit in a rusty teakettle? No, no, there's nothing to be gained by burdening our fabrications with impieties. Enough that the skin of the world is littered with our contentious artifice, lepered with the stigmata of human aggression and despair, without suffering our songs to be flatted by savagery. Back to the poker.

o   o   o

'Thank you,' he says, smiling down at her, her haunches gleaming golden over the shadowed grass. 'But, tell me, how did you know to kiss it?' 'Call it woman's intuition,' she replies, laughing lightly, and rises with an appreciative glance. 'But the neglected state that it was in, it must have tasted simply dreadful,' he apologizes, and kisses her gently on the cheek. 'What momentary bitterness I might have suffered,' she responds, 'has been more than indemnified by the sweetness of your disenchantment.' 'My disenchantment? Oh no, my dear, there *are* no disenchantments, merely progressions and styles of possession. To exist is to be spell-bound.' She collapses, marvelling, at his feet.

o   o   o

Karen, alone on the path to the mansion, pauses. Where is her sister? Has something distracted her? Has she strayed? Perhaps she has

gone on ahead. Well, it hardly matters, what can happen on a desolate island? they'll meet soon enough at the mansion. In fact, Karen
isn't even thinking about her sister, she's staring silently, entranced,
at a small green snake, stretched across the path. Is it dozing? Or
simply unafraid? Maybe it's never seen a real person before, or
doesn't know what people can do. It's possible: few people come here
now, and it looks like a very young snake. Slender, wriggly, green,
and shiny. No, probably it's asleep. Smiling, Karen leaves the path,
circling away from the snake so as not to disturb it. To the right of
the path is a small clearing and the sun is hot there; to the left it is
cool and shadowed in the gathering forest. Karen moves that way, in
under the trees, picking the flowers that grow wildly here. Her cardigan catches on brambles and birch seedlings, so she pulls it off, tosses
it loosely over her shoulder, hooked on one finger. She hears, not far
away, a sound not unlike soft footfalls. Curious, she wanders that
way to see who or what it is.

o   o   o

The path up to the main house, the mansion, is not even mottled, the
sun does not reach back here at all, it is dark and damp-smelling, an
ambience of mushrooms and crickets and fingery rustles and dead
brown leaves never quite dry, or so it might seem to the girl in gold
pants, were she to come this way. Where is she? His small eyes dart
to and fro. Here, beside the path, trees have collapsed and rotted,
seedlings and underbrush have sprung up, and lichens have crept
softly over all surfaces, alive and dead. Strange creatures abide here.

o   o   o

'Call it woman's intuition,' she says with a light laugh. He appraises
her fineboned features, her delicate hands, her soft maidenly breasts
under the ruffled blouse, her firm haunches gleaming golden over the
shadowed grass. He pulls her gently to her feet, kisses her cheek.
'You are enchantingly beautiful, my dear!' he whispers. 'Wouldn't
you like to lie with me here awhile?' 'Of course,' she replies, and
kisses his cheek in return, 'but these pants are an awful bother to
remove, and my sister awaits us. Come! Let us go up to the
mansion!'

o   o   o

A small green snake lies motionless across the path. The girl approaching does not see it, sees only the insects flicking damply, the girl in tight pants which are still golden here in the deep shadows. Her hand flutters ceaselessly before her face, it was surely the bugs that drove these people away from here finally, 'Karen, is this the right way?', and she very nearly walks right on the snake, which has perhaps been dozing, but which now switches with a frantic whip of its shiny green tail off into the damp leaves. The girl starts at the sudden whirring shush at her feet, spins around clutching her hands to her upper arms, expecting the worst, but though staring wide-eyed at the sound, she can see nothing. Why did she ever let her sister talk her into coming here? *'Karen!'* She runs, ignoring the webs now, right through all the gnats and flies, on up the path, crying out her sister's name.

o   o   o

The caretaker's son, poised gingerly on a moss-covered rock, peeking through the thick branches, watches the girl come up the path. Karen watches the caretaker's son. From the rear, his prominent feature is his back, broad and rounded, humped almost, where tufts of dark hair sprout randomly. His head is just a small hairy lump beyond the mound of heavy back. His arms are as long as his legs are short, and the elbows, like the knees, turn outwards. Thick hair grows between his buttocks and down his thighs. Smiling, she picks up a pebble to toss at him, but then she hears her sister call her name.

o   o   o

Leaning against his raised knee, smoking his pipe, the tall man on the parapet stares out on the wilderness, contemplating the island's ruin. Trees have collapsed upon one another, and vast areas of the island, once cleared and no doubt the stage for garden parties famous for miles around, are now virtually impassable. Brambles and bunchberries grow wildly amid saxifrage and shinleaf, and everything in sight is mottled with moss. Lichens: the symbiotic union, he recalls, of fungi and algae. He smiles and at the same moment, as though it has been brought into being by his smile, hears a voice on the garden path. A girl. How charming, he's to have company, after all! At least two, for he heard the voice on the path behind the mansion, and below him, slipping surefootedly through the trees and bushes, moves another creature in a yellow dress, carrying a beige sweater over her shoulder. She looks a little simple, not his type really, but then dis-similar organisms can, at times, enjoy mutually advantageous part-nerships, can they not? He knocks the ashes from his pipe and refills the bowl.

o   o   o

At times, I forget that this arrangement is my own invention. I begin to think of the island as somehow real, its objects solid and intrac-table, its condition of ruin not so much an aesthetic design as an his-torical denouement. I find myself peering into blue teakettles, batting at spiderwebs, and contemplating a greenish-grey growth on the side of a stone parapet. I wonder if others might wander here without my knowing it; I wonder if I might die and the teakettle remain. 'I have brought two sisters to this invented island,' I say. This is no extrava-gance. It is indeed I who burdens them with curiosity and history, appetite and rhetoric. If they have names and griefs, I have provided them. 'In fact,' I add, 'without me they'd have no cunts.' This is not (I interrupt here to tell you that I have done all that I shall do. I return here to bring you this news, since this seemed as good a place as any. Though you have more to face, and even more to suffer from me, this is in fact the last thing I shall say to you. But can the end be in the middle? Yes, yes, it always is ...) meant to alarm, merely to make a truth manifest – yet *I* am myself somewhat alarmed. It is one thing to discover the shag of hair between my buttocks, quite another to find myself tugging the tight gold pants off Karen's sister. Or perhaps it is the same thing, yet troubling in either case. Where does this illusion come from, this sensation of 'hardness' in a blue teakettle or an iron poker, golden haunches or a green piano?

o   o   o

In the hexagonal loggia of the mansion stands a grand piano, painted bright green, though chipped and cracked now with age and abuse. One can easily imagine a child at such a piano, a piano so glad and ready, perhaps two children, and the sun is shining – no, rather, there is a storm on the lake, the sky is in a fury, all black and pitching, the children are inside here out of the wind and storm, the little girl on the right, the boy on the left, pushing at each other a bit, staking out property lines on the keys, a grandmother, or perhaps just a lady, yet why not a grandmother? sitting on a window-bench gazing out on the frothy blue-black lake, and the children are playing *Chopsticks*, laughing, a little noisy surely, and the grandmother, or lady, looks over from time to time, forms a patient smile if they chance to glance up at her, then – well, but it's only a supposition, who knows whether there were children or if they cared a damn about a green piano even on a bad day, *Chopsticks* least of all? No, it's only a piece of fancy, the kind of fancy that is passing through the mind of the girl in gold pants who now reaches down, strikes a key. There is no sound, of course. The ivory is chipped and yellowed, the pedals dismembered, the wires torn out and hanging like rusted hairs. The girl wonders at her own unkemptness, feels a lock loose on her forehead, but there are no mirrors. Stolen or broken. She stares about her, nostalgically absorbed for some reason, at the elegantly timbered roof of the loggia, at the enormous stone fireplace, at the old shoe in the doorway, the wasps' nests over one broken-out window. She sighs, steps out on the terrace, steep and proud over the lake. 'It's a sad place,' she says aloud.

o   o   o

The tall man in the navy-blue jacket stands, one foot up on the stone parapet, gazing out on the blue sunlit lake, drawing meditatively on his pipe, while being sketched by the girl in the tight gold pants. 'I somehow expected to find you here,' she says. 'I've been waiting for you,' replies the man. Her three-quarters view of him from the rear allows her to include only the tip of his nose in her sketch, the edge of his pipebowl, the collar of his white turtleneck shirt. 'I was afraid there might be others,' she says. 'Others?' 'Yes. Children perhaps. Or somebody's grandmother. I saw so many names everywhere I went, on walls and doors and trees and even scratched into that green piano.' She is carefully filling in on her sketch the dark contours of his navy-blue jacket. 'No,' he says, 'whoever they were, they left here long ago.' 'It's a sad place,' she says, 'and all too much like my own life.' He nods. 'You mean, the losing struggle against inscrutable blind forces, young dreams brought to ruin?' 'Yes, something like that,' she says. 'And getting kicked in and gutted and shat upon.' 'Mmm.' He straightens. 'Just a moment,' she says, and he resumes his pose. The girl has accomplished a reasonable likeness of the tall man, except that his legs are stubby (perhaps she failed to centre her drawing properly, and ran out of space at the bottom of the paper) and his buttocks are bare and shaggy.

o   o   o

'It's a sad place,' he says, contemplating the vast wilderness. He turns to find her grinning and wiggling her ears at him. 'Karen, you're mocking me!' he complains, laughing. She props one foot up on the stone parapet, leans against her leg, sticks an iron poker between her teeth, and scowls upon the lake. 'Come on! Stop it!' he laughs. She puffs on the iron poker, blowing imaginary smoke-rings, then turns it into a walking stick and hobbles about imitating an old granny chasing young children. Next, she puts the poker to her shoulder like a rifle and conducts an inspection of all the broken windows facing on the terrace, scowling or weeping broadly before each one. The man has slumped to the terrace floor, doubled up with laughter. Suddenly, Karen discovers an unbroken window. She leaps up and down, does a somersault, pirouettes, jumps up and clicks her heels together. She points at it, kisses it, points again. 'Yes, yes!' the man laughs, 'I see it, Karen!' She points to herself, then at the window, to herself again. 'You? You're like the window, Karen?' he asks, puzzled, but still laughing. She nods her head vigorously, thrusts the iron poker into his hands. It is dirty and rusty and he feels clumsy with the thing. 'I don't understand ...' She grabs it out of his hands and – *crash* – drives it through the window. 'Oh no, Karen! No, no ... !'

o   o   o

It's a sad place.' Karen has joined her sister on the terrace, the bal-cony, and they gaze out at the lake, two girls alone on a desolate island. 'Sad and yet all too right for me, I suppose. Oh, I don't regret any of it, Karen. No, I was wrong, wrong as always, but I don't regret it. It'd be silly to be all pinched and morbid about it, wouldn't it, Karen?' The girl, of course, is talking about the failure of her third marriage. 'Things are done and they are undone and then we get ready to do them again.' Karen looks at her shyly, then turns her gentle gaze back out across the lake, blue with a river's muted blue under this afternoon sun. 'The sun!' the girl in gold pants exclaims, though it is not clear why she thought of it. She tries to explain that she is like the sun somehow, or the sun is like her, but she becomes confused. Finally, she interrupts herself to blurt out: 'Oh, Karen! *I'm so miserable!*' Karen looks up anxiously: there are no tears in her sister's eyes, but she is biting down painfully on her lower lip. Karen offers a smile, a little awkward, not quite understanding perhaps, and finally her sister, eyes closing a moment, then fluttering open, smiles

wanly in return. A moment of grace settles between them, but Karen
turns her back on it clumsily.

o   o   o

'No, Karen! Please! Stop!' The man, collapsed to the terrace floor,
has tears of laughter running down his cheeks. Karen has found an
old shoe and is now holding it up at arm's length, making broad
silent motions with her upper torso and free arm as though declaiming upon the sadness of the shoe. She sets the shoe on the terrace
floor and squats down over it, covering it with the skirt of her yellow
dress. 'No, Karen! No!' She leaps up, whacks her heels together in
midair, picks up the shoe and peers inside. A broad smile spreads
across her face, and she does a little dance, holding the shoe aloft.
With a little curtsy, she presents the shoe to the man. 'No! Please!'
Warily, but still laughing, he looks inside. 'What's this? Oh no! A
flower! Karen, this is too much!' She runs into the mansion, returns
carrying the green piano on her back. She drops it so hard, one leg
breaks off. She finds an iron poker, props the piano up with it, sits
down on an imaginary stool to play. She lifts her hands high over
her head, then comes driving down with extravagant magisterial
gestures. The piano, of course, has been completely disemboweled,
so no sounds emerge, but up and down the broken keyboard Karen's
stubby fingers fly, arriving at last, with a crescendo of violent flou-
rishes, at a grand climactic coda, which she delivers with such force
as to buckle the two remaining legs of the piano and send it all crashing to the terrace floor. 'No, Karen! Oh my God!' Out of the wreck-
age a wild goose springs, honking in holy terror, and goes flapping
out over the lake. Karen carries the piano back inside, there's a
splintering crash, and she returns wielding the poker. 'Careful!' She
holds the poker up with two hands and does a little dance, toes
turned outwards, hippety-hopping about the terrace. She stops abruptly over the man, thrusts the poker in front of his nose, then
slowly brings it to her own lips and kisses it. She makes a wry face.
'Oh, Karen! Whoo! Please! You're killing me!' She kisses the handle,
the shaft, the tip. She wrinkles her nose and shudders, lifts her skirt
and wipes her tongue with it. She scowls at the poker. She takes a firm
grip on the poking end and bats the handle a couple of times against
the stone parapet as though testing it. 'Oh, Karen! Oh!' Then she
lifts it high over her head and brings it down with all her might —
WHAM! — POOF! it is the caretaker's son, yowling with pain. She lets
go and spins away from him, as he strikes out at her in distress and

fury. She tumbles into a corner of the terrace and cowers there, whimpering, pale and terrified, as the caretaker's son, breathing heavily, back stooped and buttocks tensed, circles her, prepared to spring. Suddenly, she dashes for the parapet and leaps over, the caretaker's son bounding after, and off they go, scrambling frantically through the trees and brambles, leaving the tall man in the white turtleneck shirt alone and limp from laughter on the terrace.

o   o   o

There is a storm on the lake. Two children play *Chopsticks* on the green piano. Their grandmother stirs the embers in the fireplace with an iron poker, then returns to her seat on the windowbench. The children glance over at her and she smiles at them. Suddenly a strange naked creature comes bounding into the loggia, grinning idiotically. The children and their grandmother scream with terror and race from the room and on out of the mansion, running for their lives. The visitor leaps up on the piano bench and squats there, staring quizzically at the ivory keys. He reaches for one and it sounds a note – he jerks his hand back in fright. He reaches for another – a different note. He brings his fist down – BLAM! Aha! Again: BLAM! Excitedly, he leaps up and down on the piano bench, banging his fists on the piano keyboard. He hops up on the piano, finds wires inside, and pulls them out. TWANG! TWANG! He holds his genitals with one hands and rips out the wires with the other, grunting with delight. Then he spies the iron poker. He grabs it up, admires it, then bounds joyfully around the room, smashing windows and wrecking furniture. The girl in gold pants enters and takes the poker away from him. 'Lust! That's all it is!' she scolds. She whacks him on the nates with the poker, and, yelping with pain and astonishment, he bounds away, leaping over the stone parapet, and slinks off through the brambly forest.

o   o   o

'Lust!' she says, 'that's all it is!' Her sketch is nearly complete. 'And they're not the worst ones. The worst ones are the ones who just let it happen. If they'd kept their caretaker here ...' The man smiles. 'There never was a caretaker,' he explains. 'Really? But I thought!—!' 'No,' he says, 'that's just a legend of the island.' She seems taken aback by this new knowledge. 'Then ... then I don't understand ...' He relights his pipe, wanders over to appraise her

sketch. He laughs when he sees the shaggy buttocks. 'Marvellous!'
he exclaims, 'but a poor likeness, I'm afraid! Look!' He lowers his
dark slacks and shows her his hindend, smooth as marble and hair-
less as a movie starlet's. Her curiosity is caught, however, not by
his barbered buttocks, but by the hair around his genitals: the tight
neat curls fan out in both directions like the wings of an eagle, or a
wild goose . . .

o   o   o

The two sisters return to the loggia, their visit nearly concluded, the
one in gold pants still trying to explain about herself and the sun,
about consuming herself with an outer fire, while harbouring an ice-
cold centre within. Her gaze falls once more on the green piano. It
is obvious she still has something more to say. But now as she
declaims, she has less of an audience. Karen stands distractedly before the green piano. Haltingly, she lifts a finger, strikes a key. No
note, only a dull thuck. Her sister reveals a new insight she has just
obtained about it not being the people who steal or even those who
wantonly destroy, but those who let it happen, who just don't give a
proper damn. She provides instances. Once, Karen nods, but maybe
only at something she has thought to herself. Her finger lifts, strikes.
Thuck! Again. Thuck! Her whole arm drives the strong blunt finger.
Thuck! Thuck! There is something genuinely beautiful about the girl
in gold pants and silk neckscarf as she gestures and speaks. Her eyes
are sorrowful and wise. Thuck! Karen strikes the key. Suddenly, her
sister breaks off her message. 'Oh, I'm sorry, Karen!' she says. She
stares at the piano, then runs out of the room.

o   o   o

I am disappearing. You have no doubt noticed. Yes, and by some no
doubt calculable formula of event and pagination. But before we drift
apart to a distance beyond the reach of confessions (though I warn
you: like Zeno's turtle, I am with you always), listen: it's just as I
feared, my invented island is really taking its place in world geo-
graphy. Why, this island sounds very much like the old Dahlberg
place on Jackfish Island up on Rainy Lake, people say, and I wonder:
can it be happening? Someone tells me: I understand somebody
bought the place recently and plans to fix it up, maybe put a resort
there or something. On my island? Extraordinary! – and yet it seems
possible. I look on the map: yes, there's Rainy Lake, there's Jack-

fish Island. Who invented this map? Well, I must have, surely. And the Dahlbergs, too, of course, and the people who told me about them. Yes, and perhaps tomorrow I will invent Chicago and Jesus Christ and the history of the moon. Just as I have invented you, dear reader, while lying here in the afternoon sun, bedded deeply in the bluegreen grass like an old iron poker ...

o   o   o

There is a storm on the lake and the water is frothy and black. The wind howls around the corner of the stone parapet and the pine trees shake and creak. The two children playing *Chopsticks* on the green piano are arguing about the jurisdiction of the bench and keyboard. 'Come over here,' their grandmother says from her seat by the window, 'and I'll tell you the story of "The Magic Poker" ...'

o   o   o

Once upon a time, a family of wealthy Minnesotans bought an island on Rainy Lake up on the Canadian border. They built a home on it and guest cabins and boat houses and an observation tower. They installed an electric generator and a sewage system with indoor toilets, maintained a caretaker, and constructed docks and bath houses. Did they name it Jackfish Island, or did it bear that name when they bought it? The legend does not say, nor should it. What it does say, however, is that when the family abandoned the island, they left behind an iron poker, which, years later, on a visit to the island, a beautiful young girl, not quite a princess perhaps, yet altogether equal to the occasion, kissed. And when she did so, something quite extraordinary happened ...

o   o   o

One upon a time there was an island visited by ruin and inhabited by strange woodland creatures. Some thought it had once had a care-taker who had either died or found another job elsewhere. Others said, no, there was never a caretaker, that was only a childish legend. Others believed there was indeed a caretaker and he lived there yet and was in fact responsible for the island's tragic condition. All this is neither here nor there. What is certainly beyond dispute is that no one who visited the island, whether searching for its legendary Magic Poker or avenging the loss of a loved one, ever came back. Only their names were left, inscribed hastily on walls and ceilings and carved on trees.

o   o   o

Once upon a time, two sisters visited a desolate island. They walked its paths with their proclivities and scruples, dreaming their dreams and sorrowing their sorrows. They scared a snake and probably a bird or two, broke a few windows (there were few left to break), and gazed meditatively out upon the lake from the terrace of the main house. They wrote their names above the stone fireplace in the hexagonal loggia and shat in the soundbox of an old green piano. One of them did anyway; the other one couldn't get her pants down. On the island, they found a beautiful iron poker, and when they went home, they took it with them.

o   o   o

The girl in gold pants hastens out of the big house and down the dark path where earlier the snake slept and past the gutted guest cabin and on down the mottled path towards the boat. To either side of her, flies and bees mumble indolently under the summer sun. A small speckled frog who will not live out the day squats staring on a stone, burps, hops into a darkness. A white moth drifts silently into the web of a spider, flutters there awhile before his execution. Suddenly, there on the path mottled with sunlight, the girl stops short, her breath coming in short gasps, looking around her. Wasn't this — ? Yes, yes, it is the place! A smile begins to form. And in fact, there it is! She waits for Karen.

o   o   o

Once upon a time there was a beautiful young Princess in tight gold pants, so very tight in fact that no one could remove them from her. Knights came from far and wide, and they huffed and they puffed, and they grunted and they groaned, but the pants would not come down. One rash Knight even went so far as to jam the blade of his sword down the front of the gold pants, striving to pry them from her, but he succeeded only in shattering his sword, much to his life-long dismay and ignominy. The King at last delivered a Proclamation. 'Whosoever shall succeed in pulling my daughter's pants down,' he declared, 'shall have her for his bride!' Since this was perhaps not the most tempting of trophies, the Princess having been married

off three times already in previous competitions, the King added:
'And moreover he shall have bestowed upon him the Magic Poker,
whose powers and prodigies are well known in the Kingdom!' 'The
Old Man's got his bloody cart before his horse,' one Knight com-
plained sourly to a companion upon hearing the Proclamation. 'If I
had the bloody Poker, you could damn well bet I'd have no trouble
gettin' the bloody pants off her!' Now, it chanced that this heedless
remark was overheard by a peculiar little gnome-like creature,
huddling naked and unshaven in the brush alongside the road, and no
sooner had the words been uttered than this strange fellow determined to steal the Magic Poker and win the beauty for himself. Such
an enterprise might well have seemed impossible for even the most
dauntless of Knights, much less for so hapless a creature as this
poor naked brute with the shaggy loins, but the truth, always
stranger than fiction, was that his father had once been the King's
Official Caretaker, and the son had grown up among the mysteries
and secret chambers of the Court. Imagine the entire Kingdom's
astonishment, therefore, when, the very next day, the Caretaker's
son appeared, squat, naked, and hirsute, before the King and with
grunts and broad gestures made manifest his intention to quit the
Princess of her pants and win the prize for himself! 'Indeed!' cried
her father. The King's laughter boomed throughout the Palace, and
all the Knights and Ladies joined in, creating the jolliest of uproars.
'Bring my daughter here at once!' the King thundered, delighted by
the droll spectacle. The Princess, amused, but at the same time somewhat afrighted of the strange little man, stepped timidly forward, her
golden haunches gleaming in the bright lights of the Palace. The
Caretaker's son promptly drew forth the Magic Poker, pointed it at
the Princess, and – POOF! – the gold pants dropped – plop! to the
Palace floor. 'Ohs!' and 'Ahs!' of amazement and admiration rose up
in excited chorus from the crowd of nobles attending this most extraordinary moment. Flushed, trembling, impatient, the Princess grasped
the Magic Poker and kissed it – POOF! – a handsome Knight in shining
armour of white and navy blue stood before her, smoking a pipe.
He drew his sword and slew the Caretaker's son. Then, smiling at
the maiden standing in her puddle of gold pants, he sheathed his
sword, knocked the ashes from his pipe bowl, and knelt before the
King. 'Your Majesty,' he said, 'I have slain the monster and rescued
your daughter!' 'Not at all,' replied the King gloomily. 'You have
made her a widow. Kiss the fool, my dear!' 'No, please!' the Knight
begged. 'Stop!'

o   o   o

'Look, Karen, look! See what I found! Do you think we can take it? It doesn't hurt, does it, I mean, what with everything else – ? It's just beautiful and I can scour off the rust and – ?' Karen glances at the poker in the grass, shrugs, smiles in assent, turns to stride on down the rise towards the boat, a small white edge of which can be glimpsed through the trees, below, at the end of the path. 'Karen – ? Could you please – ?' Karen turns around, gazes quizzically at her sister, head tilted to one side – then laughs, a low grunting sound, something like a half-gargle, walks back and picks up the poker, brushes off the insects with her hand. Her sister, delighted, reaches for it, but Karen grunts again, keeps it, carries it down to their boat. There, she washes it clean in the lake water, scrubbing it with sand. She dries it on her dress. 'Don't get your dress dirty, Karen! It's rusty anyway. We'll clean it when we get home.' Karen holds it between them a moment before tossing it into the boat, and they both smile to see it. Wet still, it glistens, sparkling with flecks of rainbow-coloured light in the sunshine.

o   o   o

The tall man stands poised before her, smoking his pipe, one hand in the pocket of his navy-blue jacket. Besides the jacket, he wears only a white turtleneck shirt. The girl in gold pants is kissing him. From the tip of his crown to the least of his toes. Nothing happens. Only a bitter wild goose taste in the mouth. Something is wrong. 'Karen!' Karen laughs, a low grunting sound, then takes hold of the man and lifts her skirts. 'No, Karen! Please!' he cries, laughing. 'Stop!' POOF! From her skirts, Karen withdraws a wrought-iron poker, long and slender with an intricately worked handle. 'It's beautiful, Karen!' her sister exclaims and reaches for it. Karen grunts again, holds it up between them a moment, and they both smile to see it. It glistens in the sunshine, a handsome souvenir of a beautiful day.

o   o   o

Soon the bay is still again, the silver fish and the dragonflies are returned, and only the slightest murmur near the shore by the old waterlogged lumber betrays the recent disquiet. The boat is already far out on the lake, its stern confronting us in retreat. The family who prepared this island does not know the girls have been here, nor would it astonish them to hear of it. As a matter of fact, with that touch of the divinity common to the rich, they have probably forgotten why they built all the things on this island in the first place, or whatever possessed them seriously to concern themselves, to squander good hours, over the selection of this or that object to decorate the newly made spaces or to do the things that had usually to be done, over the selection of this or that iron poker, for example. The boat is almost out of sight, so distant in fact, it's no longer possible to see its occupants or even to know how many there are – all just a blurred speck on the bright sheen laid on the lake by the lowering sun. The lake is calm. Here, a few shadows lengthen, a frog dies, a strange creature lies slain, a tanager sings.

Morris in Chains

We have him, I make this report to the nation. Sleepless search, intransigent effort in the common behalf: our thanks to his captors! Morris has at last surrendered. Pursued night and day through the complexity of our parksystem (Morris, old head, protested: 'But only the parks remain!' Bumpkin! know, then, that is not your crime!), tracked by the undisguisable deposit of sheepshit, ambushed in the end by a massing of passive tourists. The interrogation was brief, the confession not quite so: alexandrian impudence! It will *not* repeat *not* be made public. Morris is in chains, his sheep shot. He has requested exile – they all do! – he shall not receive it.

The hunt was long, nor was it painless: Morris trod old paths, forced a suffering of the inveterate green visions, a merciless hacking through the damp growths of our historic hebephrenia. It was perhaps an epic of its kind, our best minds were engaged, and yet this must be granted the captive: it was his own grit and cunning gave it grandeur. Much time was wasted, of course, undue risks taken. Our fundamental error here was probably in the chase itself. But once the remarkable Doris Peloris, MD, Ph D, UD, assumed command, the end came quickly. She gathered the necessary data, reined in the hunters, set a trap of mechanical crickets, and waited for the inexorable conclusion. All praise to Dr Peloris! Her wisdom is the State's blessing!

Encounters with Morris were never rare, but Morris never stayed to fight. Cowardice? who could say so? he had his sheep to care for. Loose shreds of shrill fluting would reach our ears, and, bucking the melodic rack, we would approach, encircle, converge, catch a glimpse of his beardtuft, sheepskin jerkin, leather breeches – and then: *gone!* how explain it? sheep and all. For a time: confusion, silence, group gloom. Then: a distant report of Morris' piping and the chase was on again. It was almost as though Morris were challenging us. But simple song against our science! he lost, of course. As is well known, our parks are not connected. It is not yet clear how Morris forded the concrete stretches, but on the other hand, it is no secret that he has friends in the City. Categories of the unredeemed still to be catalogued.

(slippin nightlike through their blinkerin unarkades and splashin here below through the tile sluices I tell ye if they figger to live so close atop each other they gotta excrete less it makes a grim swim of it poor old Rameses and the girls their wool all clotted with that gop and no suns to dry by and overhead the raspin scrape of steel heels needlin the concrete cobble that caterwaul of sirenshrieks the which sure ain't nothin like the nightjars scares me silly sometimes/ well a pox on em old furrylegs! it ain't the choice is mine god knows I ain't got no mission! just alfalf and lotus that's all I'm seekin and these days it's damn hard to come by I can tell ye/sure hard to figger it we swooned their old granddaddies but somethin's clear the matter with this brood ain't none of em'll let an old hero rest his achin arse or play a lay clean through and the damn sedge swarmin with them buggers by damn! blessed flock run sick and meatless their hides mangerotted and all burred and briared nothin but sour froth in the tired old teats and spite of all they'll get us they'll get us makes me plumb sick! them slickers they do mean business damn if they don't! see them jaws? see them eyes? they ain't kiddin and if you don't get em first old furrylegs them steelyglass muckers'll have an end to us so a *pox* on em you hear? a *pox* on em!)

There were early crises, these have been admitted. No one doubted the eventual outcome, of course: it was merest Morris versus the infallibility of our computers, after all. Data properly gathered and applied must sooner or later worst the wily old cock. But, perhaps due to an underestimation of the adversary's perverse vitality, those early expeditions were all too often subverted by disorder, what we can now see as undeniable disorder, were little more than a random series of spontaneous incursions of the sort that most suited Morris' own patternless and irresponsible life. He just stayed downwind, fluted a few slim echoes off our City walls, and led his panicky pursuants into one blind valley after another. The times grew serious. It ceased being a mere parlourgame. New flocks were reported forming. New pipes were heard, plaintive essays, not to be compared with Morris' mastery, to be sure, but the oldstyle harmonics was unmistakable. Rebellion threatened. Dr Doris Peloris was given command.

On a worldwide appearance, Dr Peloris reassured the citizens that there was nothing to fear. 'All possible cause for panic will be eradicated,' she affirmed with a machined precision, her words destined for immortality. 'We shall put an end to idylatry. The studied dissonance upon which our modern State is painstakingly structured will not so easily be corrupted.'

Through the tense days that followed, Dr Peloris and her hand-picked staff of highly trained urbanologists, high above the City, pored over the dossiers of previous forays. Polly and the other systems analysts made octal and symbolic corrections to the operational program, broke down old software systems and reassembled the data under new descriptors, and came up with a new standard programming package for the project, now known as Project Sheep Shape. Boris the Chartchief prepared detailed flowcharts, built three-dimensional transverse Mercator's projections of the entire park-system, and mapped out Morris' movements, but both he and the doctor agreed there was little to go on. 'Even nonpattern eventually betrays a secret system,' Dr Peloris explained confidently to all present, 'but so far that of our subject, which seems largely instinctual, is simply not apparent.' Nan, her personal aide, working out of the newly reprocessed data, reduced Morris' known personal habits, the natural objects that seemed to attract him, his own minimal needs and the needs of his beasts, manifest psychosexual behaviour, and the like, to realtime-based mathematical formulizations, but even these computations proved inconclusive. 'No, Nan,' said the doctor gravely, pencil gripped in her teeth, 'clearly for the moment the hunt itself must go on.'

She assembled the expeditionary force into emergency session, braced them for the difficult assignments that lay ahead, spoke frankly of old temptations. 'You laugh. Yet, we are already, let us admit, to a degree corrupted. As much by our own shaky starts as by Morris. We can nearly admit notes of savagery in our parks, have not yet stifled the wild optimistic call. We might yet be thrilled by the glimmer of disembodied eyes burning hot in the dark forest, by the vision of bathing naiads' bared mammaries or of nutbrown torsos with furry thighs, by the one-note calls of hemlock pipes. In short, we are not yet freed from the sin of the simple. But it is our children, to speak in the old way, whom we must consider. There must be no confusions for them between the old legends and conceivable realities. It is *they* who oblige us to grub up, once and for all, the contaminated seed of our unfortunate origins.' Enthusiastic applause. Boris recorded the intensity on his phonometer, wrote out the figure for Nan to report in her log. He nodded towards Polly, and both observed with troubled frowns her unmoved placidity, her subtle smile. 'Our strategy is divided into two parts,' Dr Peloris continued, 'the pursuit and the trap. The second of course depends on the first, which is essentially a fact-finding mission, but which at the same time may serve the complementary function of harassing and exhausting the adversary, forcing predictable pattern-reliance: the wearier, the unwarier.'

Boris and Nan spoke to the doctor after the meeting about Polly. 'Her mind wanders,' said Boris. 'Her butt's too plump,' observed Nan. Dr Peloris nodded wistfully. It was well known that Polly was one of her favourites. '*Does* she dream of the sweet bird, the bright star?' sighed the doctor. 'Well, our interest in her wanes.'

(third national they calls it but spite of that it's clear I've took a hankerin to it all right don't plot my trackin but seems as how we come on it often enough: silver poplars and old old beeches blowin wisted measures in the green breeze the mingled elms and hazels and westerlies shiftin the flickerin shadows and a clean brook for moon-bathin and drownin the lice in and wanderin ivytendrils and foxglove and colocasia mingled with the laughin acanthus and a sweet blue-grass bed halffoot spongy: ain't the happiest valley mebbe but it's happy enough/and old Rameses he savours it here too damn if he don't he's gettin old that boy why I have to damn near bullwhip him ever time to make him decamp this little old dell he sure don't cater none to these long ramblins hasty grubbins and don't say as I blame him neither/besides this place it's somethin nice well sure it's true they's some tourists here most of the time but I tell ye they ain't bad they don't really bother us none it ain't *them* that's buggin us and after all you know I *ain't* the antisocial type in fact it pleasures me no little somewhat to pipe for the younguns tickle em into dancin a round or two and their old folks they like it too don't let em kid ye otherhow /then top of all that why now and again on *lucky* days I even experiences an occasion to stick the old staff mongst the tender herbage as the poet says: a hurried little touristhumpin in the copse when the cops ain't heedin *yes* by damn! *women!* can't say as old Morris ever passed a one up; why I've took on everthin short of newborns and old corses/well ceptin for one mebbe but that there's another story a tender folklay outa the callow prepubes: it was a sunny midday in the hot bulge of spring drove the flock into a grove of massy old oaks dipped my taut untufted flesh in the cool runlet nearby reposed alongside afterwards blouse wrapped round my breech lettin old phoebus lap me dry made my first squawky boggles on a set of reeds looked up and waddaya know? seen this here little goosegirl just stretched out beside me! well I was just a youngun I jolted up and grabbed on my breeches showin forth my shiny white croup and *that* lifted a titter outa her/then snug in my leatherns I let her tug me down longside her and so we got to talkin I said it sure was a nice day wasn't it? and she said yes it sure *was* a nice day at that and I said her geese was mighty pretty and white and she said my sheep they was pretty and white too and just then one of em clumb up on another one and damn if that didn't set *both* of us to gigglin I *swan!* sure seems silly now to talk back on it/she said the sun was in her eye and pulled me down to shade her I efforted a parched kiss her sweet breath reekin of pogonias broad crescent smile starchy folds of springfrock listin over limbcurves and heftin in flushed breezes her toes to the sun old ganders circlin as if in sacred pieties lilywhite fingers fondlin my loose leatherns and grabbin hold like of a she-goat's milkswoln udder her eyes glittery brown beckonin me and me composin mad poetries in the back of my agitated skull nervous un-buttoned the flowered bodice whitebright breasts slud out of shadows my tremblin lips bent to the nubbins – foul taste! reared back! *goosebit by damn!* scarred and bloodied one blue pap flappin free and crudded under with some mucusy gop like to made me retch right there in her poor silly face it did!/clutched my mouth and backed off her pulled on my togs and all the time the little goosegirl just lay rigid by the runlet bruised boobies to the breeze and grinnin that mad as mad widetoothed moonshaped grin *jumpin juniper!* I switched my surprised flock up outa that there grove fast as they would scat just left that goosegirl alyin there them geese paradin around her in that solemn circle and you know let me tell ye I could make out the unsubtle arc of her big mounded belly a mile away till the next by god mountain cut off my view! damn! well I ain't never been back there I can certain ye that but I done some things since well who knows? mebbe even worse yeah mebbe – oh-oh! hey you know Rameses it looks like we just might have to move on damn if it don't! just seen that there little plumpbodied scout of theirs up behind that knob there! they'll be on us by – *ah!* don't look at

me like that old trouper! tain't my fault! and look we still got all
night ain't we? the third national! well odd number's god's delight
and ain't it so?)

Dr Peloris drew up a detailed set of assignments, instructed the team
on basic methodology. But before the expedition could get under way,
an unforeseen incident occurred: Polly disappeared. Nan cursed,
Boris shook his old shaggy head. An entire day was lost in the search.
We came across her at last alongside one of the park canals in the
Third National, her plump white body splayed out in a bed of plastic
nasturtiums, eyes glazed over, simpering smile on her flushed red
lips.

'Poll on the sward,' clucked Nan, and macrofilmed the scene.

'Morris?' demanded Dr Peloris of the girl.

'Morris was not here.' Polly's slow uneven voice reached us from
a hollow echoing distance. 'No. Not him.' Rugged announcement!
A man knelt, blessed himself in the blood of the wound.

'*Morris!*' cried the doctor paling, but by then the man had disappeared.

A gloomy uneasy silence settled over the group. This had been
entirely unexpected by most. Dr Peloris probed the girl, then dic-
tated a field report to her aide, detailed the apparent causes and
effects. 'And, oh, Nan,' the doctor concluded in a clear voice that
reached us all: 'seal it with a cygnet ring,' Her everready humour
broke the spell. We laughed heartily, stood eager and ready to be of
service. Cheerfully, we received our equipment, motored to our posts.
It was the beginning of the end for old Morris.

Meanwhile, the bearded sheepherder popped in one park after
another. He eluded us less frequently now. Upon sighting him, we
recorded his behaviour for approximately four hours, then made an
intentional appearance to set him trotting again. The sheep were
slow, grazed all too leisurely, slept, drank, bred, shat across the green
spaces of our public places, nubbing the last of the old hills. Could
Morris have made it without them? The question is academic. Morris
included them, they him, his speed was describable only by theirs.

(as if I ain't havin troubles enough old Rameses stages him an in-
surrection the sonuvabitch! had it in for his old buddy Morris ever
since I cropped his marbles and hell I didn't wanna do it but the
stock was multiplicatin past all reason and I had to halt it somewheres they was draggin me down to a near standstill: tried to
explain it to the old tup but he wouldn't listen had to get his daily

diddle he did so what could I do? I roasted a coupla the younger lads
and docked the old ram but no I shouldn'ta done it by damn!
shouldn'ta done it! old Rameses! whatever got into me? if I just had
time to sit down and think! if you're gonna eunuch em you gotta do
it young by damn/so that did it he sets about to right the score and
so this here afternoon we make the hard trek up into the big hills
find us a green knob and settle us down for a breather we're stag-
gerin sick from runnin and climbin just too much! had to leave a
poor old ewe behind on accounta she was just too slow from carryin
I left her with no one to care for her damn near made me cry/but
now then the sun was lowerin peaceful down in the plain the flock
grubbin the good mountain clover and me with a big slab of roast
ram outa my pack my cup frothin with snowy white milk and first
thing you know I'm noddin off dreamin of the old country the slender
maids and soft half-forgotten lays me spread out with a fancy little
phyllis of just fourteen and never yet mown and I'm just creepin in
her kirtle with her pantin fast and tonguin my ear when I wakes of a
sudden finds me in the midmost of the motherin flock one of the old
girls nudgin me in the face with her wet nose and old Rameses' bells
clangin not far off/can't see plain at first sun down and moon just a
fingernail but yes! they're buttin me towards the old ram! still got
my fuddled mind on the old country and can't arrange the landscape
straight for a moment: but then it hits me! the precipice! *them goddamn ewes is nosin me towards the precipice!* oboy I try like hell to
haul my feet under me but them bitches just knock me down again
can't hardly see nothing only just their white wool rollin spooklike
in the moonlight their hooves and black faces blocked out by the
nightdark and I keep hearin them bells like a tinny dirge gettin
nearer and nearer *jumpin juniper! a goner by god!* and my heart's
poundin and I'm mebbe even screamin and then oh my god I catch
a clear horrifical glim of the edge: pale vision of the plains way down
below/old Rameses he's slowly givin ground edgin aside to grant
me space to slip off and away and I furious grab out at the old gruff
but all I get is his damn bells and the ewes ain't pushin directly now
the old bellwether is movin aside but they're fumblin around clumsy
and confused and I know I gotta go any minute – but suddenly quick-
like I clap the bells on the nearest mother and send her flyin and
janglin off to the right and over the cliff: half the flock follows her
over before you can't hear the bell no more me clutchin at last and
hangin on to old Rameses' hind hoof/ and then finally it's over and I
stagger over by the rocks collapse grabbin for breath Rameses his

troops cut to ribbons droops in retreat to the nearby copse can't sleep all night myself but by mornin I can see the old ram and I have found our truce: what's left to trouble us won't be neither of us)

Data streamed daily into Dr Doris Peloris' skyhigh headquarters. Only rarely did Morris escape our network of observers now, and then but briefly. His least event was recorded on notepad, punchcard, film, tape. Observers reported his noises, odours, motions, choices, acquisitions, excretions, emissions, irritations, dreams. His longest disappearance lasted only three days: at the end of that time, some dead sheep were discovered in a ravine, Morris located up in the mountains, so-called, less than an hour later. The report was rushed to Dr Peloris, high above the City.

'Little matter,' the doctor replied, smiling warmly, turning from her machines. 'We have him now.'

Instructions were given to wait for a few hours, then harass him down out of the mountains. Dr Peloris moved Expedition Headquarters to a skillfully concealed bivouac area within the Third National Park. There, she prepared the reception for the old shepherd.

'You see, Nan,' she explained to her aide that evening, 'it is now certain that Morris will camp here in this valley, beside this canal and that grove, within five days. The order of his disorder, as exposed by Boris' charts and the processed data, *forces* him to do so no matter what operations his mind might undertake in order to arrive at what he would tend to think of as a decision. Unless, of course, it included the foreknowledge that we await him here. And who knows? perhaps even this knowledge would not suffice to break the power of pattern over mere mind-activity. Were the situation not so critical, I might enjoy the experiment.' Nan smiled faintly, lit the doctor's cigarette. 'Certain precautions will make our job easier, Nan. Please request that the water in the canal be generated with slightly increased velocity, and if necessary, create small obstructions that break the surface. Until Morris is captured there are to be no overcast skies. If this order conflicts seriously with some other department, you are at liberty to alter it to pertain to nights only, but under no circumstances are there to be clouds from midnight until about one hour after dawn.'

'Temperature, Doctor?'

'About seventy-five degrees, humidity slightly higher than normal.'

'Yes, Doctor. Is there any other—?'

'Once the adversary has entered the target area, see to it that fragrances of pine, myrtle, and hyacinth are emitted faintly. Take extreme caution, of course, for this can easily be overdone and put our prey on his guard. The mechanical crickets should be turned on at sunset, but only one by one, reaching full strength about five AM. Make a public announcement about the same time, in order to clog up the park exits a bit. At six, we close in.'

Nan looked up, met the doctor's grey-eyed gaze. They nodded, smiled knowingly at each other. Six.

(so by damn whaddaya know? brought out a brandnew little lamb this evening just as old phoeb was rollin in for the night him lendin a soft goldreddish glow to the occasion the little ewe just a youngun too: her first – how is it they mother so sweet the first time? it's the pain and fright in it I guess – but *damn!* I knew that! known it for ages just forgot it I guess forgettin ever damn thing forgettin all the old songs too I am/mind wearying down with all this cussed pasture-hoppin that's it! we just ain't made for it are we Rameses? gettin old you are Morris by damn if you ain't! well of course I still got a *little* jism left in my jumpers I ain't givin it up *yet* I can tell ye but I'm sure as hell on the peterin off side of the old lifearc yes yes time it wastes *all* things and ain't it so!/sure is pretty here tonight must be a million stars up there! you know I set to countin them once well hell I was young and had silly ideas I thought they was always the same number of em up there can you imagine? just didn't know nothin/ hey! listen at them crickets! why I ain't heard crickets like that since I was a boy! got the idea somewheres they'd extincted the little buggers but I guess they don't give up that easy I guess nothin does leastly you and me eh Rameses?/well you know old wether we just shouldn'ta come back here I feel disaster in my bones I do but it seems like it don't matter somehow – no: when you figger they'da got us one place as another you might just as well go out grubbin the green herbs as gaggin on garbage in the alleys don't you reckon?/ and hey! just smell that spring old eunuch! just listen at them bawdy crickets! makes a body wanna pipe one of the *old* songs!)

> Her hairs was black as silver snails
> Her teeth was white as gold
> The copse were green as nightingales
> The runlet fresh as mould
> The runlet fresh as mould

Her ears they twinkled merrily
Her eyes hearked all I said
How lovely life, sang I, would be
If only we was dead
If only we was dead

She quite agreed and plunged her knife
Into my bleeding breast
Sweet maid, you've given me new life
Pray, let me have the rest
Pray, let me have the rest

Once her I laid, twice her I laid
I laid her three times o'er
So though she died a virgin maid
We buried her a whore
We buried her a whore

Now if my tune obscure should seem
The meaning overlong
Consider less than life a dream
And more than death a song
And more than death a song

Dawn broke at 5.55. Beside the water, alongside a grove of poplar and beech, lay the shepherd with his flock, facing the eastern sky. At precisely 6.00 AM, Dr Doris Peloris and her staff emerged from their concealments, advanced from different directions upon the shepherd. He started up, then discovered the thickening crowds of eager-eyed tourists welling up behind the doctor and her team: he offered no resistance.

'You have been herding sheep,' the doctor said.

'That figures, lady. I'm a shepherd.'

The doctor's aide snorted: 'Fruitless syllogism of eclogic!'

Dr Peloris smiled. 'My black bag, Nan.'

'Now, look here, ma'am, I don't mean no—'

'Any,' corrected Dr Peloris. She drew a stethoscope and other equipment from her black bag. 'Remove your clothes.'

'My—?'

'Let's not be impertinent! This is no less difficult for me than it is for you. I refer to those rank fulsome skins you're wearing, how do you call them? gaskins, buskins – I don't care, *but get them off!*'

Morris glared edgily at his captors, at the pressing crowd. Dr Peloris pulled a pair of scissors from her bag. Morris grumbled, removed his jerkin and breeches.

There were low whistles and the doctor's aide gasped audibly.

'What is it, Nan?'

'The ... the *legs*, doctor! the *fur*—!'

Dr Peloris smiled, hooked the stethoscope in her ears. 'I thought you knew,' she said.

While the doctor conducted her examination, her staff methodically exterminated the sheep with hypodermic injections. The beasts died quickly and, it seemed, with a certain satisfaction. Morris, nude, had grown impassive. Only the death of his lead ram seemed to affect him. A single tear formed, slid down his tawny cheek. The doctor's aide noted it in her examination record.

The examination itself did not take long: eyes, ears, nose, throat, heart, lungs, arterial pressure, routine check for hernia and piles, palpation of the prostate, various vital measurements. X-rays, blood samples, and encephalograms were taken, analysed on the spot. 'Now, a sample of your semen, please,' said the doctor turning her back, replacing the stethoscope in her black bag.

Morris, barbarian and cold-eyed, did not move.

'Nan!' said the doctor, nodding back over her shoulder towards the captive.

Her aide slipped a rubber glove on over her left hand, squeezed some oil onto it. Morris made one last desperate lunge, but Boris and another grabbed him, held him rigid. The crowd of tourists bulged closer. Nan approached him, executed three or four expert movements. Morris' bronzed and bearded face flushed yet darker, his eyes widened and lost focus, his mouth seemed to grow full of thick teeth. Nan handed the test tube to the doctor. Dr Peloris made a hasty smear, peered into the field microscope. '2-A!' she exclaimed with a soft appreciative whistle. 'Not bad for a man of his age!'

Morris now lay limp in the arms of the two men. His cheeks sagged indifferently. Defiance was over. Victory was ours!

Dr Peloris turned towards Morris, smiled gently. 'There is still a place for you in our world,' she said. 'You are more than healthy enough to warrant an attempted rehabilitation. I am in a position to recommend you. Perhaps a job at one of our mutton factories to begin with. Would you be interested?'

Morris stared numbly at the doctor. He closed his mouth. Slowly, deliberately, sullenly, he shook his head.

'Put him in chains,' the doctor ordered. She closed up her black bag, strode away, to the cheers of the gathered throng.

This, then, concludes our report. Dr Doris Peloris has received highest State honours, yet it is of course recognized by all citizens that she cannot be rewarded enough. May history grant her that which is beyond our humble means! Though he remains in chains, Morris' story may not be ended. He has been turned over to the urbanologists and a famous urbaniatrist has taken a personal interest in his case. They admit that Morris is a challenge serious beyond precedent to their young sciences, but reintegration does not seem entirely beyond possibility. We may well, in concert, wish that such might be the case!

(Doris Peloris the chorus and Morris sonorous canorous Horace scores Boris—should be able to make *somethin* outa that by juniper then there's bore us and whore us and up the old torus no not so good not so good losin the old touch I am by damn/*ahh! Rameses!* why'd they go and *do* that to ye for? it's the motherin insane are free!)

The Gingerbread House

I

A pine forest in the midafternoon. Two children follow an old man,
dropping breadcrumbs, singing nursery tunes. Dense earthy greens
seep into the darkening distance, flecked and streaked with filtered
sunlight. Spots of red, violet, pale blue, gold, burnt orange. The girl
carries a basket for gathering flowers. The boy is occupied with the
crumbs. Their song tells of God's care for little ones.

2

Poverty and resignation weigh on the old man. His cloth jacket is
patched and threadbare, sunbleached white over the shoulders, worn
through on the elbows. His feet do not lift, but shuffle through the
dust. White hair. Parched skin. Secret force of despair and guilt
seem to pull him earthward.

3

The girl plucks a flower. The boy watches curiously. The old man
stares impatiently into the forest's depths, where night seems already
to crouch. The girl's apron is a bright orange, the gay colour of freshly
picked tangerines, and is stitched happily with blues and reds and

greens; but her dress is simple and brown, tattered at the hem, and her feet are bare. Birds accompany the children in their singing and butterflies decorate the forest spaces.

4

The boy's gesture is furtive. His right hand trails behind him, letting a crumb fall. His face is half-turned towards his hand, but his eyes remain watchfully fixed on the old man's feet ahead. The old man wears heavy mud-spattered shoes, high-topped and leather-thonged. Like the old man's own skin, the shoes are dry and cracked and furrowed with wrinkles. The boy's pants are a bluish-brown, ragged at the cuffs, his jacket a faded red. He, like the girl, is barefoot.

5

The children sing nursery songs about May baskets and gingerbread houses and a saint who ate his own fleas. Perhaps they sing to lighten their young hearts, for puce wisps of dusk now coil through the trunks and branches of the thickening forest. Or perhaps they sing to conceal the boy's subterfuge. More likely, they sing for no reason at all, a thoughtless childish habit. To hear themselves. To fill the silence. Conceal their thoughts. Their expectations.

6

The boy's hand and wrist, thrusting from the outgrown jacket (the faded red cuff is not a cuff at all, but the torn limits merely, the ragged edge of the soft worn sleeve), are tanned, a little soiled, childish. The fingers are short and plump, the palm soft, the wrist small. Three fingers curl under, holding back crumbs, kneading them, coaxing them into position, while the index finger and thumb flick them sparingly, one by one, to the ground, playing with them a moment, balling them, pinching them as if for luck or pleasure, before letting them go.

7

The old man's pale-blue eyes float damply in deep dark pouches, half-shrouded by heavy upper lids and beetled over by shaggy white brows. Deep creases fan out from the moist corners, angle down past the nose, score the tanned cheeks and pinch the mouth. The old man's gaze is straight ahead, but at what? Perhaps at nothing. Some invisible destination. Some irrevocable point of departure. One thing can be said about the eyes: they are tired. Whether they have seen too much or too little, they betray no will to see yet more.

8

The witch is wrapped in a tortured whirl of black rags. Her long face is drawn and livid, and her eyes glow like burning coals. Her angular body twists this way and that, flapping her black rags — flecks of blue and amethyst wink and flash in the black tangle. Her gnarled blue hands snatch greedily at space, shred her clothes, claw cruelly at her face and throat. She cackles silently, then suddenly screeches madly, seizes a passing dove, and tears its heart out.

9

The girl, younger than the boy, skips blithely down the forest path, her blonde curls flowing freely. Her brown dress is coarse and plain, but her apron is gay and white petticoats wink from beneath the tattered hem. Her skin is fresh and pink and soft, her knees and elbows dimpled, her cheeks rosy. Her young gaze flicks airily from flower to flower, bird to bird, tree to tree, from the boy to the old man, from the green grass to the encroaching darkness, and all of it seems to delight her equally. Her basket is full to overflowing. Does she even know the boy is dropping crumbs? or where the old man is leading them? Of course, but it's nothing! a game!

10

There is, in the forest, even now, a sunny place, with mintdrop trees and cotton candy bushes, an air as fresh and heady as lemonade.

Rivulets of honey flow over gumdrop pebbles, and lollypops grow wild as daisies. This is the place of the gingerbread house. Children come here, but, they say, none leave.

II

The dove is a soft lustrous white, head high, breast filled, tip of the tail less than a feather's thickness off the ground. From above, it would be seen against the pale path – a mixture of umbers and greys and the sharp brown strokes of pine needles – but from its own level, in profile, its pure whiteness is set off glowingly against the obscure mallows and distant moss greens of the forest. Only its small beak moves. Around a bread crumb.

12

The song is about a great king who won many battles, but the girl sings alone. The old man has turned back, gazes curiously but dispassionately now at the boy. The boy, too, has turned, no longer furtive, hand poised but no crumb dropping from his fingertips. He stares back down the path by which they three have come, his mouth agape, his eyes startled. His left hand is raised, as if arrested a moment before striking out in protest. Doves are eating his breadcrumbs. His ruse has failed. Perhaps the old man, not so ignorant in such matters after all, has known all along it would. The girl sings of pretty things sold in the market.

13

So huddled over her prey is the witch that she seems nothing more than a pile of black rags heaped on a post. Her pale long-nailed hands are curled inward towards her breast, massaging the object, her head lower than her hunched shoulders, wan beaked nose poked in among restless fingers. She pauses, cackling softly, peers left, then right, then lifts the heart before her eyes. The burnished heart of the dove glitters like a ruby, a polished cherry, a brilliant, heart-shaped bloodstone. It beats still. A soft radiant pulsing. The black bony shoulders of the witch quake with glee, with greed, with lust.

14

A wild blur of fluttering white: the dove's wings flapping! Hands clutch its body, its head, its throat, small hands with short plump fingers. Its wings flail against the dusky forest green, but it is forced down against the umber earth. The boy falls upon it, his hands bloodied by beak and claws.

15

The gingerbread house is approached by flagstones of variegated wafers, through a garden of candied fruits and all-day suckers in neat little rows.

16

No song now from the lips of the girl, but a cry of anguish. The basket of flowers is dropped, the kings and saints forgotten. She struggles with the boy for the bird. She kicks him, falls upon him, pulls his hair, tears at his red jacket. He huddles around the bird, trying to elbow free of the girl. Both children are weeping, the boy of anger and frustration, the girl of pain and pity and a bruised heart. Their legs entangle, their fists beat at each other, feathers fly.

17

The pale blue eyes of the old man stare not ahead, but down. The squint, the sorrow, the tedium are vanished; the eyes focus clearly. The deep creases fanning out from the damp corners pinch inwards, a brief wince, as though at some inner hurt, some certain anguish, some old wisdom. He sighs.

18

The girl has captured the bird. The boy, small chest heaving, kneels in the patch watching her, the anger largely drained out of him. His faded red jacket is torn; his pants are full of dust and pine needles.

She has thrust the dove protectively beneath her skirt, and sits, knees apart, leaning over it, weeping softly. The old man stoops down, lifts her bright orange apron, her skirt, her petticoats. The boy turns away. The dove is nestled in her small round thighs. It is dead.

19

Shadows have lengthened. Umbers and lavenders and greens have greyed. But the body of the dove glows yet in the gathering dusk. The whiteness of the ruffled breast seems to be fighting back against the threat of night. It is strewn with flowers, now beginning to wilt. The old man, the boy, and the girl have gone.

20

The beams of the gingerbread house are liquorice sticks, cemented with taffy, weatherboarded with gingerbread, and coated with caramel. Peppermint-stick chimneys sprout randomly from its chocolate roof and its windows are laced with meringue. Oh, what a house! and the best thing of all is the door.

21

The forest is dense and deep. Branches reach forth like arms. Brown animals scurry. The boy makes no furtive gestures. The girl, carrying her flowerbasket, does not skip or sing. They walk, arms linked, eyes wide open and staring ahead into the forest. The old man plods on, leading the way, his heavy old leather-thonged shoes shuffling in the damp dust and undergrowth.

22

The old man's eyes, pale in the sunlight, now seem to glitter in the late twilight. Perhaps it is their wetness picking up the last flickering light of day. The squint has returned, but it is not the squint of weariness: resistance, rather. His mouth opens as though to speak, to rebuke, but his teeth are clenched. The witch twists and quivers, her black rags whirling, whipping, flapping. From her lean bosom, she withdraws the pulsing red heart of a dove. How it glows, how it rages, how it dances in the dusk! The old man now does not resist. Lust flattens his face and mists his old eyes, where glitter now reflections of the ruby heart. Grimacing, he plummets forward, covering the cackling witch, crashing through brambles that tear at his clothes.

23

A wild screech cleaves the silence of the dusky forest. Birds start up from branches and the undergrowth is alive with frightened animals. The old man stops short, one hand raised protectively in front of him, the other, as though part of the same instinct, reaching back to shield his children. Dropping her basket of flowers, the girl cries out in terror and springs forward into the old man's arms. The boy blanches, shivers as though a cold wind might be wetly wrapping his young body, but manfully holds his ground. Shapes seem to twist and coil, and vapours seep up from the forest floor. The girl whimpers and the old man holds her close.

24

The beds are simple but solid. The old man himself has made them. The sun is setting, the room is in shadows, the children tucked safely in. The old man tells them a story about a good fairy who granted a poor man three wishes. The wishes, he knows, were wasted, but so then is the story. He lengthens the tale with details about the good fairy, how sweet and kind and pretty she is, then lets the children complete the story with their own wishes, their own dreams. Below, a brutal demand is being forced upon him. Why must the goodness of all wishes come to nothing?

25

The flowerbasket lies, overturned, by the forest path, its wilting flowers strewn. Shadows darker than dried blood spread beneath its gaping mouth. The shadows are long, for night is falling.

26

The old man has fallen into the brambles. The children, weeping, help pull him free. He sits on the forest path staring at the boy and girl. It is as though he is unable to recognize them. Their weeping dies away. They huddle more closely together, stare back at the old man. His face is scratched, his clothes torn. He is breathing irregularly.

27

The sun, the songs, the breadcrumbs, the dove, the overturned basket, the long passage towards night: where, the old man wonders, have all the good fairies gone? He leads the way, pushing back the branches. The children follow, silent and frightened.

28

The boy pales and his heart pounds, but manfully he holds his ground. The witch writhes, her black rags fluttering, licking at the twisted branches. With a soft seductive chuckle, she holds before him the burnished cherry-red heart of a dove. The boy licks his lips. She steps back. The glowing heart pulses gently, evenly, excitingly.

29

The good fairy has sparkling blue eyes and golden hair, a soft sweet mouth and gentle hands that caress and soothe. Gossamer wings sprout from her smooth back; from her flawless chest two firm breasts with tips bright as rubies.

30

The witch, holding the flaming pulsing heart out to the boy, steps back into the dark forest. The boy, in hesitation, follows. Back. Back. Swollen eyes aglitter, the witch draws the ruby heart close to her dark lean breast, then past her shoulder and away from the boy.

Transfixed, he follows it, brushing by her. The witch's gnarled and bluish fingers claw at his poor garments, his pale red jacket and bluish-brown pants, surprising his soft young flesh.

31

The old man's shoulders are bowed earthwards, his face is lined with sorrow, his neck bent forward with resignation, but his eyes glow like burning coals. He clutches his shredded shirt to his throat, stares intensely at the boy. The boy stands alone and trembling on the path, staring into the forest's terrible darkness. Shapes whisper and coil. The boy licks his lips, steps forward. A terrible shriek shreds the forest hush. The old man grimaces, pushes the whimpering girl away, strikes the boy.

32

No more breadcrumbs, no more pebbles, no more songs or flowers. The slap echoes through the terrible forest, doubles back on its own echoes, folding finally into a sound not unlike a whispering cackle.

33

The girl, weeping, kisses the struck boy and presses him close, shielding him from the tormented old man. The old man, taken aback, reaches out uncertainly, gently touches the girl's frail shoulder. She shakes his hand off – nearly a shudder – and shrinks towards the boy. The boy squares his shoulders, colour returning to his face. The familiar creases of age and despair crinkle again the old man's face. His pale-blue eyes mist over. He looks away. He leaves the children by the last light of day.

34

But the door! The door is shaped like a heart and is as red as a cherry, always half-open, whether lit by sun or moon, is sweeter than a sugarplum, more enchanting than a peppermint stick. It is

red as a poppy, red as an apple, red as a strawberry, red as a bloodstone, red as a rose. Oh, what a thing is the door of that house!

35

The children, alone in the strange black forest, huddle wretchedly
under a great gnarled tree. Owls hoot and bats flick menacingly
through the twisting branches. Strange shapes writhe and rustle
before their weary eyes. They hold each other tight and, trembling,
sing lullabyes, but they are not reassured.

36

The old man trudges heavily out of the black forest. His way is
marked, not by breadcrumbs, but by dead doves, ghostly white in the
empty night.

37

The girl prepares a mattress of leaves and flowers and pineneedles.
The boy gathers branches to cover them, to hide them, to protect
them. They make pillows out of their poor garments. Bats screech as
they work and owls blink down on their bodies, ghostly white, young,
trembling. They creep under the branches, disappearing into the
darkness.

38

Gloomily, the old man sits in the dark room and stares at the empty
beds. The good fairy, though a mystery of the night, effuses her
surroundings with a lustrous radiance. Is it the natural glow of her
small nimble body or perhaps the star at the top of her wand? Who
can tell? Her gossamer wings flutter rapidly, and she floats, ruby-
tipped breasts downwards, legs dangling and dimpled knees bent
slightly, glowing buttocks arched up in defiance of the night. How
good she is! In the black empty room, the old man sighs and uses up
a wish: he wishes his poor children well.

39

The children are nearing the gingerbread house. Passing under
mintdrop trees, sticking their fingers in the cotton candy bushes,
sampling the air as heady as lemonade, they skip along singing
nursery songs. Nonsense songs about dappled horses and the slaying
of dragons. Counting songs and idle riddles. They cross over rivulets
of honey on gumdrop pebbles, picking the lollypops that grow as
wild as daffodils.

40

The witch flicks and flutters through the blackened forest, her livid
face twisted with hatred, her inscrutable condition. Her eyes burn
like glowing coals and her black rags flap loosely. Her gnarled
hands claw greedily at the branches, tangle in the night's webs, dig
into tree trunks until the sap flows beneath her nails. Below, the boy
and girl sleep an exhausted sleep. One ghostly white leg, with
dimpled knee and soft round thigh, thrusts out from under the
blanket of branches.

41

But wish again! Flowers and butterflies. Dense earthy greens seep-
ing into the distance, flecked and streaked with midafternoon sunlight. Two children following an old man. They drop breadcrumbs,
sing nursery songs. The old man walks leadenly. The boy's gesture is
furtive. The girl – but it's no use, the doves will come again, there are
no reasonable wishes.

42

The children approach the gingerbread house through a garden of
candied fruits and all-day suckers, hopping along on flagstones of
variegated wafers. They sample the gingerbread weatherboarding
with its caramel coating, lick at the meringue on the windowsills,
kiss each other's sweetened lips. The boy climbs up on the chocolate
roof to break off a peppermint-stick chimney, comes sliding down

into a rainbarrel full of vanilla pudding. The girl, reaching out to catch him in his fall, slips on a sugarplum and tumbles into a sticky rock garden of candied chestnuts. Laughing gaily, they lick each other clean. And how grand is the red-and-white striped chimney the boy holds up for her! how bright! how sweet! But the door: here they pause and catch their breath. It is heart-shaped and bloodstone-red, its burnished surface gleaming in the sunlight. Oh, what a thing is that door! Shining like a ruby, like hard cherry candy, and pulsing softly, radiantly. Yes, marvellous! delicious! insuperable! but beyond: what is that sound of black rags flapping?

Seven Exemplary Fictions

Dedicatoria y Prólogo a don Miguel de Cervantes Saavedra

Quisiera yo, si fuera posible (maestro apreciadísimo), excusarme de escribir este prólogo, not merely because the temerity of addressing you with such familiarity and attaching your eminence to these apprentice fictions is certain – and quite rightly – to bring on my head *el mal que han de decir de mí más de cuatro sotiles y almidonados,* but also because here we are in the middle of a book where prologues seem inappropriate. But just as your *novelas* were 'exemplary,' in the simplest sense, because they represented the different writing ideas you were working with from the 1580s to 1612, so do these seven stories – along with the three 'Sentient Lens' fictions also included in this volume represent about everything I invented up to the commencement of my first novel in 1962 able to bear this later exposure, and I felt their presence here invited interpolations.

Ejemplares you called your tales, because '*si bien lo miras, no hay ninguna de quien no se pueda sacar un ejemplo provechoso*', and I hope in ascribing to my fictions the same property, I haven't strayed from your purposes, which I take to be manifold. For they are *ejemplares*, too, because your intention was '*poner en la plaza de nuestra república una mesa de trucos, donde cada uno pueda llegar a entretenerse sin daño de barras. Digo, sin daño del alma ni del cuerpo, porque los ejercicios honestos y agradables antes aprovechan que dañan*' – splendid, *don* Miguel! for as our mutual friend *don* Roberto S. has told us, fiction 'must provide us with an imaginative experience which is necessary to our imaginative well-being ... We need all the imagination we have, and we need it exercised and in good condition' – and thus your *novelas* stand as exemplars of responsibility to that most solemn and pious charge placed upon this vocation: they tell good stories and they tell them well.

And yet there is more, if I read you rightly. For your stories also exemplified the dual nature of all good narrative art: they struggled against the unconscious mythic residue in human life and sought to synthesize the unsynthesizable, sallied forth against adolescent thought-modes and exhausted art forms, and returned home with new complexities. In fact, your creation of a synthesis between poetic analogy and literal history (not to mention reality and illusion, sanity and madness, the erotic and the ludicrous, the visionary and the scatalogical) gave birth to the Novel – perhaps above all else your works were exemplars of a revolution in narrative fiction, a revolution which governs us – not unlike the way you found yourself abused by the conventions of the Romance – to this very day.

Never mind whether it was Erasmus or Aristotle or that forgettable Italian who caused your artist's eye to focus – not on Eternal Values and Beauty – but on Character, Actions of Men in Society, and Exemplary Histories, for it was the new Age of Science dawning, and such a shift was in the air. No longer was the City of Man a pale image of the City of God, a microcosmic reflection of the macrocosm, but rather it was all there was, neither micro- nor macrocosm, yet at the same time full of potential, all the promise of what man's mind, through Science, might accomplish. The universe for you, *Maestro*, was opening up; it could no longer be described by magical numbers or be contained in a compact and marvellously designed sphere. Narrative fiction, taking a cue from Lazarillo and the New World adventurers, became a process of discovery, and to this day young authors sally forth in fiction, like majestic – indeed divinely ordained! – *pícaros* to discover again and again, their manhood.

But, *don* Miguel, the optimism, the innocence, the aura of possibility you experienced have been largely drained away, and the universe is closing in on us again. Like you, we, too, seem to be standing at the end of one age and on the threshold of another. We, too, have been brought into a blind alley by the critics and analysts; we, too, suffer from a 'literature of exhaustion', though ironically our nonheroes are no longer tireless and tiresome Amadises, but hopelessly defeated and bed-ridden Quixotes. We seem to have moved from an open-ended, anthropocentric, humanistic, naturalistic even – to the extent that man may be thought of as making his own universe

– optimistic starting point, to one that is closed, cosmic, eternal, supernatural (in its soberest sense), and pessimistic. The return to Being has returned us to Design, to microcosmic images of the macrocosm, to the creation of Beauty within the confines of cosmic or human necessity, to the use of the fabulous to probe beyond the phenomenological, beyond appearances, beyond randomly perceived events, beyond mere history. But these probes are above all – like your Knight's sallies – challenges to the assumptions of a dying age, exemplary adventures of the Poetic Imagination, high-minded journeys towards the New World and never mind that the nag's a pile of bones.

You teach us, *Maestro*, by example, that great narratives remain meaningful through time as a language-medium between generations, as a weapon against the fringe-areas of our consciousness, and as a mythic reinforcement of our tenuous grip on reality. The novelist uses familiar mythic or historical forms to combat the content of those forms and to conduct the reader (*lector amantísimo!*) to the real, away from mystification to clarification, away from magic to maturity, away from mystery to revelation. And it is above all to the need for new modes of perception and fictional forms able to encompass them that I, barber's basin on my head, address these stories. If they seem slight for such a burden as this prolix foreword, please consider them, in turn, *don* Miguel, as a mere preface to all that here flowers about this little book-within-a-book, to the other works that have already preceded them in print, and to all that is yet to come. '*Mucho prometo con fuerzas tan pocas como las mías; pero ¿quien pondrá rienda a los deseos?*' I only beg you to remark: *que pues yo he tenido osadía de dirigir estas ficciones al gran Cervantes, algún misterio tienen escondido, que las levanta. Vale.*

o   o   o

I

Panel Game

Situation: television panel game, live audience. Stage strobelit and cameras insecting about. Moderator, bag shape corseted and black suited, behind desk/rostrum, blinking mockmodesty at lens and lamps, practised pucker on his soft mouth and brows arched in mild goodguy astonishment. Opposite him, the panel: Aged Clown, Lovely Lady, and Mr America, fat as the continent and bald as an eagle. There is an empty chair between Lady and Mr A, which is now filled, to the delighted squeals of all, by a spectator dragged protesting from the Audience, nondescript introduced as Unwilling Participant, or more simply, Bad Sport. Audience: same as ever, docile, responsive, good-natured, terrifying. And the Bad Sport, you ask, who is he? fool! thou art!

'*Welcome!*' greets the merry Moderator, arms flung wide, and the Audience, cued to Thunderous Response, responds thunderingly: 'TO THE BIG QUESTION!'

You squirm, viced by Lady (who excites you) and America (who does not, but bless him all the same), but your squirms are misread: Lovely Lady lifts lashes, crosses eyes, and draws breath excitedly through puckered mouth as though sucking milkshakes through a straw, and, seemingly at the other end of the straw, the Moderator ingests: 'Tsk, tsk!' and, gently reproving, waggles his dewlaps. Audience howls happily the while and who can blame them? You, Sport, resign yourself to pass the test in peace and salute them with a timid smile, squirm no more.

A moment then of calm, but Aged Clown spoils it, quips in an old croak: 'Very bad comma Sport!'

Audience roars again. Cameras swing, bend, spring forward, recoil. Lights boil up, dim, pivot, strike.

'Reminds me of the old story of the three-spined stickleback!' Clown cackles.

Howls and chants. Moderator reacts with flushed giggle and finger to soft lips. No, no! Winks at Audience.

Mr America nudges you and mutters under the others' noise: 'Detail! Detail! Game's built on it, don't miss it!' A friend, after all.

So think. Stickleback. Freshwater fish. Freshwater fish: green seaman. Seaman: semen. Yes, but green: raw? spoiled? vigorous? Stickle: stubble. Or maybe scruple. Back: Bach: Bacchus: baccate: berry. Raw berry? Strawberry? Maybe. Sticky berry in the raw? In the raw: bare. Bare berry: beriberi. Also bearberry, the dog rose, dogberry. Dogberry: the constable, yes, right, the constable in ... what? *Comedy of Errors!* Yes! No.

'And so this here boy stickleback he shimmies up to the girl stickleback and she displays him her crimson belly. Hoo boy! That does it! Zam! They scoot down to his pad!'

Hooting and howling. Moderator collapses into easy laughter. Lamps pulse. Lovely Lady shyly reveals belly. Not crimson at all, but creamy with a blush of salmon pink. Shouts and whistles. Hoo-boys and zams. Salmon: semen. There we are again. Stickle: tickle. Belly: bag. Lovely one, too.

'I do believe,' chuckles the Moderator loosely, 'we might begin.'

'Too late, bub!' croaks Clown. 'Sport's done commenced!'

Horselaughs and catcalls. You forgo any further search for clues in Lovely's navel, shrink before the noise, before the jut of lenses, strike of strobes: Eyes of the World. On you, Sport.

'Think!' whispers America. 'She reveals! She reveals!'

Scoot: scute. But what: scales? shield? bone or horn? Scut is tail and pad is paw: an animal! Yes! But crimson: why not just red? Because crimson comes from kermes: insect – but more! *dried female insect bodies!* Shimmy: chemise, or a shimmer of light. But pad is stuff: female bellies dried and stuffed? Dryden-stuffed. It's possible. Stickle: stick: stich – a poem here, that's obvious. And some animal. Light. And Dogberry from—?

A hush ...

'Are you ready?' demands the Moderator, and the Audience replies: 'We are!'

Ready: red-dy. Red bone. Green semen. Naval: navel. Salmon pink.

'Then let us proceed!' Rounded syllables, dried and stuffed. 'I am quite reasonably certain – that is,' Moderator coughs and titters, 'I *believe* – MAY I HAVE THAT PRIVILEGE?'

'Yes! Yes!' cries the Audience.

'Of course he may,' whispers Mr America. 'He only asks out of malice.'

'Yes,' sighs the Moderator, solemnizing, 'for reasonable certainty is but the repercussion and ritornelle of belief!'

Vigorous applause, reverently paced.

'Huzzah!' hoots Aged Clown and the fat man nods. It could be so.

'Therefore, if you will allow me, I *believe*,' the Moderator continues, 'with what constitutes an almost categorical certitude—' swooping upwards on '-tude' till his voice cracks like a young boy's, extracting a jubilant '*Aaah!*' and easy laughter like a loose cough from the spectators, '– I beg your pardon!'

Gentle approving laughter.

'And so you *should*, son!' the old Clown cracks. Laughter. 'That ain't nice!' Larger laughter. 'You keep it clean now!' Gross laughter.

'Hint! Hint!' wheezes fat America.

Clean. Immaculate. Virgin. Verges. Aha! the headborough with

Dogberry in—? *The Merry Wives!* No. Verges: verger: verdure: hmmm, back to green again. Green scutes: greenhorns. Immaculate belly. Dogberry pink. Steal a glance: still there. Nice. Don't touch it, though. Eyes of the World. Keep it immaculate.

'Believe, then, as a certifiable category—'

'That's better, son.' More laughter and applause.

'Thank you.'

'Not at all, bub.' Clown grimaces. Laughter.

'—That all of you on our panel are well apprized of the precepts and procedures of our little – our – wonderfully *delightful* little game.'

From the masses packed beyond the lights: an explosion of cheering, an enthusiasm clearly insisting against demurrals, but you say: 'I'm not.'

Hush. Hostile maybe.

Moderator, into the silence, as though disbelieving: 'I beg your pardon?'

'Sport ain't!' hollers the Clown and you jump.

'Sport isn't,' Moderator corrects.

'That's what I said, he ain't!' responds Aged Clown. Crash of laughter. Nothing serious. All a joke.

'The one who has most money wins,' mutters Mr America under his breath, which is coming heavier now. Excitement? Not likely. Growth. Yes, expanding still, the old lard, some accretion process turned on early and the safety valve plugged, cells piling up, and rapidly, for your own rump is skidding perceptibly under pressure along the bench towards the Lady. She is self-absorbed, powdering her nose and her bosom, using a camera lens for a mirror. Eyes of the World: white globes and pupils pink as raspberries.

She turns, lifts bodice, smiles at you. 'Isn't what?' she asks, cooing.

'Isn't got it!' quips the old showman on the other side of her. Does he have his old gnarled fist between her legs? From the Audience: the usual response. They love him. Shrunken and yellowed, mapped with wrinkles, quaking with palsy, white-haired and brown-toothed, Clown's a remnant from the Great Tradition. But not much help. On the contrary.

'Got what?' pursues Lovely Lady. 'Come on, boys! You're teasing me! Hasn't got what?'

'My dear ... !' pleads the Moderator, giggling softly but with brows lifted in tender supplication. Whoops and whistles from the Audience.

'Oh, really!' laughs Lady sweetly. 'You can tell me! Is it something I can wear?'

'You're warm!' crows Clown mid the laughter and whacks her behind.

'Mind on your business!' whispers America, now in possession of at least half the whole bench, his eyes lost in puffing fleshfolds, suitseams parting, buttons popping. 'Here it comes!'

'Would I wear it, more likely, above the waist,' Lady asks, then reddens and lowers lashes, 'or below?'

'Depends on your scruples!' Clown squawks and the crowd roars.

Hah! Scruple: stickle: stickleback. Getting warm now. Warm indeed: flush against the Lovely Lady. Are those her toes under your pantleg? Don't jump to conclusions. Couldn't put it past the old Clown, for example, not if there was a laugh in it.

Big A groans faintly, snorting and sucking like a team of trotters, flesh pushing out as the suit tears. Wear and tear. Wear: bear. Bearberry: Dogberry: the dog rose. Paw and tail. But what of the scute? The dog rose and – what? Rose and scrupled? Rose: rows: stichs: stickleback. Going in circles. 'Depends—!' gasps America. Can't last long now. Own cells against him. Flesh dogbane pink. 'Depends—!'

Depends: hangs. But what hangs or hangs on what?

Old Clown hunches, trembling uncontrollably over knotted knuckles. Humour.

Lady: beauty, excitement, life itself.

America: hard to guess. Prestige maybe, or justice. Inclusion.

The team.

And Bad Sport? Ah, clearly, it's your *mind* they're after. Humour, passion, sobriety, and truth. On *you*, then, it depends, they depend, they all depend. They all hang. It may be so.

Odd silence. You look up to discover the Moderator drumming his ringed fingers on the rostrum and staring blankly at you. Yes, yes, the moment's come! They want to know! Cameras plunge, withdraw. Lamps blaze. You, pinned, sweat. Chilled by America's enveloping blubber, heated by the Lady pink as salmon. Pink as dog rose. As dogberry. *All's Well That Ends Well?* Hardly.

Still, in the silence, or so you tell yourself, so it seems: an aura of hope. Moderator relaxed, smiling kindly. Lifts brows in calm anticipation. Audience suppressed to a patient murmur. Will he do it? Will you do it? Fat man, perishing, balloons and snorts. Lovely Lady watches, admires. Encourages. They need you. You take strength from their need, and clear your throat.

'Oh, come, *come!*' exclaims the Moderator. 'Reckon you not this

old refrain? To replicate is but to repent and lost is less recalled!'
Applause and cheers greet his eloquence, accepting which he preens
and smiles. But what does it mean? *what does it mean?* 'Muteness is
mutinous and the mutable inscrutable!' cries the Moderator, warming to the moment now, riding on waves of grand hosannas. 'Inflex-
ibly same and *the lex of the game!*'

Nothing, nothing there at all. Think back. Wear and tear. Wary.
Tarry. Salmonberry. Faster! Sticklestuff and Dryden's belly. Crowd
roars. Moderator stands to bow. Crimson semen green as – ? Green
as – ? *Faster!* Could she wear it? Bear it? Bare it! That's it! Keep it
going! Keep it—!

'Too—!' gasps Mr America, blind and flaccid, nearly faceless,
and he has no breath to finish, yet his mouth gapes, struggling.

You speak: 'I think—'

'*Admirable!*' smiles the Moderator grimly, bringing caustic laughter from the Audience. 'So what?'

'—That, if the subject is animal—'

Unexpected crash of laughter. Lady blushes, lowers lashes. Moderator, crimson with giggling and with tears in his eyes, cries: 'Good
God! I should hate to conceive of it otherwise!' Whoop! goes the
Audience, louder than ever, and even the cameras twitch spasmodically.

'Keep it clean, son!' cackles the Aged Clown.

'But—!'

'I said, *keep it clean!*'

Immaculate butt? Incredible!

'—Late!' concludes the fat man, releases wind, and dies. Dead. Only
friend in the house. No loss felt, but no relief either. The challenge
is still the same one.

'Come, *come*, sir!' cries the Moderator, much amused, but rising
now and pressing forward. 'You *must* have contrived some concrete
conjunctions from the incontrovertible commentary *qua* commentary
just so conspicuously constituted!' Deafening applause.

Dig in! Tie it up! The truth is: 'The truth is—'

'The truth is,' shouts the Moderator, jabbing at him with an angry
finger, '*you have lost!*'

'But I haven't even—!'

'*Why are you here,*' the Moderator explodes, losing all patience,
'if not to endeavour to disentangle this entanglement? In short, Bad
Sport, you would be wise to remember that THE SAGA OF SAGACITY IS
THE PURSE OF PERSPICACITY!' Wild applause, cheers, hoots, screams.
'REASON IS THE RESIN, THE COLLEGE OF KNOWLEDGE!' Uncontrollable

uproar. Moderator rips off bowtie and flings it like a rose to the stamping shrieking crowd. Lamps flame up. 'FAILED! YOU HAVE FAILED! AND YOU MUST PAY THE CONSEQUENCES!'

'But the truth is—'

'The truth is,' crows the old Clown and leaps upon the table; Lovely Lady takes his quaking claw and hops up to join him:

> *'There once was a young bellydancer—'*

Lady strips to half chemise as Audience whistles and heaves coins to the stage. Somewhere a brass band plays Eastern music. With her thumbs, she pushes the chemise to half-mast on her hips. Wear it: bare it, bright as berries, and the old dog rose . . .

> *'Who supposed that her art was the answer—'*

Above or below? Waist: waste. Scruples, pink as salmon. Crimson. Female belly, darts and thrusts . . .

> *'But one night in a bump,*
> *She fractured her rump—'*

Lovely Lady halts abruptly, knees bent out, twitching like a spastic, navel aimed at you: Eye of the World — then staggers, thus in mid-bump, about the table, eyes wide and mouth puckered, to the convulsive delight of the entire world, then drops — BAM! — stiff as a scute to the table . . .

> *'—And perished grotesquely of cancer!'*

Audience paroxysms reach new frenzies as Lady vibrates in last throes and ossifies, legs up towards the lenses.

'Yes, the truth is,' gasps the guffawing Moderator when he's able, wiping his eyes with a linen cloth:

> *'Don't twiddle or piddle*
> *Or diddle your middle*
> *While riding a riddle, old Sport—'*

Lovely Lady miraculously revives, and with a wink of the Eye of the World, lures you to the tabletop. Laughs crash and thunder. Whistles, catcalls, hostile hoots. Cameras crouch, pounce, jab, retract. The fat man, you see, was not Mr America after all, but Mr Amentia. Should have known. Changes everything ...

> '—For the frame is the same
> In fame or in shame
> And the name of the game—'

Clown and Lady grip an arm apiece. A noose descends – yes, yes, it all depends ...

> '—is La Mort!'

'I thought—' But the Audience drowns you out. Well, they are happy, think about that. The noose is fitted.

'You thought—?' asks the Moderator and the crowd subsides.

'I thought it was all for fun.'

'That is to say,' smiles the Moderator wearily, 'much ado about nothing.'

'That's it! *that's it!* Yes! *that's* what I was *trying* to—!'

The Moderator shakes his head. At heart, a tough old boy. 'Sorry.' He rests his chins in his pudgy fist, smile informed by a surfeit of knowledge. Nods gravely at Clown and Lady.

'Keep it clean, son!' rattles the old Clown, jabbing you good-humouredly with his elbow. Well of laughter. Always the laughter. A second constant.

Noose is scratchy. Tickles your throat. Swallow. Can't swallow.

Lovely Lady's scented breath is in your ear. 'Don't be gone long, darling,' she coos and dispatches you with a parting goose. *Whoop!* Off you go!

The dog rose and there depended

Lamps expand – WHAP!

burst into crimson flares ...

Eyes of the

So long, Sport.

o   o   o

2

The Marker

Of the seven people (Jason, his wife, the police officer, and the officer's four assistants), only Jason and his wife are in the room. Jason is sitting in an armchair with a book in his hand, a book he has doubtless been reading, although now he is watching his wife get ready for bed. About Jason: he is tall and masculine, about 35, with strong calloused hands and a sensitive nose; he is deeply in love with his wife. And she: she is beautiful, affectionate, and has a direct and charming manner of speaking, if we were to hear her speak. She seems always at ease.

Nude now, she moves lightly about the room, folding a sweater into a drawer, hanging up Jason's jacket which he had tossed on the bed, picking up a comb from the floor where it had fallen from the chest of drawers. She moves neither pretentiously nor shyly. Whatever meaning there might be in her motion exists within the motion itself and not in her deliberations.

At last, she folds back the blankets of the bed (which is across the room from Jason), fluffs her short blonde hair, crawls onto the fresh sheets on her hands and knees, pokes gently at the pillows, then rolls down on her back, hands under her head, gazing across the room at Jason. She watches him, with the same apparent delight in least motions, as he again picks up his book, finds his place in it, and inserts a marker. He stands, returns her gaze for almost a minute without smiling, and then does smile, at the same time placing his book on the table. He removes his clothes, hooking his trousers over the back of the armchair and tossing the other things on the seat cushion. Before extinguishing the light behind his chair, he glances across the room at his wife once more, her tanned body gay and relaxed, a rhythm of soft lines on the large white canvas of the bed. She smiles, in subtle recognition perhaps of the pleasure he finds in her. He snaps out the light.

In the darkness, Jason pauses a moment in front of the armchair. The image of his wife, as he has just seen her, fades slowly (as when, lying on a beach, one looks at the reflection of the sun on the curving back of the sea, then shuts tight his eyes, letting the image of the reflected sun lose its brilliance, turn green, then evaporate slowly into the limbo of uncertain associations), gradually becoming transformed from that of her nude body crackling the freshness of the laundered sheets to that of Beauty, indistinct and untextured, as though still emerging from some profound ochre mist, but though without definition, an abstract Beauty that contains somehow his wife's ravaging smile and musical eyes. Jason, still facing the bed, walks steadily towards it, his right hand in front of him to feel for it in the dark. When he has reached the spot where he expects the bed, he is startled not to find it. He retraces his steps, and stumbles into ... what? the chest of drawers! Reoriented now by the chest of drawers, he sets out again and, after some distance, touches a wall. He starts to call out to his wife, but hears her laugh suddenly: she is up to some kind of joke, he says to himself with a half-smile. He walks boldly towards the laugh, only to find himself – quite by surprise – back at the armchair! He fumbles for the lamp and snaps the switch, but the light does not turn on. He snaps the switch several times, but the lamp definitely does not work. She has pulled the plug, he says to himself, but without really believing it, since he could not imagine any reason she would have for doing so. Once again, he positions himself in front of the armchair and crosses the room towards the bed. This time, however, he does not walk confidently, and although almost expecting something of the sort, is no less alarmed when he arrives at, not the bed, but a door. He gropes along the wall, past a radiator and a wastebasket, until he reaches a corner. He starts out along the second wall, working methodically now, but does not take more than five steps when he hears his wife's gentle laugh right in his ear. He turns around and finds the bed ... just behind him!

Although in the strange search he has lost his appetite for the love act, he quickly regains it at the sound of her happy laugh and the feel, in the dark, of her cool thighs. In fact, the experience, the anxiety of it and its riddles, seems to have created a new urgency, an almost brutal wish to swallow, for a moment, reason and its inadequacies, and to let passion, noble or not, have its hungry way. He is surprised to find her dry, but the entry itself is relaxed and gives way to his determined penetration. In a moment of alarm, he wonders if this is really his wife, but since there is no alternative possibility, he rejects his misgivings as absurd. He leans down over her to kiss her, and as he does so notices a strange and disagreeable odour.

At this moment, the lights come on and the police officer and his four assistants burst into the room.

'Really!' cries the police officer, pulling up short. 'This is *quite* disgusting.'

Jason looks down and finds that it is indeed his wife beneath him, but that she is rotting. Her eyes are open, but glazed over, staring up at him, without meaning, but bulging as though in terror of him. The flesh on her face is yellowish and drawn back towards her ears. Her mouth is open in a strangely cruel smile and Jason can see that her gums have dried and pulled back from her teeth. Her lips are black and her blonde hair, now long and tangled, is splayed out over the pillow like a urinal mop spread out to dry. There is a fuzzy stuff like mould around the nipples of her shrunken breasts. Jason tries desperately to get free from her body, but finds to his deepest horror that he is stuck!

'This woman has been dead for three weeks,' says the officer in genuine revulsion.

Jason strikes wildly against the thighs in his effort to free himself, jolts one leg off the bed so that it dangles there, disjointed and swinging, the long yellow toenails scratching on the wooden floor. The four assistants seize Jason and wrench him forcibly away from the corpse of his dead wife. The body follows him punishingly in movement for a moment, as a sheet of paper will follow a comb after the comb has been run through hair; then, freed by its own weight, it falls back in a pile on the badly soiled sheets. The four men carry Jason to the table where his book still lies with its marker in it. They hold him up against the table and the police officer, without ceremony, pulls Jason's genitals out flat on the tabletop and pounds them to a pulp with the butt of his gun.

He leaves Jason writhing on the floor and turns to march out, along with his four assistants. At the door he hesitates, then turns back to Jason. A flicker of compassion crosses his face.

'You understand, of course,' he says, 'that I am not, in the strictest sense, a traditionalist. I mean to say that I do not recognize tradition *qua* tradition as sanctified in its own sake. On the other hand, I do not join hands with those who find inherent in tradition some malignant evil, and who therefore deem it of terrible necessity that all custom be rooted out at all costs. I am personally convinced, if you will permit me, that there is a middle road, whereon we recognize that innovations find their best soil in traditions, which are justified in their own turn by the innovations which created them. I believe, then, that law and custom are essential, but that it is one's constant task to review and revise them. In spite of that, however, *some things still make me puke!*' He turns, flushed, to his four assistants. '*Now get rid of that fucking corpse!*' he screams.

After wiping his pink brow with a handkerchief, he puts it to his nose and turns his back on the bed as the men drag away, by the feet, the unhinged body of Jason's wife. The officer notices the book on the table, the book Jason has been reading, and walks over to pick it up. There is a slight spattering of blood on it. He flips through it hastily with one hand, the other still holding the handkerchief to his nose, and although his face wears an expression of mild curiosity, it is difficult to know if it is sincere. The marker falls to the floor beside Jason. The officer replaces the book on the table and walks out of the room.

'*The marker!*' Jason gasps desperately, but the police officer does not hear him, nor does he want to.

o   o   o

3

The Brother

right there right there in the middle of the damn field he says he wants to put that thing together him and his buggy ideas and so me I says 'how the hell you gonna get it down to the water?' but he just focuses me out sweepin the blue his eyes rollin like they do when he gets het on some new lunatic notion and he says not to worry none about that just would I help him for God's sake and because he don't know how he can get it done in time otherwise and though you'd have to be loonier than him to say yes I says I will of course I always would crazy as my brother is I've done little else since I was born and my wife she says 'I can't figure it out I can't see why you always have to be babyin that old fool he ain't never done nothin for you God knows and you got enough to do here fields need ploughin it's a bad enough year already my God and now that red-eyed brother of yours wingin around like a damn cloud and not knowin what in the world he's doin buildin a damn boat in the country my God what next? you're a damn fool I tell you' but packs me some sandwiches just the same and some sandwiches for my brother Lord knows *his* wife don't have no truck with him no more says he can go starve for all she cares she's fed up ever since the time he made her sit out on a hill-side for three whole days rain and everything because he said she'd see God and she didn't see nothin and in fact she like to die from hunger nothin but berries and his boys too they ain't so bright neither but at least they come to help him out with his damn boat so it ain't just the two of us thank God for *that* and it ain't no god-

damn fishin boat he wants to put up neither in fact it's the biggest
damn thing I ever heard of and for weeks *weeks* I'm tellin you we
ain't doin nothin but cuttin down pine trees and haulin them out to
his field which is really pretty high up a hill and my God *that's* work
lemme tell you and my wife she sighs and says I am crazy *r-e-a-l-l-y*
crazy and her four months with a child and tryin to do my work and
hers too and still when I come home from haulin timbers around all
day she's got enough left to rub my shoulders and the small of my
back and fix a hot meal her long black hair pulled to a knot behind
her head and hangin marvellously down her back her eyes gentle but
very tired my God and I says to my brother I says 'look I got a lotta
work to do buddy you'll have to finish this idiot thing yourself I
wanna help you all I can you know that but' and he looks off and he
says 'it don't matter none your work' and I says 'the hell it don't
how you think me and my wife we're gonna eat I mean where do you
think this food comes from you been puttin away man? you can't
eat this goddamn boat out here ready to rot in that bastard sun' and
he just sighs long and says 'no it just don't matter' and he sits him
down on a rock kinda tired like and stares off and looks like he
might even for God's sake cry and so I go back to bringing wood up
to him and he's already started on the keel and frame God knows
how *he* ever found out to build a damn boat lost in *his* fog where he
is Lord he was twenty when I was born and the first thing I remember was havin to lead him around so he didn't get kicked by a damn
mule him who couldn't never do nothin in a normal way just a huge
oversize fuzzyface boy so anyway I take to gettin up a few hours
earlier every day to do my farmin my wife apt to lose the baby if
she should keep pullin around like she was doin then I go to work on
the boat until sundown and on and on the days hot and dry and my
wife keepin good food in me or else I'd of dropped sure and no
matter what I say to try and get out of it my brother he says 'you
come and help now the rest don't matter' and we just keep ham-
merin away and my God the damn thing is big enough for a hundred
people and at least I think at *least* it's a place to live and not too
bad at that at least it's good for somethin but my wife she just sighs
and says no good will come of it and runs her hands through my
hair but she don't ask me to stop helpin no more because she knows
it won't do no good and she's kinda turned into herself now these
days and gettin herself all ready and still we keep workin on that
damn thing that damn boat and the days pass and my brother he says
we gotta work harder we ain't got much time and from time to time
he gets a coupla neighbours to come over and give a hand them

sucked in by the size and the novelty of the thing makin jokes some
but they don't stay around more than a day or two and they go away
shakin their heads and swearin under their breath and disgusted they
got weaseled into the thing in the first place and me I only get about
half my place planted and see to my stock as much as I can my wife
she takes more care of them than I can but at least we won't starve
we say if we just get some rain and finally we get the damn thing
done all finished by God and we cover it in and out with pitch and put
a kinda fancy roof on it and I come home on that last day and I ain't
never goin back ain't *never* gonna let him talk me into nothin again
and I'm smellin of tar and my wife she cries and cries and I says to
her not to worry no more I'll be home all the time and me I'm cryin a
little too though she don't notice just thinkin how she's had it so
lonely and hard and all and for one whole day I just sleep the whole
damn day and the rest of the week I work around the farm and one
day I get an idea and I go over to my brother's place and get some
pieces of wood left over and whaddaya know? they are all livin on
that damn boat there in the middle of nowhere him and his boys and
some women and my brother's wife she's there too but she's madder
than hell and carpin at him to get outa that damn boat and come
home and he says she's got just one more day and then he's gonna
drug her on the boat but he don't say it like a threat or nothin more
like a fact a plain fact tomorrow he's gonna drug her on the boat
well I ain't one to get mixed up in domestic quarrels God knows so
I grab up the wood and beat it back to my farm and that evenin I
make a little cradle a kinda fancy one with little animal figures cut
in it and polished down and after supper I give it to my wife as a
surprise and she cries and cries and holds me tight and says don't
never go away again and stay close by her and all and I feel so damn
good and warm about it all and glad the boat thing is over and we
get out a little wine and we decide the baby's name is gonna be either
Nathaniel or Anna and so we drink an extra cup to Nathaniel's
health and we laugh and we sigh and drink one to Anna and my wife
she gently fingers the little animal figures and says they're beautiful
and really they ain't I ain't much good at that sorta thing but I
know what she means and then she says 'where did you get the
wood?' and I says 'it's left over from the boat' and she don't say
nothin for a moment and then she says 'you been over there again
today?' and I says 'yes just to get the wood' and she says 'what's he
doin now he's got the boat done?' and I says 'funny thing they're all
living in the damn thing all except the old lady she's over there
hollerin at him how he's gettin senile and where does he think he's

sailin to and how if he ain't afraid of runnin into a octypuss on the
way he oughta get back home and him sayin she's a nut there ain't
no water and her sayin *that's* what she's been tellin *him* for six
months' and my wife laughs and it's the happiest laugh I've heard
from her in half a year and I laugh and we both have another cup of
wine and my wife she says 'so he's just livin on that big thing all
by hisself?' and I says 'no, he's got his boys on there and some young
women who are maybe wives of the boys or somethin I don't know
I ain't never seen them before and all kindsa damn animals and birds
and things I ain't never seen the likes' and my wife she says 'animals?
what animals?' and I says 'oh all kinds I don't know a whole damn
menagerie all clutterin and stinkin up the boat *God* what a mess'
and my wife laughs again and she's a little silly with the wine and
she says 'I bet he ain't got no pigs' and 'oh yes I seen them' I says
and we laugh thinkin about pigs rootin around in that big tub and
she says 'I bet he ain't got no jackdaws' and I says 'yes I seen a
couple of them too or mostly I heard them you couldn't hardly hear
nothin else' and we laugh again thinkin about them crows and his
old lady and the pigs and all and my wife she says '*I* know what he
ain't got I bet he ain't got no lice' and we both laugh like crazy
and when I can I says 'oh yes he does less he's took a bath' and
we both laugh till we're cryin and we finish off the wine and my
wife says 'look now I know what he *ain't* got he ain't got no termites' and I says 'you're right I don't recollect no termites maybe
we oughta make him a present' and my wife she holds me close
quiet all of a sudden and says 'he's really movin Nathaniel's really
movin' and she puts my hand down on her round belly and the little
fella is kickin up a terrific storm and I says kinda anxious 'does it
hurt? do you think that – ' and 'no' she says 'it's good' she says and
so I says with my hand on her belly 'here's to you Nathaniel' and
we drain what's left in the bottom of our cups and the next day
we wake up in each other's arms and it's rainin and *thank God* we
say and since it's rainin real good we stay inside and do things
around the place and we're happy because the rain has come just in
time and in the evenin things smell green and fresh and delicious
and it's still rainin a little but not too hard so I decide to take a
walk and I wander over by my brother's place thinkin I'll ask him if
he'd like to take on some pet termites to go with his collection and
there by God is his wife on the boat and I don't know if he drug
her on or if she just finally come by herself but she ain't sayin
nothin which is damn unusual and the boys they ain't sayin nothin
neither and my brother he ain't sayin nothin they're just all standin

up there on top and gazin off and I holler up at them 'nice rain ain't
it?' and my brother he looks down at me standin there in the rain
and still he don't say nothin but he raises his hand kinda funny
like and then puts it back on the rail and I decide not to say
nothin about the termites and it's startin to rain a little harder again
so I turn away and go back home and I tell my wife about what
happened and my wife she just laughs and says 'they're *all* crazy
he's finally got them *all* crazy' and she's cooked me up a special
pastry with fresh meat and so we forget about them but by God
the next day the rain's still comin down harder than ever and water's
beginnin to stand around in places and after a week of rain I can see
the crops is pretty well ruined and I'm havin trouble keepin my stock
fed and my wife she's cryin and talkin about our bad luck that we
might as well of built a damn boat as plant all them crops and still
we don't figure things out I mean it just don't come to our minds
not even when the rain keeps spillin down like a ocean dumped
upsidedown and now water is beginnin to stand around in big
pools really big ones and water up to the ankles around the house
and leakin in and pretty soon the whole damn house is gettin fulla
water and I keep sayin maybe we oughta go use my brother's boat
till this blows over but my wife she says 'never' and then she starts
cryin again so finally I says to her I says 'we can't be so proud I'll
go ask him' and so I set out in the storm and I can hardly see where
I'm goin and I slip up to my neck in places and finally I get to where
the boat is and I holler up and my brother he comes out and he
looks down at where I am and he don't say nothin that bastard he
just looks at me and I shout up at him I says 'hey is it all right for
me and my wife to come over until this thing blows over?' and still
he don't say a damn word he just raises his hand in that same silly-
ass way and I holler 'hey you stupid sonuvabitch I'm soakin wet
goddamn it and my house is fulla water and my wife she's about
to have a kid and she's apt to get sick all wet and cold to the bone
and all I'm askin you—' and right then right while I'm still talkin
he turns around and he goes back in the boat and I can't hardly
believe it me his brother but he don't come back out and I push up
under the boat and I beat on it with my fists and scream at him
and call him ever name I can think up and I shout for his boys and
for his wife and for anybody inside and nobody comes out 'GOD*damn*
you' I cry out at the top of my lungs and half sobbin and sick and
then feelin too beat out to do anythin more I turn around and head
back for home but the rain is thunderin down like mad now and
in places I gotta swim and I can't make it no further and I recollect

a hill nearby and I head for it and when I get to it I climb up on top of it and it feels good to be on land again even if it is soggy and greasy and I vomit and retch there awhile and move further up and the next thing I know I'm wakin up the rain still in my face and the water halfway up the hill towards me and I look out and I can see my brother's boat is floatin and I wave at it but I don't see nobody wave back and then I quick look out towards my own place and all I can see is the top of it and of a sudden I'm scared scared about my wife and I go tearin for the house swimmin most all the way and cryin and shoutin and the rain still comin down like crazy and so now well now I'm back here on the hill again what little there is left of it and I'm figurin maybe I got a day left if the rain keeps comin and it don't show no signs of stoppin and I can't see my brother's boat no more gone just water how *how* did he know? that bastard and yet I gotta hand it to him it's not hard to see who's crazy around here I can't see my house no more I just left my wife inside where I found her I couldn't hardly stand to look at her the way she was

o   o   o

4

In a Train Station

At 9.27 Alfred purchases a ticket from the Stationmaster for the 10.18 Express Train to Winchester.

Here's Alfred: squat, work-stooped, thick white moustache on his upper lip, pale blue eyes, white hair nearly gone on top, face and neck tanned and leathery, appears to be about fifty-two. He wears an unfashionable grey suit, loose on him and stained from the knees down, a blue checked shirt buttoned at the neck without tie, bulky thick-soled brown shoes caked with field mud. In his left hand (gold ring on it) he carries his squarish soft-billed cap, while he conducts the ticket transaction with his right. He stuffs the ticket into his coat pocket, then picks up the small bag at his feet.

The 10.18 Express Train to Winchester: it is not now in the station, and little need be said about it. It is mainly for passengers and happens to be electric. It leaves always at 10.18 from Track 2.

Now, assuming both Alfred and the Express Train to be real (to say nothing of the contract of the ticket), it will perhaps seem strange to some that when the train departs for Winchester exactly fifty-one minutes after Alfred buys his ticket – that is to say, on time – Alfred is not on it.

But to return . . .

After obtaining his ticket, pocketing it with that old man's whole-hand-into-pocket gesture, and picking up the small bag, Alfred shuffles heavily a few feet from the ticket window to a bench which faces the gate to Track 2 and the clock over it. The station is empty except for Alfred and the Stationmaster. A couple ceiling lamps glow dully. A bare bulb umbrella'd by a green metal shade brightens harshly the Stationmaster's small office. The station smells of musty wood.

Alfred puts his bag on the bench and sits down beside it. As he sits, he sighs, as though the mere act of sitting is an awful strain on him. Once seated, he sighs again and gazes straight ahead of him at the Track 2 gate, his cap in his lap.

Behind him, the Stationmaster writes something in a large elongated ledger, and as he does so, glances up at the clock over the Track 2 gate. 9.29. 'Nice evenin',' he says.

'Yep, nice enough at that,' says Alfred. 'May rain tomorra.'

'Low pressure area movin' in, I hear tell.'

'Yep. Good for the crops, though,' says Alfred.

'Been doin' much fishin' lately?'

'Nope, I ain't. Been too blamed hot for fishin'.'

'What d'ye catch mostly?'

'Oh, smallmouth. Bluegills.' All the while, Alfred continues to stare at the gate to Track 2, sitting slumped and expressionless, his cap in his lap.

'Oh, that so? Fish for bluegill, do ye?'

'Yep,' says Alfred. 'They're small, but they make good eatin'.'

'Yep, so they do. Well. And how's the family?'

'Cain't complain. Wife's been a bit poorly, but she's gittin' on better, now the summer's come on.'

'Oh? Ain't been nothin' serious, I hope.'

'Nope,' says Alfred. 'Jist female troubles.'

'Them's pretty fine lookin' vittles,' the Stationmaster continues, his voice pitched slightly louder. 'Your wife put 'em up for ye?'

Alfred fumbles nervously in his bag, produces a greasy brown paper sack. From it, he now draws an apple, an egg, a jackknife, and a small chicken leg wrapped in wax paper. He puts the apple, the knife, and the egg in his upturned cap, drops the paper sack beside the bag, and unwraps the chicken. It has already been partly eaten. His hands are trembling. 'Yep,' he says faintly. 'She's one good cook.' He hesitates, then bites resolutely into the chicken.

'That's a lucky man who's got him a good woman and good food and good work,' the Stationmaster says.

Alfred tears off a bite of chicken leg and chews it slowly, absently. So far, he has not veered his gaze from the gate to Track 2. The clock above it reads 9.33. He stops chewing, opens his mouth as though to speak, but does not.

The Stationmaster looks up at him through the ticket window. After a moment, he says: 'And a . . .'

'And a . . .' says Alfred, his mouth still full of half-chewed chicken leg. But his eyes are puzzled and he does not continue.

'And a good . . .'

'And a good wife!' cries Alfred. Both men laugh. Alfred returns to his chewing.

'Well, it looks like the old 10.18 will be in on time tonight,' says the Stationmaster, returning to his ledger.

'Good,' replies Alfred. 'Good. Don't wanna git home late. Not on a Sattiday night.' He wraps the leg of chicken in the wrinkled wax paper, returns it to the paper sack, along with the apple and the egg. The apple has a few bites taken from it and the cavities have turned brown. It has been a long time since the apple has been tried. The egg is still whole. He reopens the canvas bag on the bench beside him, peers inside, stuffs the paper sack back into it, closes the bag. He sighs. Then he notices the jackknife still in the cap in his lap. He stares sullenly at it. Then, suddenly, as though terrified, he grabs up the knife, reopens the bag, thrusts the knife inside, snaps the bag shut. Visibly shaken, he sits back and, staring once more at the Track 2 gate, continues to chew mechanically on his unswallowed bite of chicken leg.

Both men are silent for a while. The Stationmaster, finally, closes his ledger, squints up at the clock. 9.42. 'How's the tomaters doin' this year?' he asks.

'Aw, well as kin be expected. Need a – look!' Alfred spins suddenly around to confront the Stationmaster, his pale blue eyes damp as though with tears. 'Don't ye think maybe this time I could – ?'

'Need a little . . .' intones the Stationmaster softly, firmly.

Alfred sighs, turns back towards the gate, works his jaws over the chicken. 'Need a little rain,' he says glumly.

'Whole area could use some rain,' responds the Stationmaster.

Just then, at 9.44, the door of the station bangs open and a man stumbles in. He is tall and thin with uncombed dark hair, a couple days' growth of beard. Khaki pants, grey undershirt, tennis shoes, the laces broken and reknotted. He introduces with him a large odour of stale alcohol, and his eyes, though blue and as if thoughtful, focus on no fixed thing. He lurches for a bench, misses, smashes up against a wall. Leaning there, he breathes deeply, his eyes rolling back.

Alfred, all the while, is watching him. His face has blanched, his hands quaver. The Stationmaster is watching Alfred.

'Belovéd!' cries the intruder, grinning foolishly, heaving himself away from the wall. He weaves. 'The su'jeck f'my dishcoursh is ...' He slams back against the wall again, gasping brokenly. Alfred watches, paralysed. 'The su'jeck ... the su'jeck ... aw, *fuck it!*' and the man careens away from the wall, collapses over the back of the bench nearest him.

Alfred glances anxiously at the Stationmaster, who is still observing him calmly, back at the tall man folded over the bench, up at the clock (9.45), back at the man.

The stranger slowly lifts his head, braces himself half-erect with his hands against the bench, looks toward Alfred, but blearily, without focus. 'Our fazher,' he cries out, then sucks the spittle off his lips and swallows it, 'our fazher whish art 'n heaven ... 'n heaven ... *is eating hish own goddamn chil'ren!*' And, staring down appalled at the bench under him, the man vomits all over it, rolls off to the floor, lies there with his hands over his face.

Alfred, chewing frantically, fumbles with the bag, looks up at the clock. 10.01.

The man on the floor shudders, then with great effort pulls himself to his feet. His eyes cross and a string of vomit drips from his mouth. He wipes his mouth, then drops his hands limply to his sides. He twitches as though with unresolved retchings. His face is white. The stubble on his chin glistens. He takes an uncertain step towards Alfred, pauses, takes another. Alfred unsnaps the bag. 'So *help* me!' cries the tall man, focusing that instant on Alfred – then he reels, his eyes rolling back, and topples over towards Alfred. Alfred drops the bag, reaches out, catches the man in his fall, eases him to his back on the floor. In the excitement, he has unwittingly swallowed the bite of chicken leg. He looks guiltily at his own hands, then down at his feet. His lower lip is trembling.

'Alfred!' scolds the Stationmaster. 'Alfred! Shame, *shame!*'

There are tears in Alfred's eyes. He turns his head upward towards the clock, brushes the tears aside. 10.13. He utters a short pained cry, grabs up the canvas bag, scratches desperately through it. He tears out the paper sack, pokes inside it, pitches it away. Again he searches through the canvas bag, draws out the jackknife, throws the bag away, crouches over the fallen man. 10.14.

'Well?' demands the Stationmaster harshly. 'Well, Alfred?'

Alfred squeezes shut his eyes, takes a long desperate breath. Opening his eyes again, he drops quickly down over the man on the floor. He clicks open the knife, grasps the fallen man's hair. The man is sleeping fitfully. Under his white moustache, Alfred's lips are parted, his teeth clenched. A faint whining animal complaint escapes between them. As though struggling against an unseen hand, he presses the knifeblade downwards, touches it finally to the man's throat, but, with a short anguished cry, withdraws it.

'It is 10.16, Alfred,' announces the Stationmaster quietly. Outside, one can indeed hear the 10.18 Express Train to Winchester arriving.

The knife drops from Alfred's hand. He is crying. He presses his hands to his face.

The Stationmaster emerges from his office, kneels down beside Alfred, picks up the knife. 'Now, watch, Alfred,' he says. 'Watch!'

Alfred peeks through his hands, weeping, whimpering, as the Stationmaster severs the tall stranger's head with three quick strokes. The eyes on the head pop open suddenly and the body jerks spasmodically for a moment. Blood gurgles out of the man's neck, staining Alfred's trousers where he kneels on the floor. Alfred continues to weep beside the long body, which twitches still with small private reflexes of its own, as the Stationmaster carries the head into his office. He returns, lifts the body up on his shoulders, and carries it out the door. The carcass can be heard tumbling down steps.

When the Stationmaster returns, Alfred is still kneeling on the floor, weeping. The clock above the gate to Track 2 says 10.18, and one can hear a train outside sound its whistle, then pull away. The Stationmaster looks down at Alfred, sighs shortly, shakes his head, then walks over towards the Track 2 gate. There is a chair there, which the Stationmaster now slides under the clock. He stands on the chair, opens the glass that protects the clock dial, moves the hands around until they read 9.26. He steps down from the chair, slides it back to its former position, returns to his office. Alfred studies the clock, shudders, wearily gathers up his scattered possessions and places them once again in the canvas bag. The Stationmaster reopens the ledger. Alfred walks up to the ticket window, his cap in his hand.

o   o   o

5

Klee Dead

Klee, Wilbur Klee, dies. Is dead, rather. I know I know: too soon. It should come, after a package of hopefully ingenious preparations, at the end: and thus, gentle lector, Wilbur Klee is gathered to his fathers. But what's to be done? He's already gone. The city clerk has, with customary dispatch, shifted his file, just before lunch in fact, and the city clerk, public toady that he is, is not one to suffer any meddler's disturbance of things as they are and – as he would put in – must be. Not even for a bribe, certainly not for any kind of bribe that I could offer, not even for tickets to the circus. The city clerk, in short, is a surly sonuvabitch, quite beyond the touch of human sops; and so Klee is, irretrievably, dead.

In some languages, it is possible to say: *to die oneself*, as in: I die myself, you will die yourself, he would have died himself, and so on, cunningly planting the idea that one's own hand was perhaps involved. (Which, if I may say so in passing, would seem to have been the case with Wilbur Klee.) But unluckily I don't know any of these other languages – God knows I wouldn't be bludgeoning you with my insufferable English if I did – and even if I did know them it would be inconceivable I should know them well, conjugations above all, in which case my circumlocutions would only make you laugh and forget that the point of the matter is that *Klee is dead and he quite likely did it himself*, to hell with friends, family, lovers, employers, gods, countries, and anyone else who had designs on him. Providing he was in fact encumbered with any of these, and who on this earth can doubt that he was?

Yet, contrarily, old Millicent Gee is not dead, either by her own hand or any other. Perhaps you don't know Millicent Gee . . . ? Well, I can't blame you for that. She lives, in a manner of speaking, on State Street between Twelfth and Fourteenth Avenues, the absence of a Thirteenth Avenue being a preclusion, not an oversight, of our City Fathers who had every reason to expect a little bad luck, lives there in a multistory unrenovated brownstone. Millie, a believable if somewhat scabby old lady, well into her dotage, keeps house alone in the basement along with her old ram whom she tactlessly calls Lothario, her stagnant aquariums, and her vast – and for our purposes, nameless – assemblage of interfiliated cats, who provide Millie a little vicarious pleasure to lighten the daily press of care: little fuckers! Millie has been heard (her windows are always open, winter and summer, little square windows down at ground level, yet, from the inside, above Millie's reach, which helps account for the fact she has never closed them – what, in this makeshift world, is not hopelessly flawed?) to cackle from time to time, and one must assume she is referring to the cats. The fish have been dead for some time.

What Millie keeps on the several floors aboveground can only be guessed, and for my part it's her own business. Rumours are rife, but not to be trusted. Above all: not to be encouraged. The Constitution says enough about the promulgation of rumours, no need for lectures here. Thank God for the Constitution. What*ever* she keeps up there, though, one thing is certain: it is not likely to be or have been human. Millie wouldn't stand for it. And perhaps there is nothing up there at all. To be sure, we seem impulsively driven to load up empty spaces, to plump some goddamn thing, any object, real, imagined, or otherwise, where now there might happily be nothing, a peaceful unsullied and unpeopled emptiness, and maybe that's what she hides up there, who knows?

But, not to be taken in by our own biases, this much needs to be said: Millie, all efforts to the contrary notwithstanding, is not entirely divorced from humankind, and there is reason therefore to doubt that she has let all that upper space go for nothing. Her son – God knows how she came by him – has no part to play in her life, apparently his own choice. He no longer lives with old Millie, but resides elsewhere in an efficiency apartment. He passes by here occasionally to attend the seasonal devotions, in which he participates in all good humour and kindness, finely done up in his clover-green suit and stovepipe hat with its ostrich feather, which, I'm told on good authority, has something to do with his profession and is not, therefore, to be laughed at. There is no point saying much more about him, even were I capable of it, he never visits his mother, smiles at the idea of duty or obligations, and perhaps is not really her son at all, merely the victim of well-intentioned but wrongheaded gossip. To tell the truth, I wish I hadn't brought him up in the first place. Please forget I mentioned him, if you can. What's more, I'm not entirely sure why I told you about Millie. Certainly, she can have nothing to do with Wilbur Klee. In fact, I smile to think of it, that unconscious old nanny. Perhaps it was merely to demonstrate, before facing up to Klee, that I could tell a story without bringing the hero to some lurid sensational end, and who but Millie could that hero be? In any case, whatever it was led me this way, let me say in conclusion: God preserve old Millicent Gee! it's the least I can do.

As for Wilbur Klee, I've not much more to say about him either, you'll be glad to know, just this: that he jumped from a high place and is now dead. I think you can take my word for it. The proof is, as it were, here in the pudding. Need I tell you from *what* high place? Your questions, friend, are foolish, disease of the western mind. On the other hand, if you wish to assume a cause-and-effect relationship —that he is dead *because* he jumped from a high place—well, you are free to do so, I confess it has occurred to me more than once and has coloured my whole narration. Certainly, there is *some* relationship: the remains of Klee, still moist, are splattered out in their now several and discontinuous parts from a point directly below the high place from which he jumped only a moment before. But that's as far as I'll go, thank you. I refuse to be inveigled into any of the almost endless and no doubt learned arguments which so gratify and absorb the nation's savants. I don't mean to belittle, a man must take his pleasures where he finds them, it's only that, if I weren't careful, one would think before they'd had done with me that Klee had died to save physics. That Klee is dead, however, leaves less room for dissent: he'll never be the same again and only the worst sort of morbid emotionalism could imagine a suitable future for him in his present condition. So here is where I'll stand my ground: Klee is dead. As for the rest of it, if you wish to believe as I do that he took his own life, fine! It certainly will make it easier for me as we wind this up. But I won't be dogmatic about it.

Who was Klee, you ask? I do not know, I do not care. (*If* I knew do you think I would have broken silence for such a matter as this — or any man's — death? Really, my friend, you do me an injustice and forget my vows. Though this is no disparagement. I confess, I forget them frequently myself.) Wilbur Klee was Wilbur Klee, that's where it starts and ends. And already I may have pushed too far, perhaps that's not his name at all, I may have made it up, very likely in fact, given my peculiar and unprincipled penchant for logogriphics — but no matter! Whether it was his name or not, it will do as well as any other.

But enough of Klee! It's time for an assessment of some kind, time, as it is so enigmatically put by the storybook people, to wrap it up and call it thirty, to prophesy by the clouds and sign off ... but I am reminded for no clear cause of the case of Orval Nulin Evachefsky. Let us hope for some link, some light, and drive on.

Orval was born exactly forty-two years ago today, the second son of Felix and Ilse Evachefsky, on a small Eastern farm which Felix had acquired with the savings of his deceased immigrant parents. Orval's early years were largely uneventful. A strong but timid boy of average intelligence, he passed through Porter County High School as a popular athlete and incurious student. Times were difficult, the world was large and redoubtable, and the family farm was deeply mortgaged, so Orval and his two brothers, Perk and Willie, the first older than Orval, the second younger (the only sister Marge was married and living some distance away in Huffam County), stayed on after high school to help their father. Old Felix had lost his right arm in a threshing-machine accident and doubtless would have lost the farm as well, had not Perk, Orval, and young Willie pitched in. He lost it anyway, as it turned out, not many months after all three boys were drafted into service during the war, they having failed to declare their status as farmworkers. Felix died two years later, a broken and disillusioned man, entirely dependent upon state relief. Even at that, some might say he was fortunate in not living long enough to learn of the lacklustre in-the-service-of-their-country deaths of his sons Perk and Willie. Only Orval returned from the wars, though not entirely whole: an otherwise well-meaning buddy had introduced him to Maggie Wilson, who in turn had introduced him to Treponema Pallidum, and the cure was long and physically debilitating. For several months after his discharge, Orval lived isolated and unshaven in his mother's apartment (she had moved here to the City after Felix died), and had the old lady not been totally impervious to all external phenomena, she might have discovered in her son a tendency towards morbid melancholia. But luckily an old friend encouraged Orval to take advantage of governmental education handouts to veterans, and Orval went off to business school, soon forgetting – apparently anyway – his worries. At school, he met Sissy Ann Madison, rescued her from the humdrum of the business world and introduced her to the humdrum of housewifery, though not without suffering a few weeks of strange and irrational panic just before the ceremony. Orval and Sissy Ann were painfully slow at reaching a state of what people call perfect union, and in fact, much too slow for Sissy Ann, who grew increasingly nervous about the delay, and who would certainly have sought her own solutions had she had enough imagination to do so. Meanwhile, though lacking most of the businessman's arts, and often the gull of unscrupulous colleagues, Orval developed steadily into a dependable and conscientious salesman, unimpeachably loyal to the Company and embarrassingly honest in his negotiations. Then, as oftentimes happens, as Orval's self-confidence grew, Sissy Ann came to enjoy him more, and finally, with appropriate gaiety, surprised him on the night of their ninth wedding anniversary with the news that a child was expected. A kind of delirium possessed Orval. He! A father! For the first time in at least sixteen years, he thought of his own father, that morose but proud old man, and on the day after Sissy Ann had told him, he impulsively bought cigars for everyone at the Company, even though he still had nearly eight months to wait. Well, such things are understood and, more often than not, forgiven in the business world. His sales soared over the next few months, his self-confidence climbed to a new and exhilarating peak, and in short, life was extraordinarily bountiful to Orval Nulin Evachefsky ... until one day, late in the autumn, Sissy Ann, only a month away from parturition, developed a strange red splotch on her face. She thought nothing of it, in spite of feeling a little funny, but then a second one appeared a day later, and she began to grow alarmed. Yet her alarm was the purest serenity, compared to what was happening to Orval. He did not need the second splotch, that first one was quite enough to dredge up all the forgotten and unconfessed fears of his troubled past, and in particular to call up the grinning spectre of Maggie Wilson and her spirochaete. He staggered away from the breakfast table, forgetting his hat and briefcase, and hours later found himself stumbling blindly about in the port area of the City, a piece of cold toast in his hands. With the aid of three gin rickeys, he was able to pull himself together by nightfall and find his way home, but his sleep was shattered by terribly biological visions. The next day, hardly noticing the second splotch on Sissy Ann's face, he left without hat, briefcase, credit cards, or tie. Whether or not he went to the office is unfortunately not known. But at 12.47, Orval took the elevator to the thirty-seventh floor of the Federal Building, and at 12.52, without the slightest hesitation, leaped from a west window to his death, impaling himself on a parking meter in the street below, to the immense horror of Carlyle Smith, schoolteacher, age thirty-six, who was about to put a penny in the meter. Just before learning of his death, his wife Sissy Ann was told by her obstetrician that she had a fairly acute case of infectious erysipelas. He gave her a shot of penicillin in the bottom and ordered her to bed.

Their lunch – an indescribable amalgam of black meat, greenish-brown gravy, and thick wet wads of some uncertain doughy matter – concluded at last, the city firemen emerge belching from Jenny's Home Cooking Cafe, cross the small square, and, armed with putty knives and plastic buckets of soapy water, begin to remove Klee, once and for all, from our sight, and thus, let us hope, from our minds. The Chief, a withered crowfaced career man with a bent bluish nose and a citywide reputation for strict interpretation of the Laws, is shrieking obscene commands into a microphone hooked up to a public-address system with three oversize speakers and an unholy howl (a fourth speaker is present, but disconnected).

The growing bulge of spectators huddles about the accident, so-called, staring with astonishingly blank faces at the sweating black-slickered firemen. One of these latter, an enormous fireman whose uniform is, literally, splitting apart where sewn, stamps furiously up to the — what do you call it? — the point of impact, and as though in protest against the pressing dull-faced crowd, stoops and farts indelicately, yet, as it turns out, wholly unintentionally: though the crowd is visibly delighted, his own fat face reddens perceptibly, and he ducks to the task at hand with exaggerated interest. What he is doing is merely collecting in a small pouch the fragments of Klee's dentures, which lie scattered over the pavement like ... ah ... like miniature milestones, let us say, marking the paths of his spilt life's blood. Well, we could say more, but the direction is dangerous.

But mark this detail: a small scrap of paper, completely illegible and perhaps even blank, lies not far from us in the fringe splatter of the main impact, weighted by a finger joint. *Is it possible that for some time past the destructive elements in Klee's character were few and effectively — though with great effort — submerged, but that Klee perversely guarded the notes and themes provided in despairing moments by these elements, and that these notes, all too honest, all too unanswerable, eventually contributed decisively to his inevitable but no less abrupt and disturbing end?* Hmmm, but perhaps I betray my trust. For the piece of paper may well have been there on the pavement before Klee arrived so melodramatically, and would so be a circumstance of no account. In fact, I confess, it looks more like a handbill. The streets are always cluttered with them, more so today. What is life, after all, but a caravan of lifelike forgeries?

All of Klee has now been gathered up and stuffed into a wax-lined shopping bag — strange how little of him there was that it should all fit! — and the firemen are hard at work with water and scrub-brushes. Pretty dull stuff. Hardly the kind of show to keep crowds about, especially when there's a circus in town, and it goes without saying that they're all moving on. So may we. It only remains to be observed that Orval Nulin Evachefsky suffered from a mental disturbance marked by melancholy and irrational terrors, more or less sat upon, which, when given licence over him as a consequence of Sissy Ann's splotches, drove him hastily to his self-annihilation. Whether Klee's suicide, however, was the result of a mere disease of his private reason, or if, more simply, reason itself *was* Klee's disease, we will, I am sorry to say, never know. And even if we should find out somehow, though I cannot imagine it, even then it'd be damned little consolation to Klee. The best we can do, finally, is to impose the soothing distortion of individuation on the luckless bastard, and I for one feel we deserve more than that, whether he does or not. We didn't start all this just to search out a comforting headstone, God knows. No, no, in the end, in truth, we are left virtually with nothing: an overlooked eyetooth, the PA left howling, a stained and broken ostrich feather, the faint after-odour of the fireman's fart. Abandoned. And a good fifteen, twenty minutes shot to hell.

I'm sorry. What can I say? Even I had expected more. You are right to be angry. Here, take these tickets, the city clerk, obsequious fool that he is, refused them, you might as well go. I owe you something and this is all I have.

o   o   o

6

J's Marriage

It began not otherwise than one might expect. After an excessive period of unlicensed self-humiliation, ecstatic protests of love, fear, despair, and the total impossibility of any imaginable kind of ultimate happiness (to all of which she replied and usually in kind, though rarely with such intensity), J at last determined, or perhaps this had been his determination all the while, the rest mere poetry, to marry her. Slow, but then there were admittedly substantial drawbacks to the affair: he was much older for one thing. And though she was certainly intelligent and imaginative, he was far more broadly educated. In fact, it wouldn't be unkind to say, and he brought himself to confess it in the torment of his most rational moments, that a good many of the most beautiful things he said to her she failed to understand, or rather, she understood not the sense of them, but merely the apparent emotion, the urgency, the adoration behind them. And did he adore her, or the objectification of a possible adorable? To search out *this* answer, J frankly did not trust himself. And, more generally and therefore more significantly, all of his most oppressive fears about the ultimate misery of an existence, the inevitable disintegration of love, the hastening process of physical and mental rot, the stupidity of human passion, and so on, these fears were entirely real, in fact, more than fears, they were his lot and he knew it. But there was no alternative short of death, so he decided to marry her.

To his great embarrassment, however, she was shocked by his proposal, apparently so at least, and pleaded for time. Only much later did he come to understand that a new kind of fear had burgeoned in her, a fear that no doubt cowered beneath the surface all the time, but which had always been placated by the suspicion that J himself was really nothing more physically substantial than his words, words which at times pierced the heart, true, kindled the blood, powerful words, even at times painful; but their power and their pain did not, *could not* pin one helplessly to the earth, could not bring actual blood.

At the time misconstruing her behaviour, however, J grew angry, pressed his affections, with atypical peevishness. She tore away, spat out at him hatefully. He withdrew, collapsed into a prolonged and somewhat morbid melancholy, unable to lift a hammer or turn a blade. She sought him out. She wept, embraced him, tried pathetically to explain. He again misunderstood and renewed his assault. She screamed in terror and escaped. Again he fell back in remorseful confusion. He grew ill. She cared for him. And on and on, thus it dragged, until, in summary, it at last became apparent to him that although she did love him and had a healthy longing for motherhood, at least in the abstract, she was nevertheless panic-stricken by the prospect of the loveact itself.

What was it? a lifetime of misguided dehortations from ancient deformed grannies, miserable old tales of blood and the tortures of the underworld (which the woman's very position in the event must give one thoughts upon), or some early misadventure, perhaps a dominant father? It hardly mattered. For, in the instant of the present act, the past in all its troubling complexities becomes irrelevant. This is what J believed anyway, and once the immediate cause of their problems had finally been made manifest to him, he felt immense relief. Not only was his pride assuaged, but more to the case, there was now no longer any obstacle to their marriage. At the level where they two existed, he explained to her, his voice appropriately muted, eyes darkened, brow furrowed, Truth his domain where he might guide her, at this level sex could not be comprehended without love, but love could be distinguished without reference to sex; in short, that one was the whole, the other a mere part, contributing to the perfection of the whole, to be sure, but not indispensable, not indispensable. More precisely, he added: whatever his terms, he could not imagine life without her, and if later they came to share in the natural act of lovers, well, so much the better of course, but they would arrive there, if at all, only with her express encouragement and at her own pace.

It was true (just at that moment anyway) all that he said, she accepted it, even if it did fail to take into account the processes of human action as she understood them, doubtless more accurately than he. But aside from this and more important: she suddenly grasped, more by intuition than by reason, that with this man, and possibly with no other, she would always enjoy the upper hand in this singular matter of, though the word was not hers, sex. All right, she said. All right, yes, she would marry him, and not long after she did.

Their wedding night was in all truth a thing of beauty: the splendour of the celebrations, the hushed intimacy of a private walk together under the cryptic light of a large moon, the unexpected delight discovered in the reflection of a candle's flicker in a decanter of aged wine, finally the silent weeping in each other's arms through a night that seemed infinite in its innumerable dimensions. Towards dawn, J, sitting on the side of the bed (both of them still dressed, of course; it would take some while yet to learn the first art of nakedness), overflowing with profound affection, began to caress her temples, and with the first thin light of the new day, she fell asleep beside him, and J wept again to realize the meaning and the importance of her sleep.

In spite of all his doubts, fears, his submerged impatience with the qualifications, to say nothing of his general view of the universe, not exactly, as shown, a reassuring one, J nevertheless enjoyed for several months an incredible happiness. Everything became remarkably easy for him, the dullest detail of existence provided him an immense delight: a parade of ants, for example, or the colour of a piece of wood or a pebble, her footprint in the dust. Merely to watch her hand reach for a cup or place a comb in her hair left him breathless. Every act was dedicated to her being, her mere being. The bed he made for her with his own hands, the table as well which never lacked her gifts to him, little flutes and puppets, too, and the chairs she sat on, he also made these. Almost from the outset, they encountered an emotional harmony inexpressibly beautiful, and even the last, God knows: *minor*, obstacle to their complete happiness seemed certain, ultimately, to give way to their all-consuming love.

J, confident of his own sexual attractiveness, even as old as he was, which was not too old after all – no, not over much should be made of his age – was patient, infinitely patient, and she seemed, at least much of the time, as desirous as he to consummate, in the proper time, their marriage.

One evening, just before sunset, J happened to be down by the sea. He had forgotten why he was there, perhaps nothing more than an idle wandering before supper, but yet it seemed altogether necessary that he *should* be there, just at that instant, just as the dying sun melted, viscous and crimson into the sullen sea, just as the distant mountains blinked from orange-green to blue, just as the first stirring of the night awoke the pines over his head. It was not, it was *not* beautiful, no, it would be absurd to think of this or any other natural composite as beautiful, but it was as though it *could* be beautiful, as though somewhere there resided within it the potentiality of beauty, not previously existent, *some spark after all*, only illusion of course, but – and he turned just in time to see his wife coming towards him down the path. Paralysed, he stood rooted, unspeaking, utterly entranced by her graceful motion, by the pale light playing over her slender body, and, above all, by her eyes, smilingly returning his awkward stare. Oh my God I love you! he managed to whisper, when she was near enough to hear. And that night, in feverish exultation, he buried his face in her breasts and caressed them, and she allowed it. Then, finally, overcome with an excess of emotion, he fell into a deep sleep full of wonderful dreams, which unfortunately he could never later recall.

The actual process of increasing intimacy was an elaborate sequence of advances and reversals, which need not be enumerated here. At moments, J would be greatly encouraged, perhaps by a sudden act on her part, a stroking of his naked back while he was bent over his lathe, a pressing of his hand to her breast, a soft folding into his arms while still half asleep beside him in their bed. But other times he would unwittingly shock her, set her to crying or running from the room, or would wake her with a hand too insistent on her thighs. And, in fact, it actually seemed that his worst fears had been justified, that he would indeed pass the rest of his years tossing sleeplessly, tortured, alongside her marvellous but utterly impenetrable body. At such times, he found himself envying the water she bathed in or the chair he was carving for her to sit on, found himself weeping bitterly and alone, his face in a piece of her clothing.

But then, one evening after supper, utterly without warning, he entered the bedroom to find her standing, undressed, beside the bed. She was astonishingly beautiful, lovelier than he had imagined in his most distraught and fanciful dreams. He gasped, unbelieving, took a faltering step toward her. She blushed, cast her eyes down. With trembling fingers he tore off his shirt, ran to her, pressed her to his chest, no, she was no mere apparition, he tearfully kissed her ears, her hair, her eyes, her neck, her breasts. He was delirious, feared he might faint. His hands searched desperately, clumsily, swept over her smooth back, burrowed down between — Don't, she said. Please don't. It was somehow the way she said it, not the words, which were clearly meaningless, but the way she *formed* the words, as though carving them with consummate skill and certainty, and placing them, like great stone tablets, between them. Bewildered, he fumbled a moment, stepped back, and I don't — was all he could find for himself to say. I am expecting a baby, she said.

What happened in the moments, and for that matter in the weeks, that followed is, of course, a common kind of story, and not a particularly entertaining one at that. J took ill, suffered frequently from delirium, and she patiently nursed him back to health. She now undressed freely in front of him, but with a self-preoccupation and indifference to his presence that would have permanently deranged a younger man, not so well equipped for life as J. She explained to him simply that her pregnancy was an act of God, and he had to admit against all mandates of his reason that it must be so, but he couldn't imagine whatever had brought God to do such a useless and, well, yes, in a way, almost vulgar thing. J always thought about everything a great deal, even trivia that others might either sensibly ignore, or observe and forget in the very act of observing, and about *this*, to be sure, he thought even more than usual. Every day while prostrate in bed, he turned it over and over, and in feverish dreams the mystery set his brain on fire and caused tiny painful explosions behind his eyes that sometimes kept going off even after he was awake. But no power of mental effort provided a meaningful answer for him; it was simply unimaginable to him that any God would so involve himself in the tedious personal affairs of this or any other human animal, so unutterably unimportant were they to each other. Finally, he simply gave in to it, dumped it in with the rest of life's inscrutable absurdities, and from that time on began to improve almost daily.

And to his credit it must be said that one of the reasons he began to find his way back to health was her own worsening condition. She said little about it, behaved towards him as generously as ever, smiled no less frequently, but there was no mistaking her suffering, quiet or no: it was not and would not be easy. Compassion drove him to forget his own wretchedness, and daily, though he seemed to grow even older, he seemed as well to assume greater and greater stature. He returned to his carpentry with renewed dedication, secretly saved aside small portions of food as insurance for her against the approaching winter, learned to comprehend in his day's activities many of the tasks they once took for granted as hers. The last month was particularly bitter, the great misfortune of the ill-timed trip, the strange cruelty of the elements, and so on, but she took it with great courage, greater even than his own; suffered with dignity the flesh-ripping agony of birth, writhing on the dirt floor like a dying beast, yet noble, beautiful. It was — that moment of the strange birth — J's most mystic moment, his only indisputable glimpse of the whole of existence, yet one which he later renounced, needless to say, later understood in the light of his overwrought and tortured emotions. And it was also the climax of his love for her; afterwards, they drifted quietly and impassively apart, until in later years J found himself incapable even of describing her to himself or any other person.

The marriage itself, as a formal fact, lasted on to the end (in this case, J's), which did not come early, lasted for the most part because nothing was done to stop it. The boy played but a small part in the process, did of course draw away the mother's attention for quite some while, but little more. As for J, in spite of his general willingness to love the boy, he could never do so in any thoroughgoing manner, and for this or other reasons, the boy showed complete indifference to J from an early age. Just as well; J grew to prefer not being bothered to any other form of existence.

One thing did happen, though perhaps too trivial even to report here, maybe not even true as a number no doubt hold, even though J himself talked of it freely to those close to him (or perhaps he dreamt it, he could never deny it, it might have been one of those beautiful dreams from that earlier magical night, though forgotten): namely, that some four or five months after the boy came, J did at last consummate his marriage. He had frankly forgotten about doing so, had come to take life as it oddly was for granted (a carryover from his prolonged illness and consequent cure), had turned in, weary from work, when she came into the room, her breasts still exposed from having nursed the baby, and sat down on the bed beside him. She smiled wanly, perhaps not even at him, he couldn't be sure, didn't even wonder, and then she began to bathe her breasts with a small damp sponge she had brought along for the purpose. J rose up casually, as he might have done time after time, took the sponge from her hands (she surrendered it willingly, sleepily), washed her breasts (it was curious they held so little interest for him: had he kissed them with such terrible rapture so recently? it was really very long ago) and then her neck and back. He undressed her, her exhausted body compliant, went out to the well, still unclothed himself (later this struck him as extraordinary, lent the odd element that caused him doubts about the event's reality), dipped the sponge in fresh cool water, returned to complete her bath. As though nothing more than the rest of a customary routine, he then penetrated her, had a more or less satisfactory emission, rolled over, and slept until morning. She had fallen asleep some moments before.

J died, thus ending the marriage, unattractively with his face in a glassful of red wine on a tavern table many years later, and not especially appropriately, since not even in his advanced years was he much of a drinker. He just remarked to somebody sitting near him (keeping to himself the old bubbling wish that there might have been a child for him that time, a kind of testimonial for him to leave) that life had turned out to be nothing more or less than he had expected after all, he was now very inept at his carpentry, had a chestful of consumption, was already passing whole days without being able to remember them afterwards, urinated on the hour and sometimes in his pants, separately or additively could make no sense of any day of his life, and so on, a tavern-type speech, in short, but he added that the one peculiarity he had not accurately forseen, and perhaps it was the most important of all, was that, in spite of everything, there was nothing tragic about it, no, nothing there to get wrought up about, on the contrary. Then, without transition, a mental fault more common to him in later years, he had a rather uncharacteristic thought about the time she, the wife, fell asleep, or apparently so, that morning following the wedding night; he laughed (that high-pitched rattle of old men), startling the person who had been listening, and died as described above in a fit of consumptive coughing.

7

The Wayfarer

I came upon him on the road. I pulled over, stepped out, walked directly over to him where he sat. On an old milestone. His long tangled beard was a yellowish grey, his eyes dull with the dust of the road. His clothes were all of a colour and smelled of mildew. He was not a sympathetic figure, but what could I do?

I stood for a while in front of him, hands on hips, but he paid me no heed. I thought: at least he will stand. He did not. I scuffed up a little dust between us with the toe of my boot. The dust settled or disappeared into his collection of it. But still, he stared obliviously. Vacantly. Perhaps (I thought): mindlessly. Yet I could be sure he was alive, for he sighed deeply from time to time. He is afraid to acknowledge me, I reasoned. It may or may not have been the case, but it served, for the time being, as a useful premise. The sun was hot, the air dry. It was silent, except for the traffic.

I cleared my throat, shifted my feet, made a large business of extracting my memo-book from my breast pocket, tapped my pencil on it loudly. I was determined to perform my function in the matter, without regard to how disagreeable it might prove to be. Others passed on the road. They proffered smiles of commiseration, which I returned with a pleasant nod. The wayfarer wore a floppy black hat. Tufts of yellow-grey hair poked out of the holes in it like dead wheat. No doubt, it swarmed. Still he would not look at me.

Finally, I squatted and interposed my face in the path of his stare. Slowly – painfully, it would seem – his eyes focused on mine. They seemed to brighten momentarily, but I am not sure why. It could have been joy as easily as rage, or it could have been fear. Only that: his eyes brightened; his face remained slack and inexpressive. And it was not a glow, nothing that could be graphed, it was just a briefest spark, a glimmer. Then dull again. Filmy as though with a kind of mucus smeared over. And he lost the focus. I don't know whether or not in that instant of perception he noticed my badge. I wished at the time that he would, then there could be no further ambiguities. But I frankly doubted that he did. He has travelled far, I thought.

I had begun with the supposition that he feared me. It is generally a safe supposition. Now I found myself beset with doubt. It could have been impatience, I reasoned, or anger – or even *contempt!* The thought, unwonted, jolted me. I sat back in the dust. I felt peculiarly light, baseless. I studied my memo-book. It was blank! my God! *it was blank!* Urgently, I wrote something in it. There! Not so bad now. I began to recover. Once again, I supposed it was fear. I was able to do that. I stood, brushed the dust off my trousers, then squatted down once again. And now: with a certain self-assurance. Duty, a proper sense of it, is our best teacher: my catechism was coming back to me. He would enjoy no further advantages.

I asked him about himself, received no answers. I recorded his silence in my book. I wrote the word *aphonia*, then erased it. True, I could have determined the matter, a mere palpation of the neck cords, but the prospect of dipping my fingers into the cavities behind that mouldy beard revolted me, and the question, after all, was not of primary concern. Moreover, a second method then occurred to me: if I could provoke a sound out of him, any sound, it would prove that the vocal mechanism was still intact. Of course, if he uttered no sound, it would not establish that he was mute, but I felt confident I could provoke a sound and have an end to the problem.

I unstrapped my rifle from my back and poked the barrel under his nose. His gaze floated unimpeded down the barrel through my chest and out into indeterminate space. I asked him his name. I asked him the President's name. I asked him my name. I reminded him of the gravity of his violation and of my own unlimited powers. I asked him what day it was. I asked him what place it was. He was adamant. I lowered the barrel and punched it into his chest. The barrel thumped in the thick coats he wore and something cracked but he said nothing. Not so much as a whisper. He did not even wince. I was becoming angry. Inwardly, I cautioned myself. And still that old man refused – I say *refused*, although it may not have been a question of volition; in fact, it *was* not, *could not have been* – to look at me. I lowered the barrel and punched it into his groin. I might as well have been poking a pillow. He seemed utterly unaware of my attentions.

I stood impatiently. I knew, of course, that much was at stake. How could I help but know it? Those passing were now less sympathetic, more curious, more – yes: more reproving. I felt the sweat under my collar. I loosened my tie. I shouted down at him. I ordered him to stand. I ordered him to lie down. I shook the rifle in front of his nose. I ordered him to remove his hat. I fired a shot over his head. I kicked dust into his face. I stomped down on his old papery shoes with my boots. I ordered him to look at me. I ordered him to lift one finger. *He would not even lift one finger!* I screamed at him. I broke his nose with my rifle butt. But still he sat, sat on that old milestone, sat and stared. I was so furious I could have wept.

I would try a new tack. I knelt down in front of him. I intruded once more into the line—if so vague a thing could be called that—of his gaze. I bared my teeth. I ordered him to sit. I ordered him to stare vacantly. I ordered him not, under threat of death, to focus his eyes. I ordered the blood to flow from his pulpy nose. He obeyed. Or, rather: he remained exactly as he was before. I was hardly gratified. I had anticipated a certain satisfaction, a partial restoration of my confidence, but I was disappointed. In fact, I felt more frustrated than ever. I no longer looked at those passing. I knew their reproachful eyes were on me. My back sweat from the intensity of their derision.

I set my teeth. It was time. I told him if he did not speak, I would carry out my orders and execute him on the spot. My orders, to be precise, did not specify this place, but on the other hand they did not exclude it, and if he would not move, what choice did I have? Even as I asked him to speak, I knew he would not. Even while I was forming and emitting the very words, I already was contemplating the old dilemma. If I shot him in the chest, there was a fair chance I would miss or only graze the heart. He would die slowly. It could take several days. I am more humane than to take pleasure in that thought. On the other hand, if I shot him in the head, he would surely die instantly, but it would make a mess of his countenance. I do not enjoy the sight of mutilated heads. I do not. I have often thought, myself, when the time came, I would rather receive it in the chest. The chest seems to me farther away than the head. In fact, I could almost enjoy dying, allowed the slow dreamy regard of my chest distantly fountaining blood. Contrarily, the thought of the swift hard knock in the skull is an eternal torment to me. Given these considerations, I shot him in the chest.

As I had feared, he did not die immediately. He did not even, for the moment, alter either his expression or his posture. His coats were thick and many. I could see the holes drilled by the rifle shells, but saw no blood. What could that mean? I was shaken by a sudden violent fever of impatience. Only by strenuous self-control was I able to restrain myself from tearing his clothes off to inspect the wound. I thought: if I don't see blood immediately, *I shall lose it again!* I was trembling. I wiped my mouth with the back of my hand. Then slowly, a dark stain began to appear in the tatters. In the nick of time! It spread. I sighed. I sat back and lay the rifle across my knees. Now there was only to wait. I glanced towards the road from time to time and accepted without ceremony the commendatory nods.

The stain enlarged. It would not take long. I sat and waited. His coats were soon soaked and the blood dripped down the milestone between his legs. Suddenly, his eyes fixed on mine. His lips worked, his teeth chewed his beard. I wished he would end it quickly. I even considered firing a second shot through his head. And then he spoke. He spoke rapidly, desperately, with neither punctuation nor sentence structure. Just a ceaseless eruption of obtuse language. He spoke of constellations, bone structures, mythologies, and love. He spoke of belief and lymph nodes, of excavations, categories and prophecies. Faster and faster he spoke. His eyes gleamed. Harmonics! Foliations! Etymology! Impulses! Suffering! His voice rose to a shriek. Immateriality patricide ideations heat-stroke virtue predication – I grew annoyed and shot him in the head. At last, with this, he fell.

My job was done. As I had feared, he was a mess. I turned my back to him, strapped my rifle securely on my back, reknotted my tie. I successfully put his present condition out of my mind, reconstructing my earlier view of him still whole. It was little better, I admit, but it was the first essential step towards forgetting him altogether. In the patrol car, I called in details of the incident and ordered the deposition squad to the scene. I drove a little farther down the road, parked, jotted down the vital data in my memo-book. I would make the full report out later, back at the station. I noted the exact time.

This done, I returned my memo-book to my breast pocket, leaned back, and stared absently out the window. I was restless. My mind was not yet entirely free of the old man. At times, he would loom in my inner eye larger than the very landscape. I supposed that this was due to my having stooped down to his level: my motives had been commendable, of course, but the consequences of such a gesture, if practised habitually, could well prove disastrous. I would avoid it in the future. The rifle jammed against my spine. I slid down farther to relieve the obtrusion, resting my head against the back of the seat. I watched the traffic. Gradually, I became absorbed in it. Uniformly it flowed, quietly, possessed of its own unbroken grace and precision. There was a variety in detail, but the stream itself was one. One. The thought warmed me. It flowed away and away and the unpleasant images that had troubled my mind flowed away with it. At last, I sat up, started the motor, and entered the flow itself. I felt calm and happy. A participant. I enjoy my work.

The Elevator

Every morning without exception and without so much as reflecting upon it, Martin takes the self-service elevator to the fourteenth floor, where he works. He will do so today. When he first arrives, however, he finds the lobby empty, the old building still possessed of its feinting shadows and silences, desolate though mutely expectant, and he wonders if today might not turn out differently.

It is 7.30 AM: Martin is early and therefore has the elevator entirely to himself. He steps inside: this tight cell! he thinks with a kind of unsettling shock, and confronts the panel of numbered buttons. One to fourteen, plus 'B' for basement. Impulsively, he presses the 'B' — seven years and yet to visit the basement! He snorts at his timidity.

After a silent moment, the doors rumble shut. All night alert waiting for this moment! The elevator sinks slowly into the earth. The stale gloomy odours of the old building having aroused in him an unreasonable sense of dread and loss, Martin imagines suddenly he is descending into hell. *Tra la perduta gente*, yes! A mild shudder shakes him. Yet, Martin decides firmly, would that it were so. The old carrier halts with a quiver. The automatic doors yawn open. Nothing, only a basement. It is empty and nearly dark. It is silent and meaningless.

Martin smiles inwardly at himself, presses the number '14'. 'Come on, old Charon,' he declaims broadly, 'Hell's the other way!'

2

Martin waited miserably for the stench of intestinal gas to reach his nostrils. Always the same. He supposed it was Carruther, but he could never prove it. Not so much as a telltale squeak. But it was Carruther who always led them, and though the other faces changed, Carruther was always among them.

They were seven in the elevator: six men and the young girl who operated it. The girl did not participate. She was surely offended, but she never gave a hint of it. She possessed a surface detachment that not even Carruther's crude proposals could penetrate. Much less did she involve herself in the coarse interplay of men. Yet certainly, Martin supposed, they were a torment to her.

And, yes, he was right — there it was, faint at first, almost sweet, then slowly thickening, sickening, crowding up on him —

'Hey! Who fahred thet shot?' cried Carruther, starting it.

'Mart fahred-it!' came the inexorable reply. And then the crush of loud laughter.

'*What!* Is that Martin fartin' again?' bellowed another, as their toothy thicklipped howling congealed around him.

'Aw *please*, Mart! *don't fart!*' cried yet another. It would go on until they left the elevator. The elevator was small: their laughter packed it, jammed at the walls. 'Have a heart, Mart! don't *part* that fart!'

It's not me, *it's not me*, Martin insisted. But only to himself. It was no use. It was fate. Fate and Carruther. (More laughter, more brute jabs.) A couple of times he had protested. 'Aw, Marty, you're just modest!' Carruther had thundered. Booming voice, big man. Martin hated him.

One by one, the other men filed out of the elevator at different floors, holding their noses. 'Old farty Marty!' they would shout to anyone they met on their way out, and it always got a laugh, up and down the floor. The air cleared slightly each time the door opened.

In the end, Martin was always left alone with the girl who operated the elevator. His floor, the fourteenth, was the top one. When it all began, long ago, he had attempted apologetic glances toward the girl on exiting, but she had always turned her shouder to him. Maybe she thought he was making a play for her. Finally he was forced to adopt the custom of simply ducking out as quickly as possible. She would in any case assume his guilt.

Of course, there was an answer to Carruther. Yes, Martin knew it, had rehearsed it countless times. The only way to meet that man was on his home ground. And he'd do it, too. When the time came.

3

Martin is alone on the elevator with the operator, a young girl. She is neither slender nor plump, but fills charmingly her orchid-coloured uniform. Martin greets her in his usual friendly manner and she returns his greeting with a smile. Their eyes meet momentarily. Hers are brown.

When Martin enters the elevator, there are actually several other people crowded in, but as the elevator climbs through the musky old building, the others, singly or in groups, step out. Finally, Martin is left alone with the girl who operates the elevator. She grasps the lever, leans against it, and the cage sighs upwards. He speaks to her, makes a lighthearted joke about elevators. She laughs and

Alone on the elevator with the girl, Martin thinks: if this elevator should crash, I would sacrifice my life to save her. Her back is straight and subtle. Her orchid uniform skirt is tight, tucks tautly under her blossoming hips, describes a kind of cavity there. Perhaps it is night. Her calves are muscular and strong. She grasps the lever.

The girl and Martin are alone on the elevator, which is rising. He concentrates on her round hips until she is forced to turn and look at him. His gaze coolly courses her belly, her pinched and belted waist, past her taut breasts, meets her excited stare. She breathes deeply, her lips parted. They embrace. Her breasts plunge softly against him. Martin has forgotten whether the elevator is climbing or not.

4

Perhaps Martin will meet Death on the elevator. Yes, going out for lunch one afternoon. Or to the drugstore for cigarettes. He will press the button in the hall on the fourteenth floor, the doors will open, a dark smile will beckon. The shaft is deep. It is dark and silent. Martin will recognize Death by His silence. He will not protest.

He *will* protest! oh God! no matter what the
the sense of emptiness underneath breath lurching out
The shaft is long and narrow. The shaft is dark.
He will not protest.

5

Martin, as always and without so much as reflecting upon it, takes the self-service elevator to the fourteenth floor, where he works. He is early, but only by a few minutes. Five others join him, greetings are exchanged. Though tempted, he is not able to risk the 'B', but presses the '14' instead. Seven years!

As the automatic doors press together and the elevator begins its slow complaining ascent, Martin muses absently on the categories. This small room, so commonplace and so compressed, he observes with a certain melancholic satisfaction, this elevator contains them all: space, time, cause, motion, magnitude, class. Left to our own devices we would probably discover them. The other passengers chatter with self-righteous smiles (after all, they are on time) about the weather, the elections, the work that awaits them today. They stand, apparently motionless, yet moving. Motion: perhaps that's all there is to it after all. Motion and the medium. Energy and weighted particles. Force and matter. The image grips him purely. Ascent and the passive reorganization of atoms.

At the seventh floor, the elevator stops and a woman departs it. Only a trace of her perfume remains. Martin alone remarks – to himself, of course – her absence, as the climb begins again. Reduced by one. But the totality of the universe is suffused: each man contains all of it, loss is inconceivable. Yet, if that is so – and a tremor shudders coolly through Martin's body – then the totality is as nothing. Martin gazes around at his four remaining fellow passengers, a flush of compassion washing in behind the tremor. One must always be alert to the possibility of action, he reminds himself. But none apparently need him. If he could do the work for them today, give them the grace of a day's contemplation ...

The elevator halts, suspended and vibrant, at the tenth floor. Two men leave. Two more intermediate stops, and Martin is alone. He has seen them safely through. Although caged as ever in his inexorable melancholy, Martin nonetheless smiles as he steps out of the self-service elevator on the fourteenth floor. 'I am pleased to participate,' he announces in full voice. But, as the elevator doors close behind him and he hears the voided descent, he wonders: Wherein now is the elevator's totality?

6

The cable snaps at the thirteenth floor. There is a moment's deadly motionlessness – then a sudden breathless plunge! The girl, terrified, turns to Martin. They are alone. Though inside his heart is bursting its chambers in terror, he remains outwardly composed. 'I think it is safer lying on your back,' he says. He squats to the floor, but the girl remains transfixed with shock. Her thighs are round and sleek under the orchid skirt, and in the shadowed – 'Come,' he says. 'You may lie on me. My body will absorb part of the impact.' Her hair caresses his cheek, her buttocks press like a sponge into his groin. In love, moved by his sacrifice, she weeps. To calm her, he clasps her heaving abdomen, strokes her soothingly. The elevator whistles as it drops.

7

Martin worked late in the office, clearing up the things that needed to be done before the next day, routine matters, yet part of the uninterrupted necessity that governed his daily life. Not a large office, Martin's, though he needed no larger, essentially neat except for the modest clutter on top of his desk. The room was equipped only with that desk and a couple chairs, bookcase lining one wall, calendar posted on another. The overhead lamp was off, the only light in the office being provided by the fluorescent lamp on Martin's desk.

Martin signed one last form, sighed, smiled. He retrieved a cigarette, half-burned but still lit, from the ashtray, drew heavily on it, then, as he exhaled with another prolonged sigh, doubled the butt firmly in the black bowl of the ashtray. Still extinguishing it, twisting it among the heap of crumpled filters in the ashtray, he glanced idly at his watch. He was astonished to discover that the watch said twelve-thirty – and had stopped! Already after midnight!

He jumped up, rolled down his sleeves, buttoned them, whipped his suit jacket off the back of his chair, shoved his arms into it. Bad enough twelve-thirty – but my God! how much *later* was it? The jacket still only three-quarters of the way up his back, tie askew, he hastily stacked the loose papers on his desk and switched off the lamp. He stumbled through the dark room out into the hallway, lit by one dull yellow bulb, pulled his office door to behind him. The thick solid catch knocked hollowly in the vacant corridor.

He buttoned his shirt collar, straightened his tie and the collar of his jacket, which was doubled under on his right shoulder, as he hurried down the passageway past the other closed office doors of the fourteenth floor to the self-service elevator, his heels hammering away the stillness on the marble floor. He trembled, inexplicably. The profound silence of the old building disturbed him. Relax, he urged himself; we'll know what time it is soon enough. He pushed the button for the elevator, but nothing happened. Don't tell me I have to walk down! he muttered bitterly to himself. He poked the button again, harder, and this time he heard below a solemn rumble, a muffled thump, and an indistinct grinding plaint that grieved progressively nearer. It stopped and the doors of the elevator opened to receive him. Entering, Martin felt a sudden need to glance back over his shoulder, but he suppressed it.

Once inside, he punched the number '1' button on the self-service panel. The doors closed, but the elevator, instead of descending, continued to climb. Goddamn this old wreck! Martin swore irritably, and he jiggled the '1' button over and over. Just this night! The elevator stopped, the doors opened, Martin stepped out. Later, he wondered why he had done so. The doors slid shut behind him, he heard the elevator descend, its amused rumble fading distantly. Although here it was utterly dark, shapes seemed to form. Though he could see nothing distinctly, he was fully aware that he was not alone. His hand fumbled on the wall for the elevator button. Cold wind gnawed at his ankles, the back of his neck. Fool! wretched fool! he wept, there is no fifteenth floor! Pressed himself against the wall, couldn't find the button, couldn't even find the elevator door, and even the very wall was only

8

Carruther's big voice boomed in the small cage.

'Mart fahred-it!' came the certain reply. The five men laughed. Martin flushed. The girl feigned indifference. The fetor of fart vapours reeked in the tight elevator.

'Martin, damn it, cut the fartin'!'

Martin fixed his cool gaze on them. 'Carruther fucks his mother,' he said firmly. Carruther hit him full in the face, his glasses splintered and fell, Martin staggered back against the wall. He waited for the second blow, but it didn't come. Someone elbowed him, and he slipped to the floor. He knelt there, weeping softly, searched with his hands for his glasses. Martin tasted the blood from his nose, trickling into his mouth. He couldn't find the glasses, couldn't even see.

'Look out, baby!' Carruther thundered. 'Farty Marty's jist tryin' to git a free peek up at your pretty drawers!' Crash of laughter. Martin felt the girl shrink from him.

9

Her soft belly presses like a sponge into his groin. No, safer on your back, love, he thinks, but pushes the thought away. She weeps in terror, presses her hot wet mouth against his. To calm her, he clasps her soft buttocks, strokes them soothingly. So sudden is the plunge, they seem suspended in air. She has removed her skirt. How will it feel? he wonders.

10

Martin, without so much as reflecting on it, automatically takes the self-service elevator to the fourteenth floor, where he works. The systematizing, that's what's wrong, he concludes, that's what cracks them up. He is late, but only by a few minutes. Seven others join him, anxious, sweating. They glance nervously at their watches. None of them presses the 'B' button. Civilities are hurriedly interchanged.

Their foolish anxiety seeps out like a bad spirit, enters Martin. He finds himself looking often at his watch, grows impatient with the elevator. Take it easy, he cautions himself. Their blank faces oppress him. Bleak. Haunted. Tyrannized by their own arbitrary regimentation of time. Torture self-imposed, yet in all probability inescapable. The elevator halts jerkily at the third floor, quivering their sallow face-flesh. They frown. No one has pushed the three. A woman enters. They all nod, harumph, make jittery little hand motions to incite the doors to close. They are all more or less aware of the woman (she has delayed them, damn her!), but only Martin truly remarks – to himself – her whole presence, as the elevator resumes its upward struggle. The accretion of tragedy. It goes on, ever giving birth to itself. Up and down, up and down. Where will it end? he wonders. Her perfume floats gloomily in the stale air. These deformed brow-beaten mind-animals. Suffering and insufferable. Up and down. He closes his eyes. One by one, they leave him.

He arrives, alone, at the fourteenth floor. He steps out of the old elevator, stares back into its spent emptiness. There, only there, is peace, he concludes wearily. The elevator doors press shut.

II

Here on this elevator, my elevator, created by me, moved by me, doomed by me, I, Martin, proclaim my omnipotence! In the end, doom touches all! MY doom! I impose it! TREMBLE!

12

The elevator shrieks insanely as it drops. Their naked bellies slap together, hands grasp, her vaginal mouth closes spongelike on his rigid organ. Their lips lock, tongues knot. The bodies: how will they find them? Inwardly, he laughs. He thrusts up off the plummeting floor. Her eyes are brown and, with tears, love him.

13

But — ah! — the doomed, old man, the DOOMED! What are they to us, to ME? ALL! We, I love! Let their flesh sag and dewlaps tremble, let their odours offend, let their cruelty mutilate, their stupidity enchain — but let them laugh, father! FOREVER! let them cry!

14

but hey! theres this guy see he gets on the goddamn elevator and its famous how hes got him a doodang about five feet long Im not kiddin you none five feet and he gets on the — yeah! can you imagine a bastard like that boardin a friggin public I mean public elevator? hoohah! no I dont know his name Mert I think or Mort but the crux is he is possessed of this motherin digit biggern ole Rahab see — do with it? I dont know I think he wraps it around his leg or carries it over his shoulder or somethin *jeezuss!* what a problem! why I bet hes *killt* more poor bawdies than I ever dipped my poor worm in! once he was even a — listen! Carruther tells this as the goddamn truth I mean he respects that bastard — he was even one a them jack-off gods I forgot how you call them over there with them Eyetalians

after the big war see them dumb types when they seen him furl out
this here five foot hose of his one day – he was just tryin to get the
goddamn knots out Carruther says – why they thought he musta
been a goddamn jackoff god or somethin and wanted to like employ
him or whatever you do with a god and well Mort he figgered it to
be a not so miserable occupation dont you know better anyhow
than oildrillin with it in Arabia or stoppin holes in Dutch dikes like
hes been doin so the bastard he stays on there a time and them little
quiff there in that Eyetalian place they grease him up with hogfat
or olive oil and all workin together like vested virgins they pull him
off out there in the fields and spray the crops and well Mort he says
he says its the closest hes ever got to the real mccoy jeezuss! hes
worth a thousand laughs! and they bring him all the old aunts
and grannies and he splits them open a kinda stupendous euthanasia
for the old ladies and he blesses all their friggin procreations with a
swat of his doodang and even does a little welldiggin on the side but
he gets in trouble with the Roman churchers on accounta not bein
circumcised and they wanta whack it off but Mort says no and they
cant get close to him with so prodigious a batterin ram as hes got so
they work a few miracles on him and wrinkle up his old pud with
holy water and heat up his semen so it burns up the fields and even
one day ignites a goddamn volcano and *jeezuss!* he wastes no time
throwin that thing over his shoulder and hightailin it *outa* there I
can tell you! but now like Im sayin them pastoral days is dead and
gone and hes goin up and down in elevators like the rest of us and
so here he is boardin the damn cage and theys a bunch of us bastards
clownin around with the little piece who operates that deathtrap
kinda brushin her swell butt like a occasional accident and sweet
jeezus her gettin fidgety and hot and half fightin us off and half
pullin us on and playin with that lever *zoom!* wingin up through
that scraper and just then ole Carruther jeezuss he really breaks
you up sometimes that crazy bastard he hefts up her little purple
skirt and whaddaya know! the little quiff aint wearin no skivvies!
its somethin *beautiful* man I mean a sweet cleft peach right outa
some foreign orchard and poor ole Mort he is kinda part gigglin and
part hurtin and for a minute the rest of us dont see the pointa the
whole agitation but then that there incredible thing suddenly pops
up quivery right under his chin like the friggin eye of god for crissake
and then theres this big wild rip and man! it rears up and splits outa
there like a goddamn redwood topplin *gawdamighty!* and knocks old
Carruther *kapow!* right to the deck! his best buddy and that poor
little cunt she takes one glim of that impossible rod wheelin around

in there and whammin the walls and she faints dead away and *jeeezusss!* she tumbles right on that elevator lever and man! I thought for a minute we was *all* dead

15

They plunge, their damp bodies fused, pounding furiously, in terror, in joy, the impact is

I, Martin, proclaim against all dooms the indestructible seed

Martin does not take the self-service elevator to the fourteenth floor, as is his custom, but, reflecting upon it for once and out of a strange premonition, determines instead to walk the fourteen flights. Halfway up, he hears the elevator hurtle by him and then the splintering crash from below. He hesitates, poised on the stair. Inscrutable is the word he finally settles upon. He pronounces it aloud, smiles faintly, sadly, somewhat wearily, then continues his tedious climb, pausing from time to time to stare back down the stairs behind him.

Romance of the Thin Man and the Fat Lady

Now, many stories have been told, songs sung, about the Thin Man and the Fat Lady. Not only is there something comic in the coupling, but the tall erect and bony stature of the Man and the cloven mass of roseate flesh that is the Lady are in themselves metaphors too apparent to be missed. To be sure of it, one need only try to imagine a Thin Lady paired with a Fat Man. It is not ludicrous, it is unpleasant. No, the much recounted mating of the Thin Man with the Fat Lady is a circus legend full of truth. In fact, it is hardly more or less than the ultimate image of all our common everyday romances, which are also, let us confess, somehow comic. We are all Thin Men. You are all Fat Ladies.

But such simplicities are elusive; our metaphors turn on us, show us backsides human and complex. For observe them now: the Thin Man slumps soup-eyed and stoop-shouldered, seeming not thin so much as ill, and the Fat Lady in her stall sags immobile and turned blackly into herself. A passerby playfully punches his thumb into her thigh, an innocent commonplace event, and she spits in his eye.

'Hey, lady!'

'Right in his eye! I saw her!'

'What kinda circus is this, anyway?'

'She's probably not fat, just wearing a balloon suit!'

'Come, darling, don't get too close to the Fat Lady, something's wrong with her.'

Children cry, and lovers, strangely disturbed, turn quickly away from them, seeking out the monkey cage. Whoo! the Image of all our Romances indeed!

Yet perhaps – why yes! surely! – the signs are unmistakable: a third party has intruded.

Madame Cobra the Snakecharmer?

The Incredible Man with the Double Joints?

The Missing Link?

No, our triangle is of a more sinister genius. Our villain is the Ringmaster.

'We thought he'd understand. We were open about it. The circus life is a good life, but it's a tough one, too. A man's gotta be a man.'

'Get off that diet, Fat Lady, says he. The pig. Okay, okay, I say. But he doesn't believe me. He moves in on us! Can you imagine?'

'I was in the Strong Man's tent. I had twenty-five pounds up in the air, which for a Thin Man ain't bad. I'm pretty proud of it and when he comes in I say: Hey! look at that muscle! I'll show you muscle, says he, and kicks my poor ass all over that tent. He shouldn't do that. I got a very fragile spine.'

'Tape measure, calory charts, scales, everything. Don't take his beady eyes off us day or night. I ain't allowed to sweat, my Man can't exert hisself. What're we supposed to *do*?'

'Like animals, that's how he treats us. Livestock. Checks her teeth, hefts her udders, slaps her on the bare nates when she's on the scales. No heart at all. She's crying, but does he care? Eat! he says. Eat! You gotta let a woman be a woman, I believe that.'

It comes to this, then: that not even Ultimate Heroes are free from fashion. The Thin Man has wished to develop muscles, further to excite his Fat Lady—

'Builds stamina, too. Helps your wind.'

And the Lady has attempted to reduce to be more appealing to her Man—

'And I had my heart to think about. You understand.'

Now, were the Ringmaster a philosopher, he might have avoided the catastrophe – for, as in all true romances, and surely in the Truest, there is a catastrophe. He might have been able to convince the couple with a merest syllogism of the absurdity – indeed the very contradiction! – of their respective wishes. But, far from being a philosopher, he indulges in the basest of trades (and is thus the best of villains!): he is a trafficker, a businessman, a financier, a Keeper of the Holier Books.

'Philosophy! You want philosophy? I'll give you philosophy! Okay, okay, so they're romantic symbols, I understand that, I'm not stupid, but what they symbolize, buddy, ain't Beauty. It's like that old fraud Merlin the Prestidigitator said when he came to try and softsoap me: Who can blame them if they see outside themselves symbols of their own? There's something in all of us, Mr Ringmaster, he says, that rebels against extremes. Hell, I can follow that. And *being* a symbol: who wants it anyway? Narcissism, that's all it is. *But what the fuck else do you think a circus is all about?* Philosophy! Philosophy my ass! And the same goes for human nature! Want me to wreck my goddamn business? Listen! If the Fat Lady were not the fattest and the Thin Man the thinnest in the world — we're talking first principles now, buster — no one would pay to see them. Where are all your goddamn noble abstractions when the circus collapses and we're all of us out on the streets? *Adaptation*, boys and girls! *Expediency!* And to hell with nature!'

Things do not work out as well, however, as the Ringmaster has anticipated. The Fat Lady in her gloom loses her appetite and begins to waste away. The Thin Man stops eating altogether and must be held in an upright position all day by props. And even the Ringmaster, normally of such stable even if unpleasant temper, grows inexplicably fidgety in the long fumbling nights alongside the couple's troubled bed.

'She can't sleep, the poor dear. Whimpering all night long. I try to soothe her best I can, but my hands, so to speak, are tied.'

'One squeak of the bedsprings and on come the lights!'

'The man's a nut!'

'He looks down at my Man and says: That's one muscle too many! And throws cold water on it—'

'All night in a cold wet bed!'

At last, the Ringmaster negotiates a highly favourable contract of exchange with a rival circus, by which he is to acquire an Ambassador from Mars and a small sum of money for the waning Fat Lady. Another couple weeks, he thinks, and she would have been worthless. Hoo hee! A miraculous deal, a work of genius! Giggling softly (and no doubt meanly) to himself, he drops off that night into a comfortable slumber, the first in weeks, the bed beside him heaving fretfully the while with the parting anguish of the distraught lovers.

'It wasn't murder, it was a revolution.'

'A revolution of *love!*'

As one, the entire complement of the circus arises at midnight —

'Now!'

'Freedom!'

'Equality!'

'Clobber the fuckin lech!'

—summarily executes and inters the Ringmaster alongside the deserted country road (castrating him symbolically in the process – circus people are born to symbology!), and installs the Fat Lady and the Thin Man as Representatives of the Common Proprietorship.

'We were all agreed. The Thin Man and the Fat Lady, in fact, were the last to know.'

'An Ambassador from Mars indeed! Did he think we had no pride?'

So joy reigns in the circus for weeks. Every performance concludes with a party. The two lovers' happiness seems to radiate magically, attracting new masses of spectators, all of which augments, in turn, their happiness. It is indeed a paradise. The Thin Man exercises without compunction and quickly reaps a sturdy little pair of biceps. The Fat Lady, all aglow, switches calory charts with the Thin Man, and within a week loses one of her several chins. Everyone, including the Thin Man, remarks on her beauty. Love is the word of the day. Circus people are basically good people. Their hatred for their former Ringmaster subsides, the souvenir taken from him is fed to the lions, and he is soon forgotten altogether. In a new day, there is no place for old resentments.

'I mean, you go along for years, see, thinking you got a Ringmaster on accounta you gotta have one. Ever seen a circus without a Ringmaster? No. Well, that just goes to show how history can fake you out!'

'It was beautiful! All of it just *happening!* Acts coming on spontaneously, here, there, it was wild and exciting and unpredictable!'

'Suddenly it hits you, see. All your life you been looking at circuses and you say, that's how circuses are. But what if they ain't? What if that's all a goddamn myth propagated by Ringmasters? You dig? What if it's all open-ended, and we can, if we want to, live by love?'

'We even started enjoying each other's acts!'

'I rode the elephant once!'

'Who says clowns gotta take pratfalls alla time? I learned to play in the band and train a bear and ride a horse through a fiery hoop!'

But, just when the picture is pinkest, bad news: it becames all too apparent that fewer people are visiting the stalls of the Thin Man and the Fat Lady, and those that do pass through, do so hastily and with little interest.

'Okay, so they're happy, so they're in love. So what? You see one lover, you seen 'em all.'

At first, everyone stubbornly disregards the signs. The parties go on, the songs and the celebrations. The Thin Man lifts weights as always, and the Fat Lady diets. Their glad hearts, though gnawed at a bit by apprehension, remain kindled by love and joy. One could almost say it was the romantic legend come true. But finally they can no longer ignore the black-and-white truth of the circus ledger, now in their care. Somewhere, apparently, there is a fatter lady and a thinner man. Their new world threatens to crumble.

'We didn't wanna hurt their feelings, you know. We kidded them a little, hoping they'd take the hint.'

'Why couldn't they just love each other for themselves?'

'For the good of the whole circus, we said.'

In their van one night, doubt having doused for the moment the flame of passion, they agree: the Fat Lady will restore her cast-off corpulence, the Thin Man will return his set of barbells to the Strong Man. They re-exchange calory charts. They begin in earnest to win back their public, found to be an integrant of their attachment, after all.

It is not easy. Worried by business reverses, the Fat Lady must work doubly hard to lay on each pound. And the Thin Man discovers that his little knots of muscle tend to sag instead of disappear. But they are driven by the most serious determination. The eyes of the circus are upon them. Momentary reverses only steel them more to the task.

'Chocolates! For me? It's been so long!'

'With love.'

'But now that you've seen me like this, will you truly love me when I'm fat again?'

'To be honest, dear, I ain't sure I can even tell the difference.'

The worst part of the day for the Fat Lady comes when she steps upon the scales. Disgusted by her fat, she is disgusted she has added so little of it. The Thin Man dutifully records her weight each day, and his presence comes to irritate her. He clucks his tongue when she fails to increase and sighs wistfully when she succeeds. She would cry but is afraid of the loss of anything, even tears. She refuses to submit to any activity which might make her perspire, and even demands that she be lifted in and out of the van each day.

The Thin Man steps daily before a full-length mirror. Disgusted by his thinness, he is disgusted that he still wears those little pouches under his skin. He wishes to be mere bone. Hilarious frightening unfleshed bone. The Fat Lady nags and pinches the little lumps that were once his muscles. He wonders if he has come to hate her.

'Hold up your arm there, loverboy, lemme feel that flab – hey! how cute! just like a little oyster!'

'Yeah? And so what?'

'So: oysters are a luxury, skinhead. People may pay to eat 'em, but they won't pay just to look!'

The Fat Lady, pointing out the Thin Man's bagginess, doubts he has been firm in his resolution, and snoops about for hidden food. The Man, grimly checking the Lady on the scales each day, begins to suspect her of burning off calories behind his back. They sneak into each other's stalls during the day, spy on one another at mealtimes, wrangle bitterly over the business books at night in their van. If one day the Fat Lady takes in a single dime more than the Thin Man, he must account for his obvious inconstancy of will. If a child carried past the Fat Lady's stall fails to laugh and point at her, the Thin Man uses it as proof of her deceptions. Of what use is she to the circus if not even a child is titillated? What is worse than a baggy Thin Man who can't make a dime?

'I'm sorry. I didn't build these goddamn biceps overnight, they don't shrink overnight neither. You can't exercise backwards, I tell her. You just go limp and hope for the best. But I do that and she just laughs at me. I think she's got her eye on Daredevil Dick.'

'Think of my nerves, I tell him. If they ain't fat nerves, he says, I got no use for them. All day, he's stuffing me. Even wants to add intravenous feedings. One day he brings home this dumbbell. He's got a mean glint in his eye— Nothing doing, I say. But it gives him this idea. Maybe you oughta get pregnant, he says. That'd work for nine months, I say, but then what? And he gives me this strange look.'

The situation deteriorates rapidly. The Thin Man becomes sour and morose, his shoulders stooped, head sunk in dark thoughts. The Fat Lady, immobile and glum, goes so far as to belch obscenely when a passerby remarks that she is really not so fat after all. They quarrel without cease, and their gloom spreads like wet sawdust through the whole circus. Gate receipts diminish and even the peanut sales drop off.

And then one night, the Thin Man moves abruptly to the old Ringmaster's van, something of a sacrifice on his part, since in the interim it has been used by a pair of camels. The Fat Lady bellows after him that she is glad to see him go (it's not true about Daredevil Dick, though: who could think about love in times like these?), as he stamps peevishly out of her van, the business books smuggled under his shirt. He renegotiates the old deal with the rival circus, and before anyone realizes what has happened, they have an Ambassador from Mars in their midst and the Fat Lady is gone. There are some unspecific rumbles of discontent, but since no one wishes to be sold to the rival circus, known to be on its last legs and infamous for its corrupt and tyrannical Ringmaster, these rumbles are held within discreet limits.

'Well, it was a crisis, after all. He did what he had to do. You had to think about the competition. They were all out to get us. It was the best thing for everybody.'

'She was my best friend. Everyone loved her. But no one seemed to care. I was alone. What could I say?'

'You get used to everything in this life.'

The Thin Man, in power, gains strength. He squares his shoulders and sets about getting the circus back on its feet. He is ruthless with himself as he has learned to be ruthless with others. The harder he works, the more rigorously he fasts. He will be thin, and damn the world! And even the unhappy Fat Lady, leagues distant, surrenders wearily to her fate and, doing so, finds it easy enough to expand once again.

But wait! See what we have come to! The Fat Lady separated from her inseparable Thin Man! The solution, for all the Thin Man's admirable will, cannot but fail. It is a circus without pleasure. What are three rings of determination? These are dismal shadowy tents and who can wander through their yawning flaps without a taste of dread? No, no, it is worse even than the mythological Thin Lady coupled with a Fat Man! Our metaphor, with time, has come unhinged! A rescue is called for!

Let us suppose, then, that the Thin Man is suddenly deposed, never mind why or how.

'Taking everything for himself.'

'Even started growing a moustache, bought himself a whip!'

'We had a meeting and—'

Never mind. The Ambassador from Mars, unexpectedly popular, assumes the Thin Man's functions, and the Man himself is exiled to the rival circus in exchange for a Family of Webfooted Midgets.

And so here we go! The Thin Man, all atremble and with tears springing to his eyes, here he comes, rushing pell mell into the Fat Lady's tent! All the circus people, the visiting crowds, the animals run behind, snorting, whooping, laughing giddily. Whoopee! into her arms! and she clasps him eagerly and forgivingly to her heaving bosom. Spectators weep for joy! The image is made whole!

'Beautiful! In spite of all history!'

'See how their joyful tears flow!'

'Oh! I'm all weepy and excited myself!'

'He buries his head in her lap!'

'Hold me!'

Later, when the world's love is momentarily spent and the crowds have slipped weakly away, she makes a space for him in her little van. It is rundown, like this whole decrepit circus, yet there is a corner in it still for happiness. This Ringmaster is, as all have rightly averred, a corrupt and mordant bastard, greedy beyond belief. But, by staying very fat and very thin, respectively, they satisfy his daytime proddings, and by night he is too absorbed in his ledgers to pay them notice.

Thus, though the sacrifices have been considerable, if indeed not prohibitive, we have obeyed the innocent bite in our forks and held fast to our precious metaphor.

Yet, somehow, strangely, it has lost some of its old charm. We go to the circus to see the Fat Lady and the Thin Man, and though warmed by them, perhaps even amused and incited by them still, we nevertheless return home somehow dissatisfied. Fat, yes, the Fattest, and Thin — but what is it? Maybe only that, as always, they are ludicrous, and that now, having gone to such lengths to reunite them, we are irritated to discover their limits, to find that the Ludicrous is not also Beautiful.

'Like, well, like they oughta do *more* for us somehow—'

'After all we've done for them!'

'Thin Man, Fat Lady, all right, it's cute, it's funny maybe, but ...'

Well, let us admit it, perhaps it is ourselves who are corrupted. Perhaps we have seen or been too many Ringmasters, watched too many parades, safely witnessed too many thrills, counted through too many books. Maybe it's just that we've lost a taste for the simple in a world perplexingly simple. For, see, there? There a child laughs gaily at the Thin Man's tense smile, and there a young couple giggle in front of the unctuous Fat Lady.

So, what the hell, some circus music, please! Some raging lions and white horses and the clean cracking of black whips! Crackerjacks! Peanuts! And a monkey to wrap his tail around the flagpole!

For remember: these two, magic metaphor or no, are not the whole circus. Nor — to borrow from the hoariest spiel of them all – in this matter of circuses, is life one. There are three rings—

'Lazygentamun, absolutely unique, this way, patrons of the arts, desolate wastes, deepest Injah, suckled by werewolves, nekkid and hairy—'

'Raithiswhay, folks! She's half-human, half-reptile! Yawone believe yer eyes!'

'Absolutely wild gotta stand back limited time only, getcha tickets here, before goin inta the Big Top, see him now may never get another chance lives entirely on human flesh, ya heard me right, son! and we don't know how long we can keep him alive – !'

—And then there are more. Who can grasp it all? And who, grasping, can hold it! No, we have lost many things, go on losing, and must yet lose more. Even the Thin Man will grow old and bent, the Fat Lady will shrivel and die. We can hang on to nothing. Least of all the simple.

'This way, boyzungirls, inna the Big Show startin in jusfiminnit! still plennya seats but goodwonzur goin fast! yessir mistuh and how many—?'

'Hey cottoncandy popcawn sodypop!'

'Getcha soovuhnih booklet while they last! Fittysens two quaw-tuhs of a dollah! Byootiful faw-colour alla stars take a thrills home with ya!'

'There they came! It's the parade!'

'Lass chance now folks tellyawhawgawnuhdo! limted time only fore the Big Show gets unnerway! pay tenshun madam while supply lasts one quawtuh hurry! alla thrillsnchills Big Top in faw colours one quawtuh fifferadollah add extra bonus feachuh bagga nuts! you there—!'

But listen! the losses! these too are ludicrous, aren't they? these too are part of the comedy, right? a ring around the rings! So, damn it, let us hoot and holler and thrill and eat peanuts and cheer and swill the pop and laugh and bawl! Come on! All us Thin Men! All you Fat Ladies!

'Annow lazygentamun anawyoo youngsters! (crack) whatcha all been waiting for (crack!) inna the first ring feachuh act the Tumblin Twosome from Tuskyloosa (crack!) givum a hand folks! (crack!) inna second first time this side a the Atlantic comin to us from (crack!) and riding on a unicycle (crack!) whatsat rocket you carry-ing there George watchout (crack!) and high above without a net those flirters with death (crack!) defying the lawza gravity (drum-rolls and whipcracks!) you say it's a new secret weapon yer workin on for the guvmint George? well howzit work? (crack!) nothin but her teeth folks between her and the other world! (fanfare!) and his trained thoroughbred Arabian hawses! (crack!) now don't tell me you're gonna light that big thing in here George! (crack!) and rode by the Thin Man and the Fat Lady haw haw givum a big hand folks (crack!) *look out!*'

Quenby and Ola, Swede and Carl

Night on the lake. A low cloud cover. The boat bobs silently, its motor for some reason dead. There's enough light in the far sky to see the obscure humps of islands a mile or two distant, but up close: nothing. There are islands in the intermediate distance, but their uncertain contours are more felt than seen. The same might be said, in fact, for the boat itself. From either end, the opposite end seems to melt into the blackness of the lake. It feels like it might rain.

o   o   o

Imagine Quenby and Ola at the barbecue pit. Their faces pale in the gathering dusk. The silence after the sudden report broken only by the whine of mosquitoes in the damp grass, a distant whistle. Quenby has apparently tried to turn Ola away, back towards the house, but Ola is staring back over her shoulder. What is she looking at, Swede or the cat? Can she even see either?

o   o   o

In the bow sat Carl. Carl was from the city. He came north to the lake every summer for a week or two of fishing. Sometimes he came along with other guys, this year he came alone.

He always told himself he liked it up on the lake, liked to get away, that's what he told the fellows he worked with, too: get out of the old harness, he'd say. But he wasn't sure. Maybe he didn't like it.

Just now, on a pitchblack lake with a stalled motor, miles from nowhere, cold and hungry and no fish to show for the long day, he was
pretty sure he didn't like it.

o   o   o

You know the islands are out there, not more than a couple hundred
yards probably, because you've seen them in the daylight. All you can
make out now is here and there the pale stroke of what is probably
a birch trunk, but you know there are spruce and jack pines as well,
and balsam firs and white cedars and Norway pines and even maples
and tamaracks. Forests have collapsed upon forests on these islands.

o   o   o

The old springs crush and grate like crashing limbs, exhausted trees,
rocks tumbling into the bay, like the lake wind rattling through dry
branches and pine needles. She is hot, wet, rich, softly spread. Need-
ful. 'Oh yes!' she whispers.

o   o   o

Walking on the islands, you've noticed saxifrage and bellwort,
clintonia, shinleaf, and stemless lady's slippers. Sioux country once
upon a time, you've heard tell, and Algonquin, mostly Cree and
Ojibwa. Such things you know. Or the names of the birds up here:
like spruce grouse and whiskey jack and American three-toed wood-
pecker. Blue-headed vireo. Scarlet tanager. Useless information. Just
now, anyway. You don't even know what makes that strange whistle
that pierces the stillness now.

o   o   o

'Say, what's that whistling sound, Swede? Sounds like a goddamn
traffic whistle!' That was pretty funny, but Swede didn't laugh.
Didn't say anything. 'Some bird, I guess. Eh, Swede? Some goddamn
bird.'
    'Squirrels,' Swede said finally.
    'Squirrels!' Carl was glad Swede had said something. At least
he knew he was still back there. My Jesus, it was dark! He waited
hopefully for another response from Swede, but it didn't come. 'Learn
something new every day.'

o   o   o

Ola, telling the story, laughed brightly. The others laughed with her. What had she seen that night? It didn't matter, it was long ago. There were more lemon pies and there were more cats. She enjoyed being at the centre of attention and she told the story well, imitating her father's laconic ways delightfully. She strode longleggedly across the livingroom floor at the main house, gripping an imaginary cat, her face puckered in a comic scowl. Only her flowering breasts under the orange shirt, her young hips packed snugly in last year's bright white shorts, her soft girlish thighs, slender calves: these were not Swede's.

o   o   o

She is an obscure teasing shape, now shattering the sheen of moonlight on the bay, now blending with it. Is she moving towards the shore, towards the house? No, she is in by the boats near the end of the docks, dipping in among shadows. You follow.

o   o   o

By day, there is a heavy greenness, mostly the deep dense greens of pines and shadowed undergrowth, and glazed blues and the whiteness of rocks and driftwood. At night, there is only darkness. Branches scrape gently on the roof of the guests' lodge; sometimes squirrels scamper across it. There are bird calls, the burping of frogs, the rustle of porcupines and muskrats, and now and then what sounds like the crushing footfalls of deer. At times, there is the sound of wind or rain, waves snapping in the bay. But essentially a deep stillness prevails, a stillness and darkness unknown to the city. And often, from far out on the lake, miles out perhaps, yet clearly ringing as though just outside the door: the conversation of men in fishing boats.

o   o   o

'Well, I guess you know your way around this lake pretty well. Eh, Swede?'
  'Oh yah.'
  'Like the back of your hand, I guess.' Carl felt somehow encouraged that Swede had answered him. That 'oh yah' was Swede's trademark. He almost never talked, and when he did, it was usually just 'oh yah'. Up on the 'oh', down on the 'yah'. Swede was bent down over the motor, but what was he looking at? Was he looking at the

motor or was he looking back this way? It was hard to tell. 'It looks the same to me, just a lot of trees and water and sky, and now you can't even see that much. Those goddamn squirrels sure make a lot of noise, don't they?' Actually, they were probably miles away.

Carl sighed and cracked his knuckles. 'Can you hunt ducks up here?' Maybe it was better up here in the fall or winter. Maybe he could get a group interested. Probably cold, though. It was cold enough right now. 'Well, I suppose you can. Sure, hell, why not?'

o   o   o

Quenby at the barbecue pit, grilling steaks. Thick T-bones, because he's back after two long weeks away. He has poured a glass of whiskey for himself, splashed a little water in it, mixed a more diluted one for Quenby. He hands her her drink and spreads himself into a lawnchair. Flames lick and snap at the steaks, and smoke from the burning fat billows up from the pit. Quenby wears pants, those relaxed faded bluejeans probably, and a soft leather jacket. The late evening sun gives a gentle rich glow to the leather. There is something solid and good about Quenby. Most women complain about hunting trips. Quenby bakes lemon pies to celebrate returns. Her full buttocks flex in the soft blue denim as, with tongs, she flips the steaks over. Imagine.

o   o   o

Her hips jammed against the gunwales, your wet bodies sliding together, shivering, astonished, your lips meeting – you wonder at your madness, what an island can do to a man, what an island girl can do. Later, having crossed the bay again, returning to the rocks, you find your underwear is gone. Yes, here's the path, here's the very tree – but gone. A childish prank? But she was with you all the time. Down by the kennels, the dogs begin to yelp.

o   o   o

Swede was a native of sorts. He and his wife Quenby lived year-round on an island up here on the lake. They operated a kind of small rustic lodge for men from the city who came up to fish and hunt. Swede took them out to the best places, Quenby cooked and kept the cabin up. They could take care of as many as eight at a time. They moved here years ago, shortly after marrying. Real natives, folks born and bred on the lake, are pretty rare; their 14-year-old daughter Ola is one of the few.

How far was it to Swede's island? This is a better question maybe than 'Who is Swede?' but you are even less sure of the answer. You've been fishing all day and you haven't been paying much attention. No lights to be seen anywhere, and Swede always keeps a dock light burning, but you may be on the back side of his island, cut off from the light by the thick pines, only yards away from home, so to speak. Or maybe miles away. Most likely miles.

o   o   o

Yes, goddamn it, it was going to rain. Carl sucked on a beer in the bow. Swede tinkered quietly with the motor in the stern.

What made a guy move up into these parts? Carl wondered. It was okay for maybe a week or two, but he couldn't see living up here all the time. Well, of course, if a man really loved to fish. Fish and hunt. If he didn't like the ratrace in the city, and so on. Must be a bitch for Swede's wife and kid, though. Carl knew his own wife would never stand still for the idea. And Swede was probably pretty hard on old Quenby. With Swede there were never two ways about it. That's the idea Carl got.

Carl tipped the can of beer back, drained it. Stale and warm. It disgusted him. He heaved the empty tin out into the darkness, heard it plunk somewhere on the black water. He couldn't see if it sank or not. It probably didn't sink. He'd have to piss again soon. Probably he should do it before they got moving again. He didn't mind pissing from the boat, in a way he even enjoyed it, he felt like part of things up here when he was pissing from a boat, but right now it seemed too quiet or something.

Then he got to worrying that maybe he shouldn't have thrown it out there on the water, that beercan, probably there was some law about it, and anyway you could get things like that caught in boat motors, couldn't you? Hell, maybe that was what was wrong with the goddamn motor now. He'd just shown his ignorance again probably. That was what he hated most about coming up here, showing his ignorance. In groups it wasn't so bad, they were all green and could joke about it, but Carl was all alone this trip. Never again.

o   o   o

The Coleman lantern is lit. Her flesh glows in its eery light and the starched white linens are ominously alive with their thrashing shadows. She has brought clean towels; or perhaps some coffee, a book. Wouldn't look right to put out the lantern while she's down here, but its fierce gleam is disquieting. Pine boughs scratch the roof. The springs clatter and something scurries under the cabin. 'Hurry!' she whispers.

o   o   o

'Listen, Swede, you need some help?' Swede didn't reply, so Carl stood up in a kind of crouch and made a motion as though he were going to step back and give a hand. He could barely make Swede out back there. He stayed carefully in the middle of the boat. He wasn't completely stupid.

Swede grunted. Carl took it to mean he didn't want any help, so he sat down again. There was one more can of beer under his seat, but he didn't much care to drink it. His pants, he had noticed on rising and sitting, were damp, and he felt stiff and sore. It was late. The truth was, he didn't know the first goddamn thing about outboard motors anyway.

o   o   o

There's this story about Swede. Ola liked to tell it and she told it well. About three years ago, when Ola was eleven, Swede had come back from a two-week hunting trip up north. For ducks. Ola telling the story, would make a big thing about the beard he came back with and the jokes her mother made about it.

Quenby had welcomed Swede home with a big steak supper: thick T-bones, potatoes wrapped in foil and baked in the coals, a heaped green salad. And lemon pie. Nothing in the world like Quenby's homemade lemon pie, and she'd baked it just for Swede. It was a great supper. Ola skipped most of the details, but one could imagine them. After supper, Swede said he'd bring in the pie and coffee.

In the kitchen, he discovered that Ola's cat had tracked through the pie. Right through the middle of it. It was riddled with cat tracks, and there was lemon pie all over the bench and floor. Daddy had been looking forward to that lemon pie for two weeks, Ola would say, and now it was full of cat tracks.

He picked up his gun from beside the back door, pulled some shells out of his jacket pocket, and loaded it. He found the cat in the laundryroom with lemon pie still stuck to its paws and whiskers. He picked it up by the nape and carried it outside. It was getting dark, but you could still see plainly enough. At least against the sky.

He walked out past the barbecue pit. It was dark enough that the coals seemed to glow now. Just past the pit, he stopped. He swung his arm in a lazy arc and pitched the cat high in the air. Its four paws scrambled in space. He lifted the gun to his shoulder and blew the cat's head off. Her daddy was a good shot.

o   o   o

Her mock pout, as she strides across the room, clutching the imaginary cat, makes you laugh. She needs a new pair of shorts. Last year they were loose on her, wrinkled where bunched at the waist, gaping around her small thighs. But she's grown, filled out a lot, as young girls her age do. When her shirt rides up over her waist, you notice that the zipper gapes in an open V above her hip bone. The white cloth is taut and glossy over her firm bottom; the only wrinkle is the almost painful crease between her legs.

o   o   o

Carl scrubbed his beard. It was pretty bristly, but that was because it was still new. He could imagine what his wife would say. He'd kid his face into a serious frown and tell her, hell, he was figuring on keeping the beard permanently now. Well, he wouldn't, of course, he'd feel like an ass at the office with it on, he'd just say that to rile his wife a little. Though, damn it, he did enjoy the beard. He wished more guys where he worked wore beards. He liked to scratch the back of his hand and wrist with it.

'You want this last beer, Swede?' he asked. He didn't get an answer. Swede was awful quiet. He was a quiet type of guy. Reticent, that's how he is, thought Carl. 'Maybe Quenby's baked a pie,' he said, hoping he wasn't being too obvious. Sure was taking one helluva long time.

o   o   o

He lifts the hem of his tee shirt off his hairy belly, up his chest, but she can't seem to wait for that – her thighs jerk up, her ankles lock behind his buttocks, and they crash to the bed, the old springs shrieking and thumping like a speeding subway, traffic at noon, arriving trains. His legs and buttocks, though pale and flabby, seem dark against the pure white spectacle of the starched sheets, the flushed glow of her full heaving body, there in the harsh blaze of the Coleman lantern. Strange, they should keep it burning. His short stiff beard scrubs the hollow of her throat, his broad hands knead her trembling flesh. She sighs, whimpers, pleads, as her body slaps rhythmically against his. 'Yes!' she cries hoarsely.

You turn silently from the window. At the house, when you arrive, you find Ola washing dishes.

o   o   o

What did Quenby talk about? Her garden probably, pie baking, the neighbours. About the wind that had come up one night while he'd been gone, and how she'd had to move some of the boats around. His two-week beard: looked like a darned broom, she said. He'd have to sleep down with the dogs if he didn't cut it off. Ola would giggle, imagining her daddy sleeping with the dogs. And, yes, Quenby would probably talk about Ola, about the things she'd done or said while he was away, what she was doing in sixth grade, about her pets and her friends and the ways she'd helped around the place.

Quenby at the barbecue pit, her full backside to him, turning the steaks, sipping the whisky, talking about life on the island. Or maybe not talking at all. Just watching the steaks maybe. Ola inside setting the table. Or swimming down by the docks. A good thing here. The sun now an orangeish ball over behind the pines. Water lapping at the dock and the boats, curling up on the shore, some minutes after a boat passes distantly. The flames and the smoke. Down at the kennels, the dogs were maybe making a ruckus. Maybe Ola's cat had wandered down there. The cat had a habit of teasing them outside their pen. The dogs had worked hard, they deserved a rest. Mentally, he gave the cat a boot in the ribs. He had already fed the dogs, but later he would take the steak bones down.

o   o   o

Quenby's thighs brush together when she walks. In denim, they whistle; bare, they whisper. Not so, Ola's. Even with her knees together (they rarely are), there is space between her thighs. A pressure there, not of opening, but of awkwardness.

Perhaps, too, island born, her walk is different. Her mother's weight is settled solidly beneath her buttocks; she moves out from there, easily, calmly, weightlessly. Ola's centre is still between her

narrow shoulders, somewhere in the midst of her fine new breasts,
and her quick astonished stride is guided by the tips of her hipbones,
her knees, her toes. Quenby's thick black cushion is a rich locus of
movement; her daughter still arches uneasily out and away from the
strange outcropping of pale fur that peeks out now at the inner edges
of the white shorts.

It is difficult for a man to be alone on a green island.

o   o   o

Carl wished he had a cigarette. He'd started out with cigarettes, but
he'd got all excited once when he hooked a goddamn fish, and they
had all spilled out on the wet bottom of the boat. What was worse,
the damn fish – a great northern, Swede had said – had broke his
line and got away. My Jesus, the only strike he'd got all day, and
he'd messed it up! Swede had caught two. Both bass. A poor day, all
in all. Swede didn't smoke.

To tell the truth, even more than a cigarette, he wished he had a
good stiff drink. A hot supper. A bed. Even that breezy empty lodge
at Swede's with its stale piney smell and cold damp sheets and
peculiar noises filled him with a terrific longing. Not to mention
home, real home, the TV, friends over for bridge or poker, his own
electric blanket.

'Sure is awful dark, ain't it?' Carl said 'ain't' out of deference
to Swede. Swede always said 'ain't' and Carl liked to talk that way
when he was up here. He liked to drink beer and say 'ain't' and 'he
don't' and stomp heavily around with big boots on. He even found
himself saying 'oh yah!' sometimes, just like Swede did. Up on the
'oh', down on the 'yah'. Carl wondered how it would go over back
at the office. They might even get to know him by it. When he was
dead, they'd say: 'Well, just like good old Carl used to say: oh yah!'

o   o   o

In his mind, he watched the ducks fall. He drank the whisky and
watched the steaks and listened to Quenby and watched the ducks
fall. They didn't just plummet, they fluttered and flopped. Sometimes they did seem to plummet, but in his mind he saw the ones
that kept trying to fly, kept trying to understand what the hell was
happening. It was the rough flutter sound and the soft loose splash of
the fall that made him like to hunt ducks.

o   o   o

Swede, Quenby, Ola, Carl ... Having a drink after supper, in the livingroom around the fireplace, though there's no fire in it. Ola's not drinking, of course. She's telling a story about her daddy and a cat. It is easy to laugh. She's a cute girl. Carl stretches. 'Well, off to the sack, folks. Thanks for the terrific supper. See you in the morning, Swede.' Quenby: 'Swede or I'll bring you fresh towels, Carl. I forgot to put any this morning.'

o   o   o

You know what's going on out here, don't you? You're not that stupid. You know why the motor's gone dead, way out here, miles from nowhere. You know the reason for the silence. For the wait. Dragging it out. Making you feel it. After all, there was the missing underwear. Couldn't find it in the morning sunlight either.

But what could a man do? You remember the teasing buttocks as she dogpaddled away, the taste of her wet belly on the gunwales of the launch, the terrible splash when you fell. Awhile ago, you gave a tug on the stringer. You were hungry and you were half-tempted to paddle the boat to the nearest shore and cook up the two bass. The stringer felt oddly weighted. You had a sudden vision of a cold body at the end of it, hooked through a cheek, eyes glazed over, childish limbs adrift. What do you do with a vision like that? You forget it. You try to.

o   o   o

They go in to supper. He mixes a couple more drinks on the way. The whisky plup-plup-plups out of the bottle. Outside, the sun is setting. Ola's cat rubs up against his leg. Probably contemplating the big feed when the ducks get cleaned. Brownnoser. He lifts one foot and scrubs the cat's ears with the toe of his boot. Deep-throated purr. He grins, carries the drinks in and sits down at the dining-room table.

Quenby talks about town gossip, Ola talks about school and Scouts, and he talks about shooting ducks. A pretty happy situation. He eats with enthusiasm. He tells how he got the first bird, and Ola explains about the Golden Gate Bridge, cross-pollination, and Tom Sawyer, things she's been reading in school.

He cleans his plate and piles on seconds and thirds of everything. Quenby smiles to see him eat. She warns him to save room for the pie, and he replies that he could put away a herd of elephants and still have space for ten pies. Ola laughs gaily at that. She sure has a nice laugh. Ungainly as she is just now, she's going to be a pretty girl, he decides. He drinks his whisky off, announces he'll bring in the pie and coffee.

o   o   o

How good it had felt! In spite of the musty odours, the rawness of the stiff sheets, the gaudy brilliance of the Coleman lantern, the anxious haste, the cool air teasing the hairs on your buttocks, the scamper of squirrels across the roof, the hurried by-passing of pre-liminaries (one astonishing kiss, then shirt and jacket and pants had dropped away in one nervous gesture, and down you'd gone, you in teeshirt and socks still): once it began, it was wonderful! Lunging recklessly into that steaming softness, your lonely hands hungering over her flesh, her heavy thighs kicking up and up, then slamming down behind your knees, hips rearing up off the sheets, her voice rasping: 'Hurry!' – everything else forgotten, how good, how good! And then she was gone. And you lay in your teeshirt and socks, staring half-dazed at the Coleman lantern, smoking a cigarette, thinking about tomorrow's fishing trip, idly sponging away your groin's dampness with your shorts. You stubbed out the cigarette, pulled on your khaki pants, scratchy on your bare and agitated skin, slipped out the door to urinate. The light leaking out your shuttered window caught your eye. You went to stand there, and through the broken shutter, you stared at the bed, the roughed-up sheets, watched yourself there. Well. Well. You pissed on the wall, staring up towards the main house, through the pines. Dimly, you could see Ola's head in the kitchen window.

You know. You know.

o   o   o

'Listen, uh, Swede . . .'

'Yah?'

'Oh, nothing. I mean, well, what I started to say was, maybe I better start putting my shoulder to, you know, one of the paddles or whatever the hell you call them. I – well, unless you're sure you can get it—'

'Oh yah. I'm sure.'

'Well . . .'

o   o   o

Swede, Carl, Ola, Quenby ... One or more may soon be dead. Swede or Carl, for example, in revenge or lust or self-defence. And if one or both of them do return to the island, what will they find there? Or perhaps Swede is long since dead, and Carl only imagines his presence. A man can imagine a lot of things, alone on a strange lake in a dark night.

o   o   o

Carl, Quenby, Swede, Ola ... Drinks in the living-room. An after-dinner sleepiness on all of them. Except Ola. Wonderful supper. Nothing like fresh lake bass. And Quenby's lemon pie. 'Did you ever hear about Daddy and the cat?' Ola asks. 'No!' All smile. Ola perches forward on the hassock. 'Well, Daddy had been away for two weeks ...'

o   o   o

Listen: alone, far from your wife, nobody even to play poker with, a man does foolish things sometimes. You're stretched out in your underwear on an uncomfortable bed in the middle of the night; for example, awakened perhaps by the footfalls of deer outside the cabin, or the whistle of squirrels, the cry of loons, unable now to sleep. You step out, barefoot, to urinate by the front wall of the lodge. There seems to be someone swimming down in the bay, over near the docks, across from the point here. No lights up at the main house, just the single dull bulb glittering as usual out on the far end of the dock, casting no light. A bright moon.

You pad quietly down towards the bay, away from the kennels, hoping the dogs don't wake. She is swimming this way. She reaches the rocks near the point here, pulls herself up on them, then stands shivering, her slender back to you, gazing out on the way she's come, out towards the boats and docks, heavy structures crouched in the moonglazed water. Pinpricks of bright moonlight sparkle on the crown of her head, her narrow shoulders and shoulderblades, the crest of her buttocks, her calves and heels.

Hardly thinking, you slip off your underwear, glance once at the house, then creep out on the rock beside her. 'How's the water?' you whisper.

She huddles over her breasts, a little surprised, but smiles up at you. 'It's better in than out,' she says, her teeth chattering a little with the chill.

You stoop to conceal, in part, your burgeoning excitement, which you'd hoped against, and dip your fingers in the water. Is it cold? You hardly notice, for you are glancing back up now, past the hard cleft nub where fine droplets of water, catching the moonlight, bejewel the soft down, past the flat gleaming tummy and clenched elbows, at the young girl's dark shivering lips. She, too, seems self-conscious, for like you, she squats now, presenting you only her bony knees and shoulders, trembling, and her smile. 'It's okay,' you say, 'I have a daughter just your age.' Which is pretty stupid.

o   o   o

They were drifting between two black islands. Carl squinted and concentrated, but he couldn't see the shores, couldn't guess how far away the islands were. Didn't matter anyway. Nobody on them. 'Hey, listen, Swede, you need a light? I think I still got some matches here if they're not wet—'

'No, sit down. Just be a moment . . .'

Well, hell, stop and think, goddamn it, you can't stick a lighted match around a gasoline motor. 'Well, I just thought . . .' Carl wondered why Swede didn't carry a flashlight. My Jesus, a man live up here on a lake all these years and doesn't know enough to take along a goddam flashlight. Maybe he wasn't so bright, after all.

He wondered if Swede's wife wasn't worrying about them by now. Well, she was probably used to it. A nice woman, friendly, a good cook, probably pretty well built in her day, though not Carl's type really. A little too slack in the britches. Skinny little daughter, looked more like Swede. Filling out, though. Probably be a cute girl in a couple years. Carl got the idea vaguely that Quenby, Swede's wife, didn't really like it up here. Too lonely or something. Couldn't blame her.

He knew it was a screwy notion, but he kept wishing there was a goddamn neon light or something around. He fumbled under the seat for the other beer.

o   o   o

'I asked Daddy why he shot my cat,' she said. She stood at the opposite end of the living-room, facing them, in her orange shirt and bright white shorts, thin legs apart. It was a sad question, but her lips were smiling, her small white teeth glittering gaily. She'd just imitated her daddy lobbing the cat up in the air and blowing its head off. 'Well, honey, I gave it a sporting chance,' he said. 'I threw it up in the air, and if it'd flown away, I wouldn't have shot it!' She joined in the general laughter, skipping awkwardly, girlishly, back to the group. It was a good story.

o   o   o

She slips into the water without a word, and dogpaddles away, her narrow bottom bobbing in and out of sight. What the hell, the house is dark, the dogs silent: you drop into the water – wow! sudden breathtaking impact of the icy envelope! whoopee! – and follow her, a dark teasing shape rippling the moonlit surface.

You expect her to bend her course in towards the shore, towards the house, and, feeling suddenly exposed and naked and foolish in the middle of the bright bay, in spite of your hunger to see her again, out of the water, you pause, prepare to return to the point. But, no, she is in by the boats, near the end of the docks, disappearing into the wrap of shadows. You sink out of sight, swim underwater to the docks – a long stretch for a man your age – and find her there, holding onto the rope ladder of the launch her father uses for guiding large groups. The house is out of sight, caution out of mind.

She pulls herself up the ladder and you follow close behind, her legs brushing your face and shoulders. At the gunwales, she emerges into full moonlight, and as she bends forward to crawl into the launch, drugged by the fantasy of the moment, you lean up to kiss her glistening buttocks. In your throbbing mind is the foolish idea that, if she protests, you will make some joke about your beard.

o   o   'o

He punched the can and the beer exploded out. He ducked just in time, but got part of it in his ear. 'Hey! Did I get you, Swede?' he laughed. Swede didn't say anything. Hell, it was silly even to ask. The beer had shot off over his shoulder, past the bow, the opposite direction from Swede. He had asked only out of habit. Because he didn't like the silence. He punched a second hole and put the can to his lips. All he got at first was foam. But by tipping the can almost straight up, he managed a couple swallows of beer. At first, he thought it tasted good, but a moment later, the flat warm yeasty taste sliming his mouth, he wondered why the hell he had opened it up. He considered dumping the rest of it in the lake. But, damn it, Swede would hear him and wonder why he was doing it. This time, though, he would remember and not throw the empty can away.

o   o   o

Swede, Quenby, Carl, Ola ... The story and the laughter and off to
bed. The girl has omitted one detail from her story. After her daddy's
shot, the cat had plummeted to the earth. But afterwards, there was
a fluttering sound on the ground where it hit. Still, late at night, it
caused her wonder. Branches scrape softly on the roof. Squirrels
whistle and scamper. There is a rustling of beavers, foxes, skunks,
and porcupines. A profound stillness, soon to be broken surely by
rain. And, far out on the lake, men in fishing boats, arguing, chattering, opening beercans. Telling stories.

The Sentient Lens

Scene for 'Winter'

No sound, it gets going with utter silence, no sound except perhaps an inappreciable crackle now and then, not unlike static, but our ear readily compensates for it, hears not that sound but the absence of sound, stretches itself, reaches out past any staticky imperfections there might be and finds: only the silence. And that's how it starts. Not even a wind. Merely the powderfine snow dropping silently, evenly, no more than infinitesimal flecks of light, settling icily on the quiet forest like frozen dust. The snow has folded itself into drifts, or perhaps the earth itself is ribbed beneath, cast into furrows by fallen trees and humps of dying leaves – we cannot know, we can be sure only of the surface we see now, a gently bending surface that warps and cracks the black shadows of the trees into a fretwork of complex patterns, complex yet tranquil, placed, reflective: the interlaced shadows and polygons of brightly daylit snow suggest the quavering stability of light, the imperceptible violence and motion of shadow. So close to the drifts are we that whole trees cannot be seen, only thick black trunks flecked with white and plunging branches weighted with snow, sweeping perilously near the white heaps of earth: we pass beneath them, sliding by the black trunks, over the virgin planes of groundsnow.

Brief sharp crackling sound! We pause. Different from the static.

Again! Next to us, up close: the columnar trunk of a great pine. Crack! In the wood. Yes, again! The subtle biting voice of wood freezing. We hesitate, expectant, straining to hear it again – but our attention is suddenly shaken, captured by a new sound, an irregular crumpling smashing noise that repeats itself four or five times, stops, then sounds again – yes, of course! the squeaky splashing padded unmistakable crash of snow being crushed underfoot! A motion! Now we see him – *there!* White past white, but distinct. Rabbit! Crush crush crush crush crush. Stop. Crush crush crush. Stop. Listens. Nervous twitch of wide-nostrilled nose. Gone! Diminishing crush crush beat. Stop. Then again, louder now. Stop. Ah! behind that pine! Then away again, crush crush crush crush. Finally: silence. *Sudden astonishing close-up of dog's head, small black glittering eyes, long black nose flicking swinging sniffing over the white earth, sharp triangular ears alert,* and now we see the whole dog, lean, light-coated, of noble origin, taut-bodied. Nose down, the dog slips soundlessly through the muted forest, through the soft snow's weightless fall.

We reach, forgetting the dog, what appears to be a small open space, nearly flat, the familiar chiaroscuro configurations unbroken by upspearing forms. Here we pause. Our gaze drifts upwards, through the diminishing snow, past the arch of reaching branches, towards the sky, up where the treetops lean inwards as though possessed by, drawn towards some omnipotent vanishing point. We cannot see the vanishing point, or even the sky: the snow that tumbles down and away upon us obliterates all but the static black outlines of the trees. When we look back down, we see that this open area is really a park with lamp posts standing rigid and inscrutable, wide snow-pillowed benches sprawling in the deep snow at their feet, a small weathered sign poking up, its paint all but weathered away. We can barely discern, and then at extremely close range, the word MEN on it, but there is no arrow to tell us where they might be found. The lamps are not lit: it is the bright part of day.

A road passes through the park, barely visible in the untrammelled snow, seen as a slightly recessed plane about ten feet wide and stretching into the indefinite distance. In fact, we are standing in the middle of it, and as our gaze traces its course towards the horizon – an horizon by no means defined, by the way, but muddled by the converging forest – we see a sleigh approaching, drawn by two dark horses. Noiselessly, rapidly, it comes, the horses' hooves kicking up the dry snow in a swirl of seething clouds, pounding towards us, but in silence. Fine the horses, with flying manes and tight lithe bodies, shoulders sweating, muscles rippling, mouths afroth. And then suddenly the roar of sleighbells breaks in on us, and the thunder of hooves, as the sleigh races by us, over us, in a turbulence of blinding snow!

The noise breaks off as suddenly as it began. For a moment, all is blurred. Then, as the fine powder of cold snow settles about us, we see a man left in the sleigh's wake. He is afoot, smiling, waving at the sleigh as though in recognition of it; now he follows it, walking with firm measured tread along one of the two narrow tracks left by the sleigh's runners.

The man's face is familiar, someone we know, or have at least seen before, or much *like* someone we have seen before, a rugged masculine outdoor kind of face his, with craglike brow above a bold once-broken nose, thin brows knotted, narrow pale eyes squinting against the glare, forehead lined by, it would seem, alternating casts of astonished perplexity and sustained anger, crowfeet searing deep into the temples, strong jaw thrust forward, coarse sunblanched hair blown askew. His eyes are fixed on some distant point, perhaps on the sleigh shrinking noiselessly into the horizon behind us, or maybe merely and resolutely on the horizon itself. The man continues to smile, the smile creasing his weathered cheeks with humorous deep-cut grooves. The sun's dazzling radiance is constant. The man's cheeks bear the stubble of a day's beard, small wiry hairs that poke out from their dark pockets like a plague of indefatigable parasites. A large irregular mole, the size of a black ant's head interrupts the dense growth of stubble near one of the vertical creases presently deepened by the smile. The smile gradually fades, though not entirely, and the frown deepens, but – *we are quick to note* – it is the pleasing virile frown of resolve. One peculiarity: his thin lips appear uncommonly dark, almost black, and his eyelashes are strangely prominent. A mere defect in certain skills, no doubt; we overlook it as we might ignore a misplaced word, an unwanted tear, a broken-backed shoe, static. The man wears an open leather jacket, short, over his chest and strong shoulders, swings his broad leathery hands in wide rhythmic arcs, strides vigorously through the snow, his legs wrapped tightly in coarse grey leggings. His boots tramp wilfully into the drifts, but the glaze off the snow is so blinding that these boots appear no more than black shoe-shaped stumps: only rarely do we catch a glimpse of an individual lace or a buttonhook – no, for the most part, it is just a furry tunnelling of black in and out of an unstable white.

From a distance, we watch the man marching towards us, his jaw jutting forward in a strange complex of anger and bewilderment. He is alone, utterly alone, in a vast white desolation. It is no longer snowing. The sky is clear. There are no trees, no shadows, even the sleigh tracks have disappeared — there is only this slender leather-jacketed man with wind-tossed hair striding furiously across a barren expanse of shadowless slopes. The man breaks stride now from time to time. He seems troubled, glances about uneasily, is lost perhaps. He stops. Then: three nervous disorganized steps. He stops again. Looks about. We have drawn nearer. He puts one broad hand to his brow to shade his eyes, leans out slightly from the waist, searches the horizon in a complete circle. He drops his hand, hitches his trousers, appears to sigh, frowns. He draws a pack of cigarettes from his jacket pocket, a crumpled packet containing one cigarette. He pulls it out, tamps it against the back of one hand, clamps it defiantly in his mouth. He crushes the empty packet in a quick practised gesture, flings it several feet away into the snow. Now, from the same pocket: a book of matches. He tears one out, strikes it, holds it to the end of the cigarette, his hands cupped massively around it. Smoke issues from his nose. He tosses the match away, draws deeply on the cigarette. His face is set, tense, with a purposeful rigidity; he exhales slowly, his lips pressed, eyes trained on the distance. Absently, he flicks the cigarette away, glances hurriedly about, and, thrusting his head forward, sets off again.

He has not taken more than three or four steps when, once more, he stops. He gazes about. Licks his lips. The butt of his right hand presses down against his groin. Once more he warily and now somewhat gracelessly peers around him in a full circle, left hand shielding his dark-lashed eyes. Apparently satisfied that he is alone, he unbuttons his fly and prepares to urinate.

From behind his left shoulder, past his flushed left ear, we can see down into the dazzling unbroken slope in front of him. The tension in his left temple relaxes as a certain absorption in his task — a kind of satisfaction as it were — passes over what we can see of his face: just this left side and not all of that. Moreover, the blinding radiance of what is beyond makes the face seem almost black. He writes in the snow as he relieves himself. We follow but we cannot discover the words — or, rather, we can make them out plainly, but afterwards we cannot remember them, cannot even remember if he finished the word or words before the stream of urine diminished, weakened from its initial surging onrush to a thin drooping trickle, spurted ungoverned three times, then wilted to an occasional drip. The man's shoulders are shaking and we see that he is laughing, *has been laughing throughout his performance,* laughing uncontrollably now, but we hear none of it, silence still governs our consciousness, there is only an occasional and unplaced staticky sound, which perhaps we have been hearing all along.

The man shakes out the last of it, buttons himself up, all the while continuing to laugh, his head thrown back, his mouth wide open, his white teeth bared, narrow eyes squeezed tight, the crowfeet moist and exaggerated. He collapses to his knees and scribbles in the snow with his finger

I DID THIS!

but soon is laughing so violently that he spills headfirst down into the snow and rolls about in it. *The laughter! we begin to hear it now! strong, racking, hysterical, welling up, loose and perverse, rattling louder and louder* – but though the laughter swells, we observe that the man's face is startlingly sober! He huddles in the snow, curled up in a ball of terror, his lined eyes damp, his cheeks whitened as though dusted with flour–and we see for the first time that his smile is not real, but painted: his real mouth turns down while the smile, *what we thought was a smile,* remains obstinate and impersonal, on his weeping face. The mad laughter thunders to a peak, then rattles off into the distance. Hollow. Peculiar. Now: no more than an echo. And then that silence again. A silence we know now. The man's dark lips move, over and over, as though reciting some terrible syllable, shattering the painted smile, although, as we have come to expect, we can hear none of it. Just the – but then somewhat astonishingly, we *do* distinguish a noise of some sort, a new sound resembling gagging, a sort of strangled deep-throated gagging—

Slowly *quickly* we swoop backwards from the man and the sound, leave him there coiled in the snow, helpless like a beetle on its back, slide away from the vast and blinding plain, returning gratefully to the comforting shadows of the forest, the great weighted forest with its low-slung canopy of snow-laden boughs. *For a brief but stunning moment, we suddenly see the man's hysterical face again, as though in a memory, a sudden terrorizing recollection that drives a cold and unwanted terror through us*—but we gradually perceive that it is not the man at all, no, it is only the face of the white rabbit, nothing more, its wide-nostrilled nose quivering, its rodent eyes cloudy, its mouth split in a sardonic grin. As we slip back, we discover that it is between the jaws of the lean-bodied dog. Listening carefully, we are able to hear a rhythmic crackle, not unlike soldiers marching over fragile porcelain. Louder it grows and louder, even after the dog and the rabbit it is munching on are long since out of sight. At last, nevertheless, even this sound diminishes, is absorbed into the transcendent silence of winter. Snow begins to fall.

o   o   o

2

The Milkmaid of Samaniego

Llevaba en la cabeza
una lechera el cántaro etcetera *futuro;*
mira que ni el presente está seguro.

We've nothing present to let us suppose it, except the realization perhaps of being, vaguely, in the country somewhere, yet nevertheless it is true: there is, though we do not now see her, a milkmaid approaching. Nor is her coming suggested in any way by the man's expression or position. He for his part merely sits, as a man alone might sit, at the foot of the small arched bridge, staring idly at the stream eddying by, occasionally breaking a hunk of bread from the loaf in his lap and stuffing it between his yellow teeth. He chews without much interest, the thick wads of bread forming shifting bulges in his dark unshaven cheeks. Yet, for all that, there is in fact a milkmaid approaching, on her head a tall gently curving pitcher filled with fresh milk for the market. It's almost as though there has been some sort of unspoken but well understood prologue, no mere epigraph of random design, but a precise structure of predetermined images, both basic and prior to us, that describes her to us before our senses have located her in the present combination of shapes and colours. We are, then, aware of her undeniable approach, aware somehow of the slim graceful pitcher, the red kerchief knotted about her neck, her starched white blouse and brightly flowered skirt, her firm yet jubilant stride down the dusty road, this dusty road leading to the arched bridge, past the oaks and cypresses, the twisted wooden fences, the haphazard system of sheep and cattle, alongside the occasional cottage and frequent fields, fields of clover, cabbage, and timothy, past chickens scratching in the gravel by the road, and under the untempered ardour of the summer sun.

We might not, on the other hand, have thought of the man. And even had the ambiguity of our expectations allowed a space for him, as it might allow, for example, for various dispositions of the oaks, the cypresses, the daffodils and the cabbages, we probably would not have had him just at the bridge, just where our attention might, at the wrong moment, be distracted from the maid. And, what is more, his tattered black hat, the hair curling about his ears and around his sun-blackened neck, his torn yellow shirt open down the front, his fixed and swollen right eye, nearly two fingers lower than the left: these are all surprises, too, and of a sort that might encourage us to look for another bridge and another milkmaid, were such a happy option available. But, as though conscious of our sensing him intrusive and discomposing, he suddenly starts up from his idle contemplation of the brook below him, cocks his head attentively to the right, exaggerating thereby the grotesquerie of his bad eye, and slowly, deliberately, turns to look over his right shoulder, thus guiding us directly towards the milkmaid herself, now barely visible at a turning in the road, several hundred paces away.

The maid moves gracefully, evenly, surely towards us, as if carried by a breeze, though there is none this hot day, her delicate hands in the folds of her brightly flowered apron, lifting her apron and skirt slightly to make still smoother her light-bodied stride, on her head as though mounted there for all time the tall eggshell-white pitcher, the kind used for carrying fresh milk to the market. Her feet stir small swirls of dust in the road, intensifying the general effect of midsummer haze. A white hen rears up, ruffles its feathers, then scrambles across the road in front of her, stopping to scratch in the gravel on the other side. Even from this distance, we can make out the trace of a smile on the girl's fine-boned face, and beneath the red — or rather, daffodil yellow — kerchief knotted around her neck, her full breasts, fuller perhaps than we had expected, thrust proudly forward within the white starched blouse.

As she slowly completes the long turn in the road and approaches us from directly ahead, her hips broaden perceptibly, her skirts grow fuller. The pitcher, a stoneware jug, long and smooth with a narrow mouth, is a soft absorbent white, the slightly grey colour of eggshells; it rests steadily on her auburn head, as beneath it she moves with a gliding, purely linear motion down the dusty rutted road, a smile playing suggestively on her rouged mouth, her eyes looking neither left nor right, but steadfastly upon the road several paces ahead. As she walks, her skirt flutters and twists as though caught by some breeze, though there is none. Her — but the man, this one with the tattered hat and bulging eye, he stands and – no, no! the maid, *the maid!*

Through the eddies of dust swirling about her feet, we can catch an occasional glimpse of her ankles, rather thick but flashing nimbly in the summer sun beneath her dark skirt and brightly checked apron. Her hands, though coarse and broad-palmed, are strong and self-confident, the dark calloused hands of a milkmaid, hands that curry cattle, grasp swollen teats, and shovel fodder into bins. Above the kerchief, the rich colour of goldenrods, knotted about her neck, her bemused smile exposes large even teeth, white and healthy. Her nose shifts just a bit to the left, extends slightly, and above the right nostril there appears, or has appeared, a small dark spot not unlike a wart or mole. Her narrow black eyes look neither left nor right, but stare vacantly into the road several paces ahead. Above her high-boned face, tanned dark by the unremittent summer sun, and nested securely in her peat-coloured hair is the tall pitcher, completely undisturbed by her graceful heavy-bodied stride.

The pitcher itself is a pale grey in colour, shaded darker at the neck, and etched throughout with an intricate tracery of minute rust-coloured veins. Even from extreme proximity, we are struck by its resemblance, in both hue and texture, to the shells of white eggs. In fact, as we observe yet more closely, we discover that it is not a pitcher at all, though it has seemed like one, but actually real eggs, six dozen at least, maybe seven, all nestled in a great raffia basket, the kind of basket used for carrying fresh eggs to the market. Suddenly, even as we watch, a kind of internal energy seems to take possession of the eggs: they tumble about in the basket, burst open, and a hundred chicks or more, yes! surely more! pop out one by one, fluff out their yellow down, and scurry about for the seed tossed at them by the gay excited milkmaid in her brightly flowered apron. They fluster anxiously, almost furiously, about her narrowing ankles, and the faster they run, the faster they grow – now they are fat white hens, now they are still fatter yellow sows, their bellies scraping the ground, their snouts rummaging voraciously in the superfluity of cabbage, bran and acorns, which the slender maid is flinging into their troughs. And, as we look about now for the first time, we discover still more sows, chickens, too, even cattle with their calves, all surrounding as though glorifying in the happy milkmaid with the eggshell-white pitcher on her head.

Not more than a dozen paces away, a tall lad, dark and fine-boned with flashing brown eyes and bold mouth, curries a thick-chested coal-black bull, his sturdy tanned – but no more of that! for,

in short, he looks up, they exchange charged glances, smile, she casts
her eyes down. The boy seems paralysed, he gazes at her in wonder-
ment, at her beautiful auburn hair gleaming in the fiery summer sun,
at her gently blushing fair-skinned cheeks, at her soft ripe-breasted
body in its starched white blouse and brightly flowered skirt. The
currycomb drops to the ground. He pushes past the sows and the
young calves, struggles towards her, the smile gone from his lips, his
eyes wide and astonished, his nostrils distended. His hands are on
her breasts, on her face, tearing at her dress, tangled in her hair – *no!
not – !* She wrenches free, but as she does so, she feels a sudden light-
ening, almost a sense of growth, as the pitcher of fresh milk leans forward, topples, caroms off the boy's lurching shoulders, and plummets into the dust at his fading feet. The white liquid bubbles out of
the narrow mouth, seeps futilely into the dry yellow dust of the rutted
road at the foot of the small arched bridge.

The maid stoops to right the pitcher, but too late. Gone. The milk,
the eggs, the chickens, the fatbellied sows, the cows and the calves,
that clumsy stupid beautiful boy: all gone. Tears burst down the
maid's tanned face. Gone, *gone!* In her anguish, she does not at first
notice the two dry cracked hands that are helping her set aright the
stoneware jug, but when through her tears she sees them at last, it
takes but a brief second more for her to discover the rest: the tattered
black hat and uncut hair, the dark bearded face with its bulging
bloodshot eye, the sweat-stained shirt open down to the belt. She
starts back in terror, her right hand pressed against her open mouth.
She scrambles to her feet. Her left hand comes up as though to ward
off some blow. She steps back, seems about to run. The man sets the
pitcher in the grass by the foot of the bridge, turns back to her,
smiles. She smiles faintly, wipes the tears from her cheeks, takes
another rearward step. He looks down at himself, at his torn yellow
shirt and muddy shoes, makes an apologetic gesture, bows slightly
from the waist. She nods, clutches with both hands her brightly
checked apron, smiles again, shakes her head, does not step back.
He shrugs his shoulders, gestures at the sun, at the pitcher standing
by the bridge, at the bread beside it in the grass. She smiles openly,
showing her large white teeth, shakes her head, also gestures at the
high sun and then at the road she has just travelled. He follows her
gestures, gazes with real compassion down the long dusty road, then
again at the empty pitcher, hesitates, finally reaches into his pocket
and withdraws some coins. He shows them to the maid. She steps
forward to observe them more closely: they are few, but of gold and
silver. They look, to tell the truth, like nothing less than a whole

private universe of midsummer suns in the man's strong dark hand. She smiles, casts her eyes down.

The pitcher, thought at first to be stable in the grass at the foot of the bridge, is actually, as we now can see, on a small spiny ridge: it weaves, leans, then finally rolls over in a gently curving arc, bursting down its rust-coloured veins into a thousand tiny fragments, fragments not unlike the broken shells of white eggs. Many of these fragments remain in the grass at the foot of the bridge, while others tumble silently down the hill into the eddying stream below.

o   o   o

3

The Leper's Helix

At first, in an instant half-real half-remembered, the leper is at rest; then he begins his approach, urgent across the – no, no! impossible! he has always been beginning, always approaching, it was the glare, just the glare caused the illusion: sun at its zenith and this leper coming on. Solitary flutter advancing like a crippled bird, the leper, staggering out of isolation, staggering towards us as though in amazement, joy, disbelief, here under the boiling desert sun, across the parched and desolate surface, jerking, twisting his white robe – if it is a robe – stirring starched and binding, illustrating the fault of his motion, the painful shifts of fulcrum through his abdomen, the strange uncertain gait as though he lacks the hang of it, or having had it, lost it, dazzling white this shimmery figure crossing the molten red flats, his outline blurred by the savage glare.

Our own progress, on the other hand, is precise, governed, has been from the start. The active principle, we might call it. Might mockingly call it. We are describing a great circle on the desert surface, the leper's starting position as our compass point (thus, admittedly, forcing a further reconsideration of the realities of that first idle moment – good god! must we fall foul of such riddles forever?). Since the leper is always approaching, must always approach, we compel him with this studied tour to bend his stupid bungling lope into a spiral, so regulating our own velocity as to schedule his arrival, if only he doesn't stumble, the fool, and fall (and he does not, will not), at our starting point.

He seems puzzled by our motion – hah! must look to him like flight, recoil, he unable, at such separation, to envision any shape to our career–but o constancy! he but devotes more strength to the cause, more of his failing strength, feet now pigeon-toed now splayed, arms flung like torn sails grappling for a stay, pelvis now thrust forward now twisted to one side, head swaying precariously on his thin white (is it for art's sake we prolong this miserable journey? what matter! for art or no, *let him know extremity!* – how else obtain impact for its counterpart?) neck. His approach in some other circumstances might even serve for comedy, this ungainly, high-legged, limbs-awry dance in the hot sun. It's his isolation cuts the humour. If anything is a serious thing, it must be he.

Our speed is not constant. No, were it so, we would leave him behind at the end, we would have to inscribe additional circles to catch him from the rear, a dull and pointless strategy. So our velocity diminishes, doubtless at a computable rate. He does not know that. He merely dances on, arms and legs outflung, dances on helplessly – yet full of hope, that old disease – scratching his helix across the desert floor, less true perhaps than our perfect circle, yet for that the more beautiful, his steaming white helix on the burnt red plane. His robe seems not so much a robe as a ... a winding sheet! *Death!* we cry inwardly, but beat back the (alarming!) absurdity. It's the sun, only the sun, the glare, heat – but only for a moment! it is, and to the end will be, a leper in a white tunic. And he, not we, will die.

Down the last arc segment we glide, closing it now, our task more than two-thirds done, the worst of it over. Our pace letting up, steadily – he is close enough now for us to see his eager smile: *strange* that smile! for his mouth is split apart at the corners, and even not smiling he would surely seem to. Crusted eyes protruding over shiny white cheekbones, tattered ends of his white flesh confusing themselves with (peculiar, perhaps, this sensuous digression, and just at this moment, but there's, you see, a kind of pleasure to be had in it, a need being reached) confuse themselves with his fluttering robe, flake off in a scaly dust that blurs his outline, dance lightly around him as he staggers wildly on, closing in on us. The flesh, the flesh reminds of mica: translucent layers of dead scaly material, here and there hardened into shiny nodules, here and there disturbed by deep cavities. In the beds of these cavities: a dark substance, resembling blood not so much as ... as: excrement. Well, simple illusion, blood mixed with pus and baked in the sun, that's what it is. His bare feet leave a trail of this viscous brown.

But now – oh my god! – as a mere few paces separate us, our

point of origin – and end! – just visible before us, the brute reality
slams through the barriers of our senses: *the encounter is now im-
minent!* Absorbed in our visual registrations, our meaningless mathe-
matics, our hedonistic pleasure in mere action and its power – how
could we have wasted it all! – we had forgot what was to come at
the end! had we thought, only *thought*, we could have drawn two
circles, or ten circles, postponed this ultimate experience, *could* have,
but the choice was ours just once, our impulsive first action has
become – alas! – a given, the inexorable governor of all that remains
– or has the leper had us all along? did his pace allow two circles?
and does it matter? for the encounter must come, mustn't it?
whether after one circle, two circles, or ten.

It is of no consequence. There is in us that conditions acceptance.
We turn to greet the leper.

Our hands, *my* hands, appear before us, ruddy, hairy, thick-
wristed, muscular, fine rich blood pounding through them, extended
now for the embrace. They do not tremble. The leper, tongue
dangling – *god! nearly black!* – frothing pitifully at the mouth, eyes
blank, whole wretched body oozing a kind of milky sweat, hurls
himself into our arms, smothering us, pitching us to the red clay, his
sticky cold flesh fastening to us, me, his black tongue licking my face,
blind eyes, that whine! his odours choking us, we lie, I lie helpless
under the sickening weight of his perishing flesh. Then, in the same
instant, it is over. Purged of all revulsions, we free ourselves from
him, lay him gently on the red earth, dry his final ecstatic tears. At
first, we make an effort to claw the earth with our fingers, dig a hole
large enough to conceal the blight of his gathering decay. But we
weary of it: the earth is hard, burial an old reflex. We leave him lie
and sit beside to wait. Under the desert sun. We wait, as he waited
for us, for you. Desperate in need, yet with terror. What terrible
game will *you* play with *us?* me.

A Pedestrian Accident

Paul stepped off the kerb and got hit by a truck. He didn't know what it was that hit him at first, but now, here on his back, under the truck, there could be no doubt. Is it me? he wondered. Have I walked the earth and come here?

Just as he was struck, and while still tumbling in front of the truck and then under the wheels, in a kind of funhouse gambado of pain and terror, he had thought: this has happened before. His neck had sprung, there was a sudden flash of light and a blaze roaring up in the back of his head. The hot — almost fragrant — pain: that was new. It was the *place* he felt he'd returned to.

He lay perpendicular to the length of the truck, under the trailer, just to the rear of the truck's second of three sets of wheels. All of him was under the truck but his head and shoulders. Maybe I'm being born again, he reasoned. He stared straight up, past the side of the truck, towards the sky, pale blue and cloudless. The tops of skyscrapers closed towards the centre of his vision; now that he thought about it, he realized it was the first time in years he had looked up at them, and they seemed inclined to fall. The old illusion; one of them anyway. The truck was red with white letters, but his severe angle of vision up the side kept him from being able to read the letters. A capital 'K', he could see that — and a number, yes, it seemed to be a '14'. He smiled inwardly at the irony, for he had a private fascination with numbers: fourteen! He thought he remembered having had a green light, but it didn't really matter. No way to prove it. It would have changed by now, in any case. The thought, obscurely, troubled him.

'Crazy goddamn fool he just walk right out in fronta me no respect just burstin for a bustin!'

The voice, familiar somehow, guttural, yet falsetto, came from above and to his right. People were gathering to stare down at him, shaking their heads. He felt like one chosen. He tried to turn his head towards the voice, but his neck flashed hot again. Things were bad. Better just to lie still, take no chances. Anyway, he saw now, just in the corner of his eye, the cab of the truck, red like the trailer, and poking out its window, the large head of the truckdriver, wagging in the sunshine. The driver wore a small tweed cap – too small, in fact: it sat just on top of his head.

'Boy I seen punchies in my sweet time but this cookie takes the cake God bless the labouring classes I say and preserve us from the humble freak!'

The truckdriver spoke with broad gestures, bulbous eyes rolling, runty body thrusting itself in and out of the cab window, little hands flying wildly about. Paul worried still about the light. It was important, yet how could he ever know? The world was an ephemeral place, it could get away from you in a minute. The driver had a bent red nose and coarse reddish hair that stuck out like straw. A hard shiny chin, too, like a mirror image of the hooked nose. Paul's eyes wearied of the strain, and he had to stop looking.

'Listen lays and gentmens I'm a good Christian by Judy a decent hardworkin fambly man earnin a honest wage and got a dear little woman and seven yearnin younguns all my own seed *a responsible man* and goddamn that boy what he do but walk right into me and my poor ole truck!'

On some faces Paul saw compassion, or at least a neutral curiosity, an idle amusement, but on most he saw reproach. There were those who winced on witnessing his state and seemed to understand, but there were others – a majority – who jeered.

'He asked for it if you ask me!'

'It's the idler plays the fool and the workingman's to hang for it!'

'Shouldn't allow his kind out to walk the streets!'

'What is the use of running when you are on the wrong road?'

It worsened. Their shouts grew louder and ran together. There were orations and the waving of flags. Paul was wondering: had he been carrying anything? No, no. He had only – *wait!* a book? Very likely, but ... ah well. Perhaps he was carrying it still. There was no feeling in his fingers.

The people were around him like flies, grievances were being aired, sides taken, and there might have been a brawl, but a policeman arrived and broke it up. 'All right, everybody! Stand back, please!' he shouted. 'Give this man some air! Can't you see he's been injured?'

At last, Paul thought. He relaxed. For a moment, he'd felt himself in a strange and hostile country, but now he felt at home again. He even began to believe he might survive. Though really: had he ever doubted it?

'Everybody back, *back!*' The policeman was effective. The crowd grew quiet, and by the sound of their sullen shuffling, Paul guessed they were backing off. Not that he got more or less air by it, but he felt relieved just the same. 'Now,' said the policeman, gently but firmly, 'what has happened here?'

And with that it all started up again, same as before, the clamour, the outrage, the arguments, the learned quotations, but louder and more discordant than ever. I'm hurt, Paul said. No one heard. The policeman cried out for order, and slowly, with his shouts, with his nightstick, with his threats, he reduced them again to silence.

One lone voice hung at the end: ' – for the last time, Mister, *stop goosing me!*' Everybody laughed, released.

'Stop goosing her, sir!' the policeman commanded with his chin thrust firmly forward, and everybody laughed again.

Paul almost laughed, but he couldn't, quite. Besides, he'd just, with that, got the picture, and given his condition, it was not a funny one. He opened his eyes and there was the policeman bent down over him. He had a notebook in his hand.

'Now, tell me, son, what happened here?' The policeman's face was thin and pale, like a student's, and he wore a trim little tuft of black moustache under the pinched peak of his nose.

I've just been hit, Paul explained, by this truck, and then he realized that he probably didn't say it at all, that speech was an art no longer his. He cast his eyes indicatively towards the cab of the truck.

'Listen, I asked you what happened here! Cat got your tongue, young man?'

'Crazy goddamn fool he just walk right out in fronta me no respect just burstin for a bustin!'

The policeman remained crouched over Paul, but turned his head up to look at the truckdriver. The policeman wore a brilliant blue uniform with large brass buttons. And gold epaulettes.

'Boy I seen punchies in my sweet time but this cookie takes the cake God bless the labouring classes I say and preserve us from the humble freak!'

The policeman looked down at Paul, then back at the truckdriver. 'I know about truckdrivers,' Paul heard him say.

'Listen lays and gentmens I'm a good Christian by Judy a decent hardworkin fambly man earnin a honest wage and got a dear little woman and seven yearnin younguns all my own seed *a responsible man* and goddamn that boy what he do but walk right into me and my poor ole trike. Truck, I mean.'

There was a loose tittering from the crowd, but the policeman's frown and raised stick contained it. 'What's your name, lad?' he asked, turning back to Paul. At first, the policeman smiled, he knew who truckdrivers were and he knew who Pauls were, and there was a salvation of sorts in that smile, but gradually it faded. 'Come, come, boy! Don't be afraid!' He winked, nudged him gently. 'We're here to help you.'

Paul, Paul replied. But, no, no doubt about it, it was jammed up in there and he wasn't getting it out.

'Well, if you won't help me, I can't help you,' the policeman said pettishly and tilted his nose up. 'Anybody here know this man?' he called out to the crowd.

Again a roar, a threatening tumult of words and sounds, shouts back and forth. It was hard to know if none knew him or if they all did. But then one voice, belted out above the others, came through: 'O God in heaven! It's Amory! *Amory Westerman!*' The voice, a woman's, hysterical by the sound of it, drew near. 'Amory! What ... *what* have they *done* to you?'

Paul understood. It was not a mistake. He was astonished by his own acumen.

'Do you know this young man?' the policeman asked, lifting his notebook.

'What? Know him? Did Sarah know Abraham? Did Eve know Cain?'

The policeman cleared his throat uneasily. 'Adam,' he corrected softly.

'You know who you know, I know who I know,' the woman said, and let fly with a low throaty snigger. The crowd responded with a belly laugh.

'But this young man—!' the policeman insisted, flustered.

'Who, you and Amory?' the woman cried. 'I can't believe it!' The crowd laughed and the policeman bit his lip. 'Amory! What new persecutions are these?' She billowed out above him: old, maybe even seventy, fat and bosomy, pasty-faced with thick red rouges, head haloed by ringlets of sparse orangeish hair. 'My poor Amory!' And down she came on him. Paul tried to duck, got only a hot flash in his neck for it. Her breath reeked of cheap gin. Help, said Paul.

'Hold, madame! Stop!' the policeman cried, tugging at the woman's sleeve. She stood, threw up her arms before her face, staggered backwards. What more she did, Paul couldn't see, for his view of her face was largely blocked by the bulge of her breasts and belly. There were laughs, though. 'Everything in order here,' grumped the policeman, tapping his notebook. 'Now, what's your name, please ... uh ... miss, madame?'

'My name?' She twirled gracelessly on one dropsied ankle and cried to the crowd: 'Shall I tell?'

'Tell! Tell! Tell!' shouted the spectators, clapping rhythmically. Paul let himself be absorbed by it; there was, after all, nothing else to do.

The policeman, rapping a pencil against his blue notebook to the rhythm of the chant, leaned down over Paul and whispered: ('I think we've got them on our side now!')

Paul, his gaze floating giddily up past the thin white face of the police officer and the red side of the truck into the horizonless blue haze above, wondered if alliance were really the key to it all. What am I without them? Could I even die? Suddenly, the whole world seemed to tip: his feet dropped and his head rose. Beneath him the red machine shot grease and muck, the host rioted above his head, the earth pushed him from behind, and out front the skyscrapers pointed, like so many insensate fingers, the path he must walk to oblivion. He squeezed shut his eyes to set right the world again – he was afraid he would slide down beneath the truck to disappear from sight forever.

'My name—!' bellowed the woman, and the crowd hushed, tittering softly. Paul opened his eyes. He was on his back again. The policeman stood over him, mouth agape, pencil poised. The woman's puffy face was sequined with sweat. Paul wondered what she'd been doing while he wasn't watching. 'My name, officer, is Grundy.'

'I beg your pardon?' The policeman, when nervous, had a way of nibbling his moustache with his lowers.

'Mrs Grundy, dear boy, who did you think I was?' She patted the policeman's thin cheek, tweaked his nose. 'But you can call me Charity, handsome!' The policeman blushed. She twiddled her index finger in his little moustache. 'Kootchy-kootchy-koo!' There was a roar of laughter from the crowd.

The policeman sneezed. 'Please!' he protested.

Mrs Grundy curtsied and stooped to unzip the officer's fly. 'Hello! Anybody home!'

'*Stop that!*' squeaked the policeman through the thunderous laughter and applause. Strange, thought Paul, how much I'm enjoying this.

'Come out, come out, wherever you are!'

'*The story!*' the policeman insisted through the tumult.

'Story? What——?'

'This young fellow,' said the policeman, pointing with his pencil. He zipped up, blew his nose. 'Mr, uh, Mr Westerman ... you said——'

'Mr *Who?*' the woman shook her jowls, perplexed. She frowned down at Paul, then brightened. 'Oh yes! Amory!' She paled, seemed to sicken. Paul, if he could've, would've smiled. 'Good God!' she rasped, as though appalled at what she saw. Then, once more, she took an operatic grip on her breasts and staggered back a step. 'O mortality! O fatal mischief! Done in! A noble man lies stark and stiff! Delenda est Carthago! *Sic transit glans mundi!*'

Gloria, corrected Paul. No, leave it.

'Squashed like a lousy bug!' she cried. 'And at the height of his potency!'

'Now, wait a minute!' the policeman protested.

'The final curtain! The last farewell! The journey's end! Over the hill! The last muster!' Each phrase was answered by a happy shout from the mob. 'Across the river! The way of all flesh! The last roundup!' She sobbed, then ballooned down on him again, tweaked his ear and whispered: ('How's Charity's weetsie snotkins, eh? Him fall down and bump his little putsy? Mumsy kiss and make well!') And she let him have it on the – well, sort of on the left side of his nose, left cheek, and part of his left eye: one wet enveloping sour blubbering kiss, and this time, sorrily, the policeman did not intervene. He was busy taking notes. Officer, said Paul.

'Hmmm,' the policeman muttered, and wrote. 'G - R -U - N - ah, ahem, Grundig, Grundig - D, yes, D - I - G. Now what did you——?'

The woman laboured clumsily to her feet, plodded over behind the policeman, and squinted over his shoulder at the notes he was taking. 'That's a "Y" there, buster, a "Y".' She jabbed a stubby ruby-tipped finger at the notebook.

'Grundigy?' asked the policeman in disbelief. 'What kind of a name is that?'

'No, no!' the old woman whined, her grand manner flung to the winds. 'Grundy! Grundy! Without the "-ig", don't you see? You take off your——'

'Oh, *Grundy!* Now I have it!' The policeman scrubbed the back end of his pencil in the notebook. 'Darned eraser. About shot.' The paper tore. He looked up irritably. 'Can't we just make it Grundig?'

'Grundy,' said the woman coldly.

The policeman ripped the page out of his notebook, rumpled it up angrily, and hurled it to the street. 'All right, gosh damn it all!' he cried in a rage, scribbling: 'Grundy. I have it. Now get on with it, lady!'

'Officer!' sniffed Mrs Grundy, clasping a handkerchief to her throat. 'Remember your place, or I shall have to speak to your superior!' The policeman shrank, blanched, nibbled his lip.

Paul knew what would come. He could read these two like a book. *I'm* the strange one, he thought. He wanted to watch their faces, but his streetlevel view gave him at best a perspective on their underchins. It was their crotches that were prominent. Butts and bellies: the squashed bug's-eye view. And that was strange, too: that he wanted to watch their faces.

The policeman was begging for mercy, wringing his pale hands. There were faint hissing sounds, wriggling out of the crowd like serpents. 'Cut the shit, mac,' Charity Grundy said finally. 'you're overdoing it.' The officer chewed his moustache, stared down at his notebook, abashed. 'You wanna know who this poor clown is, right?' The policeman nodded. 'Okay, are you ready?' She clasped her bosom again and the crowd grew silent. The police officer held his notebook up, the pencil poised. Mrs Grundy snuffled, looked down at Paul, winced, turned away and wept. 'Officer!' she gasped. *'He was my lover!'*

Halloos and cheers from the crowd, passing to laughter. The policeman started to smile, blinking down at Mrs Grundy's body, but with a twitch of his moustache, he suppressed it.

'We met ... just one year ago today. O fateful hour!' She smiled bravely, brushing back a tear, her lower lip quivering. Once, her hands clenched woefully before her face, she winked down at Paul. The wink nearly convinced him. Maybe I'm him after all. Why not? 'He was selling seachests, door to door. I can see him now as he was then—' She paused to look down at him as he was now, and wrinkles of revulsion swept over her face. Somehow this brought laughter. She looked away, puckered her mouth and bugged her eyes, shook one hand limply from the wrist. The crowd was really with her.

'Mrs Grundy,' the officer whispered, 'please ...'

'Yes, there he was, chapfallen and misused, orphaned by the

rapacious world, yet pure and undefiled, there: there at my door!'
With her baggy arm, flung out, quavering, she indicated the door.
'Bent nearly double under his impossible seachest, perspiration
illuminating his manly brow, wounding his eyes, wrinkling his undershirt—'

'Careful!' cautioned the policeman nervously, glancing up from
his notes. He must have filled twenty or thirty pages by now.

'In short, my heart went out to him!' Gesture of heart going out.
'And though – alas! – my need for seachests was limited—'

The spectators somehow discovered something amusing in this
and tittered knowingly. Mainly in the way she said it, he supposed.
Her story in truth did not bother Paul so much as his own fascination
with it. He knew where it would lead, but it didn't matter. In fact,
maybe that *was* what fascinated him.

'—I invited him in. Put down that horrid seachest, dear boy, and
come in here, I cried, come in to your warm and obedient Charity,
love, come in for a cup of tea, come in and rest, rest your pretty little
shoulders, your pretty little back, your pretty little ...' Mrs Grundy
paused, smiled with a faint arch of one eyebrow, and the crowd
responded with another burst of laughter. 'And it *was* pretty little,
okay,' she grumbled, and again they whooped, while she sniggered
throatily.

How was it now? he wondered. In fact, he'd been wondering all
along.

'And, well, officer, that's what he did, he *did* put down his seachest
– alas! sad to tell, right on my unfortunate cat Rasputin, dozing
there in the day's brief sun, God rest his soul, his (again, alas!)
somewhat homaloidal soul!'

She had a great audience. They never failed her, nor did they
now.

The policeman, who had finally squatted down to write on his
knee, now stood and shouted for order. 'Quiet! *Quiet!*' His moustache twitched. 'Can't you see this is a serious matter?' He's the
funny one, thought Paul. The crowd thought so, too, for the laughter mounted, then finally died away. 'And ... and then what happened?' the policeman whispered. But they heard him anyway and
screamed with delight, throwing up a new clamour in which could
be distinguished several coarse paraphrases of the policeman's question. The officer's pale face flushed. He looked down at Paul with a
brief commiserating smile, shrugged his shoulders, fluttering the
epaulettes. Paul made a try at a never-mind kind of gesture, but, he
supposed, without bringing it off.

'What happened next, you ask, you naughty boy?' Mrs Grundy shook and wriggled. Cheers and whistles. She cupped her plump hands under her breasts and hitched her abundant hips heavily to one side. 'You don't understand,' she told the crowd. 'I only wished to be a mother to the lad.' Hoohahs and catcalls. 'But I had failed to realize, in that fleeting tragic moment when he unburdened himself upon poor Rasputin, how I was wrenching his young and unsullied heart asunder! Oh yes, I know, I know—'

'This is the dumbest story I ever heard,' interrupted the policeman finally, but Mrs Grundy paid him no heed.

'I know I'm old and fat, that I've crossed the Grand Climacteric!' She winked at the crowd's yowls of laughter. 'I know the fragrant flush of first flower is gone forever!' she cried, not letting a good thing go, pressing her wrinkled palms down over the soft swoop of her blimp-sized hips, peeking coyly over one plump shoulder at the shrieking crowd. The policeman stamped his foot, but no one noticed except Paul. 'I know, I know – *yet:* somehow, face to face with little Charity, a primitive unnameable urgency welled up in his untaught loins, his pretty little—'

'*Stop it!*' cried the policeman, right on cue. 'This has gone far enough!'

'And *you* ask what happened next? I shall tell you, officer! For why conceal the truth ... from you of all people?' Though uneasy, the policeman seemed frankly pleased that she had put it this way. 'Yes, without further discourse, he buried his pretty little head in my bosom—' (Paul felt a distressing sense of suffocation, though perhaps it had been with him all the while) ' – and he tumbled me there, yes he did, there on the front porch alongside his seachest and my dying Rasputin, there in the sunlight, before God, before the neighbours, before Mr Dunlevy the mailman who is hard of hearing, before the children from down the block passing on their shiny little—'

'Crazy goddamn fool he just walk right out in fronta me no respect just burstin for a bustin!' said a familiar voice.

Mrs Grundy's broad face, now streaked with tears and mottled with a tense pink flush, glowered. There was a long and difficult silence. Then she narrowed her eyes, smiled faintly, squared her shoulders, touched a handkerchief to her eye, plunged the handkerchief back down her bosom, and resumed: '—Before, in short, the whole itchy eyes-agog world, a coupling unequalled in the history of Western concupiscence!' Some vigorous applause, which she acknowledged. 'Assaulted, but – yes, I confess it – assaulted, but *aglow*, I reminded him of—'

'Boy I seen punchies in my sweet time but this cookie takes the cake God bless the labouring classes I say and preserve us from the humble freak!'

Swivelling his wearying gaze hard right, Paul could see the truckdriver waggling his huge head at the crowd. Mrs Grundy padded heavily over to him, the back of her thick neck reddening, swung her purse in a great swift arc, but the truckdriver recoiled into his cab, laughing with a taunting cackle. Then, almost in the same instant, he poked his red-beaked head out again, and rolling his eyes, said: 'Listen lays and gentmens I'm a good Christian by Judy a decent hardworkin fambly man earnin a honest wage and got a dear little woman and seven yearnin younguns all my own seed *a responsible*—'

'*I'll responsible your ass!*' hollered Charity Grundy and let fly with her purse again, but once more the driver ducked nimbly inside, cackling obscenely. The crowd, taking sides, was more hysterical than ever. Cheers were raised and bets taken.

Again the driver's waggling head popped out: '—*man* and god—' he began, but this time Mrs Grundy was waiting for him. Her great lumpish purse caught him square on his bent red nose – ka-RAACKK! – and the truckdriver slumped lifelessly over the door of his cab, his stubby little arms dangling limp, reaching just below the top of his head. As best Paul could tell, the tweed cap did not drop off, but since his eyes were cramped with fatigue, he had to stop looking before the truckdriver's head ceased bobbing against the door.

Man and god! he thought. Of course! terrific! What did it mean? Nothing.

The policeman made futile little gestures of interference, but apparently had too much respect for Mrs Grundy's purse to carry them out. That purse was big enough to hold a bowling ball, and maybe it did.

Mrs Grundy, tongue dangling and panting furiously, clapped one hand over her heart and, with the handkerchief, fanned herself with the other. Paul saw sweat dripping down her legs. 'And so – *foo! – I ... I – puf!* – I reminded him of ... of the – *whee!* – the cup of tea!' she gasped. She paused, swallowed, mopped her brow, sucked in a deep lungful of air, and exhaled it slowly. She cleared her throat. '*And so I reminded him of the cup of tea!*' she roared with a grand sweep of one powerful arm, the old style recovered. There was a general smattering of complimentary applause, which Mrs Grundy acknowledged with a short nod of her head. 'We went inside. The air was heavy with expectation and the unmistakable aroma of catshit. One might almost be pleased that Rasputin had yielded up the spirit—'

'Now JUST STOP IT!' cried the policeman. 'THIS IS—'

'I poured some tea, we sang the now famous duet, "¡Ciérrate la bragueta! ¡La bragueta está cerrada!," I danced for him, he – '

'ENOUGH, I SAID!' screamed the policeman, his little moustache quivering with indignation. 'THIS IS ABSURD!'

You're warm, said Paul. But that's not quite it.

'Absurd?' cried Charity Grundy, aghast. 'Absurd? You call my dancing absurd?'

'I . . . I didn't say—'

'Grotesque, perhaps, and yes, a bit awesome – but absurd!' She grabbed him by the lapels, lifting him off the ground. 'What do you have against dancing, you worm? What do you have against grace?'

'P-please! Put me down!'

'Or is it, you don't believe I can dance?' She dropped him.

'N-no!' he squeaked, brushing himself off, straightening his epaulettes. 'No! I—'

'Show him! Show him!' chanted the crowd.

The policeman spun on them. 'STOP! IN THE NAME OF THE LAW!' They obeyed. 'This man is injured. He may die. He needs help. It's no joking matter. I ask for your cooperation.' He paused for effect. 'That's better.' The policeman stroked his moustache, preening a bit. 'Now, ahem, is there a doctor present? A doctor, please?'

'Oh, officer, you're cute! You're very cute!' said Mrs Grundy on a new tack. The crowd snickered. 'Is there a doctor present?' she mimicked, 'a doctor, please?'

'Now just cut it out!' the policeman ordered, glaring angrily across Paul's chest at Mrs Grundy. 'Gosh damn it now, you stop it this instant, or . . . or you'll see what'll happen!'

'Aww, you're jealous!' cried Mrs Grundy. 'And of poor little supine Rasputin! Amory, I mean.' The spectators were in great spirits again, total rebellion threatening, and the police officer was at the end of his rope. 'Well, don't be jealous, dear boy!' cooed Mrs Grundy. 'Charity tell you a weetsie bitty secret.'

'Stop!' sobbed the policeman. Be careful where you step, said Paul below.

Mrs Grundy leaned perilously over Paul and got a grip on the policeman's ear. He winced, but no longer attempted escape. 'That boy,' she said, 'he humps terrible!'

It carried out to the crowd and broke it up. It was her big line and she wambled about gloriously, her rouged mouth stretched in a flabby toothless grin, retrieving the pennies that people were pitching (Paul knew about them from being hit by them; one landed on his upper lip, stayed there, emitting that familiar dead smell common to pennies the world over), thrusting her chest forward to catch them in the cleft of her bosom. She shook and, shaking, jangled. She grabbed the policeman's hand and pulled him forward to share a bow with her. The policeman smiled awkwardly, twitching his moustache.

'You asked for a doctor,' said an old but gentle voice.

The crowd noises subsided. Paul opened his eyes and discovered above him a stooped old man in a rumpled grey suit. His hair was shaggy and white, his face dry, lined with age. He wore rimless glasses, carried a black leather bag. He smiled down at Paul, that easy smile of a man who comprehends and assuages pain, then looked back at the policeman. Inexplicably, a wave of terror shook Paul.

'You wanted a doctor,' the old man repeated.

'Yes! *Yes!*' cried the policeman, almost in tears. 'Oh, thank God!'

'I'd rather you thanked the profession,' the doctor said. 'Now what seems to be the problem?'

'Oh, Doctor, it's awful!' The policeman twisted the notebook in his hands, fairly destroying it. 'This man has been struck by this truck, or so it would appear, no one seems to know, it's all a terrible mystery, and there is a woman, but now I don't see—? and I'm not even sure of his name –'

'No matter,' interrupted the doctor with a kindly nod of his old head, 'who he is. He is a man and that, I assure you, is enough for me.'

'Doctor, that's so good of you to say so!' wept the policeman.

I'm in trouble, thought Paul. Oh boy, I'm really in trouble.

'Well, now, let us just see,' said the doctor, crouching down over Paul. He lifted Paul's eyelids with his thumb and peered intently at Paul's eyes; Paul, anxious to assist, rolled them from side to side. 'Just relax, son,' the doctor said. He opened his black bag, rummaged about in it, withdrew a flashlight. Paul was not sure exactly what the doctor did after that, but he seemed to be looking in his ears. I can't move my head, Paul told him, but the doctor only asked: 'Why does he have a penny under his nose?' His manner was not such as to insist upon an answer, and he got none. Gently, expertly, he pried Paul's teeth apart, pinned his tongue down with a wooden depresser, and scrutinized his throat. Paul's head was on fire with pain. 'Ahh, yes,' he mumbled. 'Hum, hum.'

'How ... how is he, Doctor?' stammered the policeman, his voice muted with dread and respect. 'Will ... will he ... ?'

The doctor glared scornfully at the officer, then withdrew a stethoscope from his bag. He hooked it in his ears, slipped the disc inside Paul's shirt and listened intently, his old head inclined to one side like a bird listening for worms. Absolute silence now. Paul could hear the doctor breathing, the policeman whimpering softly. He had the vague impression that the doctor tapped his chest a time or two, but if so, he didn't feel it. His head felt better with his mouth closed. 'Hmmm,' said the doctor gravely, 'yes . . .'

'Oh, please! What *is* it, Doctor?' the policeman cried.

'What is it? *What is it?*' shouted the doctor in a sudden burst of rage. 'I'll tell you *what is it!*' He sprang to his feet, nimble for an old man. 'I cannot examine this patient while you're hovering over my shoulder and mewling like a goddamn schoolboy, *that's* what *is* it!'

'B-but I only—' stammered the officer, staggering backwards.

'And how do you expect me to examine a man half buried under a damned truck?' The doctor was in a terrible temper.

'But I—'

'Damn it! I'll but-I-you, you idiot, if you don't remove this truck from the scene so that I can determine the true gravity of this man's injuries! *Have I made myself clear?*'

'Y-yes! But . . . but wh-what am I to *do?*' wept the police officer, hands clenched before his mouth. 'I'm only a simple policeman, Doctor, doing my duty before God and count—'

'Simple, you said it!' barked the doctor. 'I *told* you what to do, you God-and-cunt simpleton – *now get moving!*'

God and cunt! Did it again, thought Paul. Now what?

The policeman, chewing wretchedly on the corners of his notebook, stared first at Paul, then at the truck, at the crowd, back at the truck. Paul felt fairly certain now that the letter following the 'K' on the truck's side was an 'I'. 'Shall I . . . shall I pull him out from under —?' the officer began tentatively, thin chin aquiver.

'*Good God, no!*' stormed the doctor, stamping his foot. 'This man may have a broken neck! Moving him would *kill* him, don't you see that, you sniveling birdbrain? Now, goddamn it, wipe your wretched nose and go wake up your – your accomplice up there, *and I mean right now!* Tell him to back his truck *off* this poor devil!'

'B-back it off—! But . . . but he'd have to run *over* him again! He—'

'Don't by God run-over-him-again *me*, you blackshirt hireling, *or I'll have your badge!*' screamed the doctor, brandishing his stethoscope.

The policeman hesitated but a moment to glance down at Paul's body, then turned and ran to the front of the truck. 'Hey! Come on, you!' He whacked the driver on the head with the nightstick. Hollow *thunk!* 'Up and at 'em!'

'—DAM THAT BOY WHAT,' cried the truckdriver rearing up wildly and fluttering his head as though lost, 'HE DO BUT WALK RIGHT INTO ME AND MY POOR OLE TRICK! TRUCK, I MEAN!' The crowd laughed again, first time in a long time, but the doctor stamped his foot and they quieted right down.

'Now, start up that engine, you, right now! I mean it!' ordered the policeman, stroking his moustache. He was getting a little of his old spit and polish back. He slapped the nightstick in his palm two or three times.

Paul felt the pavement under his back quake as the truckdriver started the motor. The white letters above him joggled in their red fields like butterflies. Beyond, the sky's blue had deepened, but white clouds now flowered in it. The skyscrapers had greyed, as though withdrawing information.

The truck's noise smothered the voices, but Paul did overhear the doctor and the policeman occasionally, the doctor ranting, the policeman imploring, something about mass and weight and vectors and direction. It was finally decided to go forward, since there were two sets of wheels up front and only one to the rear (a decent kind of humanism maintaining, after all, thought Paul), but the truckdriver apparently misunderstood, because he backed up anyway, and the middle set of wheels rolled up on top of Paul.

'Stop! STOP!' shrieked the police officer, and the truck motor coughed and died. 'I ordered you to go *forwards*, you pighead, not backwards!'

The driver popped his head out the window, bulged his ping-pong-ball eyes at the policeman, then waggled his tiny hands in his ears and brayed. The officer took a fast practised swing at the driver's big head (epaulettes, or no, he still had a skill or two), but the driver deftly dodged it. He clapped his runty hands and bobbed back inside the cab.

'What oh *what* shall we ever do *now?*' wailed the officer. The doctor scowled at him with undisguised disgust. Paul felt like he was strangling, but he could locate no specific pain past his neck. 'Dear lord above! There's wheels on each side of him and wheels in the middle!'

'Capital!' the doctor snorted. 'Figure that out by yourself, or somebody help you?'

'You're making fun,' whimpered the officer.

'AND YOU'RE MURDERING THIS MAN!' bellowed the doctor.

The police officer uttered a short anxious cry, then raced to the front of the truck again. Hostility welling in the crowd, Paul could hear it. 'Okay, okay!' cried the officer. 'Back up or go forward, *please*, I don't care, but hurry! HURRY!'

The motor started up again, there was a jarring grind of gears abrading, then slowly   slowly   slowly   the middle set of wheels backed down off Paul's body. There was a brief tense interim before the next set climbed up on him, hesitated as a ferris wheel hesitates at the top of its ambit, then sank down off him.

Some time passed.

He opened his eyes.

The truck had backed away, out of sight, out of Paul's limited range of sight anyway. His eyelids weighed closed. He remembered the doctor being huddled over him, shreds of his clothing being peeled away.

Much later, or perhaps not, he opened his eyes once more. The doctor and the policeman were standing over him, some other people too, people he didn't recognize, though he felt somehow he ought to know them. Mrs Grundy, she was up there; in fact, it looked for all the world as though she had set up a ticket booth and was charging admission. Some of the people were holding little children up to see, warm faces, tender, compassionate; more or less. Newsmen were taking his picture. 'You'll be famous,' one of them said.

'His goddam body is like a mulligan stew,' the doctor was telling a reporter.

The policeman shook his head. He was a bit green. 'Do you think —?'

'Do I think what?' the doctor asked. Then he laughed, a thin raking old man's laugh. 'You mean, do I think he's going to *die?*' He laughed again. 'Good God, man, you can see for yourself! There's nothing left of him, he's a goddamn gallimaufry, and hardly an appetizing one at that!' He dipped his fingers into Paul, licked them, grimaced. 'Foo!'

'I think we should get a blanket for him,' the policeman said weakly.

'Of course you should!' snapped the doctor, wiping his stained hands on a small white towel he had brought out of his black bag. He peered down through his rimless spectacles at Paul, smiled. 'Still there, eh?' He squatted beside him. 'I'm sorry, son. There's not a damn thing I can do. Well, yes, I suppose I can take this penny off your lip. You've little use for it, eh?' He laughed softly. 'Now, let's see, there's no function for it, is there? No, no, there it is.' The doctor started to pitch it away, then pocketed it instead. The eyes, don't they use them for the eyes? 'Well, that's better, I'm sure. But let's be honest: it doesn't get to the real problem, does it?' Paul's lip tickled where the penny had been. 'No, I'm of all too little use to you there, boy. I can't even prescribe a soporific platitude. Leave that to the goddamn priests, eh? Hee hee hee! Oops, sorry son! Would you like a priest?'

No thanks, said Paul.

'Can't get it out, eh?' the doctor probed Paul's neck. 'Hmmm. No, obviously not.' He shrugged. 'Just as well. What could you possibly have to say, eh?' He chuckled drily, then looked up at the policeman who still had not left to search out a blanket. 'Don't just stand there, man! Get this lad a priest!' The police officer, clutching his mouth, hurried away, out of Paul's eye-reach. 'I know it's not easy to accept death,' the doctor was saying. He finished wiping his hands, tossed the towel into his black bag, snapped the bag shut. 'We all struggle against it, boy, it's part and parcel of being alive, this brawl, this gutterfight with death. In fact, let me tell you, son, it's *all* there is to life.' He wagged his finger in punctuation, and ended by pressing the tip of it to Paul's nose. 'That's the secret, *that's* my happy paregoric! Hee hee hee!'

KI, thought Paul. KI and 14. What could it have been? Never know now. One of those things.

'But death begets life, there's *that*, my boy, and don't you ever forget it! Survival and murder are synonyms, son, first flaw of the universe! Hee hee h – oh! Sorry son! No time for puns! Forget I said it!'

It's okay, said Paul. Listening to the doctor had at least made him forget the tickle on his lip and it was gone.

'New life burgeons out of rot, new mouths consume old organisms, father dies at orgasm, mother dies at birth, only old Dame Mass with her twin dugs of Stuff and Tickle persists, suffering her long slow split into pure light and pure carbon! Hee hee hee! A tender thought! Don't you agree, lad?' The doctor gazed off into space, happily contemplating the process.

I tell you what, said Paul. Let's forget it.

Just then, the policeman returned with a big quilted comforter, and he and the doctor spread it gently over Paul's body, leaving only his face exposed. The people pressed closer to watch.

'Back! *Back!*' shouted the policeman. 'Have you no respect for the dying? '*Back, I say!*'

'Oh, come now,' chided the doctor. 'Let them watch if they want to. It hardly matters to this poor fellow, and even if it does, it can't matter for much longer. And it will help keep the flies off him.'

'Well, Doctor, if you think . . .' His voice faded away. Paul closed his eyes.

As he lay there among the curious, several odd questions plagued Paul's mind. He knew there was no point to them, but he couldn't rid himself of them. The book, for example: did he have a book? And if he did, what book, and what had happened to it? And what about the stoplight, that lost increment of what men call history, why had no one brought up the matter of the stoplight? And pure carbon he could understand, but as for light: what could its purity consist of? KI. 14. That impression that it had happened before. Yes, these were mysteries, all right. His head ached from them.

People approached Paul from time to time to look under the blanket. Some only peeked, then turned away, while others stayed to poke around, dip their hands in the mutilations. There seemed to be more interest in them now that they were covered. There were some arguments and some occasional horseplay, but the doctor and policeman kept things from getting out of hand. If someone arrogantly ventured a Latin phrase, the doctor always put him down with some toilet-wall barbarism; on the other hand, he reserved his purest, most mellifluous toponymy for small children and young girls. He made several medical appointments with the latter. The police officer, though queasy, stayed nearby. Once, when Paul happened to open his eyes after having had them closed some while, the policeman smiled warmly down on him and said: 'Don't worry, good fellow. I'm still here. Take it as easy as you can. I'll be here to the very end. You can count on me.' Bullshit, thought Paul, though not ungratefully, and he thought he remembered hearing the doctor echo him as he fell off to sleep.

When he awoke, the streets were empty. They had all wearied of it, as he had known they would. It had clouded over, the sky had darkened, it was probably night, and it had begun to rain lightly. He could now see the truck clearly, off to his left. Must have been people in the way before.

MAGIC KISS LIPSTICK

IN

14

DIFFERENT SHADES

Never would have guessed. Only in true life could such things happen.

When he glanced to his right, he was surprised to find an old man sitting near him. Priest, no doubt. He had come after all ... black hat, long greyish beard, sitting in the puddles now forming in the street, legs crossed. Go on, said Paul, don't suffer on my account, don't wait for me, but the old man remained, silent, drawn, rain glistening on his hat, face, beard, clothes: prosopopoeia of patience. The priest. Yet, something about the clothes: well, they were in rags. Pieced together and hanging in tatters. The hat, too, now that he noticed. At short intervals, the old man's head would nod, his eyes would cross, his body would tip, he would catch himself with a start, grunt, glance suspiciously about him, then back down at Paul, would finally relax again and recommence the cycle.

Paul's eyes wearied, especially with the rain splashing into them, so he let them fall closed once more. But he began suffering discomforting visions of the old priest, so he opened them again, squinted off to the left, towards the truck. A small dog, wiry and yellow padded along in the puddles, hair drooping and bunching up with the rain. It sniffed at the tyres of the truck, lifted its legs by one of them, sniffed again, padded on. It circled around Paul, apparently not noticing him, but poking its nose at every object, narrowing the distance between them with every circle. It passed close by the old man, snarled, completed another half-circle, and approached Paul from the left. It stopped near Paul's head – the wet-dog odour was suffocating – and whimpered, licking Paul's face. The old man did nothing, just sat, legs crossed, and passively watched. Of course ... not a priest at all: an old beggar. Waiting for the clothes when he died. If he still had any. Go ahead and take them now, Paul told him, I don't care. But the beggar only sat and stared. Paul felt a tugging sensation from below, heard the dog growl. His whole body seemed to jerk upwards, sending another hot flash through his neck. The dog's hind feet were planted alongside Paul's head, and now and again the right paw would lose its footing, kick nervously at Paul's face, a buffeting counterpoint to the waves of hot pain behind his throat and eyes. Finally, something gave way. The dog shook water out of its yellow coat, and padded away, a fresh piece of flesh between its jaws. The beggar's eyes crossed, his head dipped to his chest, and he started to topple forward, but again he caught himself, took a deep breath, uncrossed his legs, crossed them again, but the opposite way, reached in his pocket and pulled out an old cigarette butt, moulded it between his yellow fingers, put it in his mouth, but did not light it. For an instant, the earth upended again, and Paul found himself hung on the street, a target for the millions of raindarts somebody out in the night was throwing at him. There's nobody out there, he reminded himself, and that set the earth right again. The beggar spat. Paul shielded his eyes from the rain with his lids. He thought he heard other dogs. How much longer must this go on? he wondered. How much longer?

The Babysitter

She arrives at 7.40, ten minutes late, but the children, Jimmy and Bitsy, are still eating supper, and their parents are not ready to go yet. From other rooms come the sounds of a baby screaming, water running, a television musical (no words: probably a dance number – patterns of gliding figures come to mind). Mrs Tucker sweeps into the kitchen, fussing with her hair, and snatches a baby bottle full of milk out of a pan of warm water, rushes out again. 'Harry!' she calls. 'The babysitter's here already!'

o   o   o

That's My Desire? I'll Be Around? He smiles toothily, beckons faintly with his head, rubs his fast balding pate. Bewitched, maybe? Or, What's the Reason? He pulls on his shorts, gives his hips a slap. The baby goes silent in mid-scream. Isn't this the one who used their tub last time? Who's Sorry Now, that's it.

o   o   o

Jack is wandering around town, not knowing what to do. His girl-friend is babysitting at the Tuckers', and later, when she's got the kids in bed, maybe he'll drop over there. Sometimes he watches TV with her when she's babysitting, it's about the only chance he gets to make out a little since he doesn't own wheels, but they have to be careful because most people don't like their sitters to have boyfriends

over. Just kissing her makes her nervous. She won't close her eyes
because she has to be watching the door all the time. Married people
really have it good, he thinks.

o   o   o

'Hi,' the babysitter says to the children, and puts her books on top
of the refrigerator. 'What's for supper?' The little girl, Bitsy, only
stares at her obliquely. She joins them at the end of the kitchen table.
'I don't have to go to bed until nine,' the boy announces flatly and
stuffs his mouth full of potato chips. The babysitter catches a glimpse
of Mr Tucker hurrying out of the bathroom in his underwear.

o   o   o

Her tummy. Under her arms. And her feet. Those are the best places.
She'll spank him, she says sometimes. Let her.

o   o   o

That sweet odour that girls have. The softness of her blouse. He
catches a glimpse of the gentle shadows amid her thighs, as she curls
her legs up under her. He stares hard at her. He has a lot of meaning
packed into that stare, but she's not even looking. She's popping her
gum and watching television. She's sitting right there, inches away,
soft, fragrant, and ready: but what's his next move? He notices his
buddy Mark in the drugstore, playing the pinball machine, and joins
him. 'Hey, this mama's cold, Jack baby! She needs your touch!'

o   o   o

Mrs Tucker appears at the kitchen doorway, holding a rolled-up
diaper. 'Now, don't just eat potato chips, Jimmy! See that he eats
his hamburger, dear.' She hurries away to the bathroom. The boy
glares sullenly at the babysitter, silently daring her to carry out the
order. 'How about a little of that good hamburger now, Jimmy?'
she says perfunctorily. He lets half of it drop to the floor. The baby
is silent and a man is singing a love song on the TV. The children
crunch chips.

o   o   o

He loves her. She loves him. They whirl airily, stirring a light breeze, through a magical landscape of rose and emerald and deep blue. Her light brown hair coils and wisps softly in the breeze, and the soft folds of her white gown tug at her body and then float away. He smiles in a pulsing crescendo of sincerity and song.

o   o   o

'You mean she's alone?' Mark asks. 'Well, there's two or three kids,' Jack says. He slides the coin in. There's a rumble of steel balls tumbling, lining up. He pushes a plunger with his thumb, and one ball pops up in place, hard and glittering with promise. His stare? to say he loves her. That he cares for her and would protect her, would shield her, if need be, with his own body. Grinning he bends over the ball to take careful aim: he and Mark have studied this machine and have it figured out, but still it's not that easy to beat.

o   o   o

On the drive to the party, his mind is partly on the girl, partly on his own high-school days, long past. Sitting at the end of the kitchen table there with his children, she had seemed to be self-consciously arching her back, jutting her pert breasts, twitching her thighs: and for whom if not for him? So she'd seen him coming out of there, after all. He smiles. Yet what could he ever do about it? Those good times are gone, old man. He glances over at his wife, who, readjusting a garter, asks: 'What do you think of our babysitter?'

o   o   o

He loves her. She loves him. And then the babies come. And dirty nappies and one goddamn meal after another. Dishes. Noise. Clutter. And fat. Not just tight, her girdle actually hurts. Somewhere recently she's read about women getting heart attacks or cancer or something from too-tight girdles. Dolly pulls the car door shut with a grunt, strangely irritated, not knowing why. Party mood. Why is her husband humming *Who's Sorry Now?* Pulling out of the drive, she glances back at the lighted kitchen window. 'What do you think of our babysitter?' she asks. While her husband stumbles all over himself trying to answer, she pulls a stocking tight, biting deeper with the garters.

o   o   o

'Stop it!' she laughs. Bitsy is pulling on her skirt and he is tickling
her in the ribs. 'Jimmy! Don't!' But she is laughing too much to stop
him. He leaps on her, wrapping his legs around her waist, and they
all fall to the carpet in front of the TV, where just now a man in a
tuxedo and a little girl in a flouncy white dress are doing a tapdance
together. The babysitter's blouse is pulling out of her skirt, showing
a patch of bare tummy: the target. 'I'll spank!'

o   o   o

Jack pushes the plunger, thrusting up a steel ball, and bends studi-
ously over the machine. 'You getting any off her?' Mark asks, and
clears his throat, flicks ash from his cigarette. 'Well, not exactly, not
yet,' Jack says, grinning awkwardly, but trying to suggest more than
he admits to, and fires. He heaves his weight gently against the
machine as the ball bounds off a rubber bumper. He can feel her
warming up under his hands, the flippers suddenly coming alive, deli-
cate rapid-fire patterns emerging in the flashing of the lights. 1000
WHEN LIT! *now!* 'Got my hand on it, that's about all.' Mark glances
up from the machine, cigarette dangling from his lip. 'Maybe you
need some help,' he suggests with a wry one-sided grin. 'Like maybe
together, man, we could do it.'

o   o   o

She likes the big tub. She uses the Tuckers' bath salts, and loves to
sink into the hot fragrant suds. She can stretch out, submerged, up
to her chin. It gives her a good sleepy tingly feeling.

o   o   o

'What do you think of our babysitter?' Dolly asks, adjusting a
garter. 'Oh, I hardly noticed,' he says. 'Cute girl. She seems to get
along fine with the kids. Why?' 'I don't know.' His wife tugs her
skirt down, glances at a lighted window they are passing, adding:
'I'm not sure I trust her completely, that's all. With the baby, I mean.
She seems a little careless. And the other time, I'm almost sure she
had a boyfriend over.' He grins, claps one hand on his wife's broad
gartered thigh. 'What's wrong with that?' he asks. Still in anklets,
too. Bare thighs, no girdles, nothing up there but a flimsy pair of
panties and soft adolescent flesh. He's flooded with vague remem-
brances of football matches and movie balconies.

o   o   o

How tiny and rubbery it is! She thinks, soaping between the boy's legs, giving him his bath. Just a funny jiggly little thing that looks like it shouldn't even be there at all. Is that what all the songs are about?

o   o   o

Jack watches Mark lunge and twist against the machine. Got her running now, racking them up. He's not too excited about the idea of Mark fooling around with his girlfriend, but Mark's a cooler operator than he is, and maybe, doing it together this once, he'd get over his own timidity. And if she didn't like it, there were other girls around. If Mark went too far, he could cut him off, too. He feels his shoulders tense: enough's enough, man ... but sees the flesh, too. 'Maybe I'll call her later,' he says.

o   o   o

'Hey, Harry! Dolly! Glad you could make it!' 'I hope we're not late.' 'No, no, you're one of the first, come on in! By golly, Dolly, you're looking younger every day! How do you do it? Give my wife your secret, will you?' He pats her on her girdled bottom behind Mr Tucker's back, leads them in for drinks.

o   o   o

8.00. The babysitter runs water in the tub, combs her hair in front of the bathroom mirror. There's a western on television, so she lets Jimmy watch it while she gives Bitsy her bath. But Bitsy doesn't want a bath. She's angry and crying because she has to be first. The babysitter tells her if she'll take her bath quickly, she'll let her watch television while Jimmy takes his bath, but it does no good. The little girl fights to get out of the bathroom, and the babysitter has to squat with her back against the door and forcibly undress the child. There are better places to babysit. Both children mind badly, and then, sooner or later, the baby is sure to wake up for a nappy change and more bottle. The Tuckers do have a good colour TV, though, and she hopes things will be settled down enough to catch the 8.30 programme. She thrusts the child into the tub, but she's still screaming and thrashing around. 'Stop it now, Bitsy, or you'll wake the baby!' 'I have to go potty!' the child wails, switching tactics. The babysitter sighs, lifts the girl out of the tub and onto the toilet, getting her skirt and blouse all wet in the process. She glances at herself in the mirror. Before she knows it, the girl is off the seat and out of the bathroom. 'Bitsy! Come back here!'

o   o   o

'Okay, that's enough!' Her skirt is ripped and she's flushed and crying. 'Who says?' 'I do, man!' The bastard goes for her, but he tackles him. They roll and tumble. Tables tip, lights topple, the TV crashes to the floor. He slams a hard right to the guy's gut, clips his chin with a rolling left.

o   o   o

'We hope it's a girl.' That's hardly surprising, since they already have four boys. Dolly congratulates the woman like everybody else, but she doesn't envy her, not a bit. That's all she needs about now. She stares across the room at Harry, who is slapping backs and getting loud, as usual. He's spreading out through the middle, so why the hell does he have to complain about her all the time? 'Dolly, you're looking younger every day!' was the nice greeting she got tonight. 'What's your secret?' And Harry: 'It's all those calories. She's getting back her baby fat.' 'Haw, haw! Harry, have a heart!'

o   o   o

'Get her feet!' he hollers at Bitsy, his fingers in her ribs, running over her naked tummy, tangling in the underbrush of straps and strange clothing. 'Get her shoes off!' He holds her pinned by pressing his head against her soft chest. 'No! No, Jimmy! Bitsy, stop!' But though she kicks and twists and rolls around, she doesn't get up, she can't get up, she's laughing too hard, and the shoes come off, and he grabs a stocking foot and scratches the sole ruthlessly, and she raises up her legs, trying to pitch him off, she's wild, boy, but he hangs on, and she's laughing, and on the screen there's a rattle of hooves, and he and Bitsy are rolling around and around on the floor in a crazy rodeo of long bucking legs.

o   o   o

He slips the coin in. There's a metallic fall and a sharp click as the dial tone begins. 'I hope the Tuckers have gone,' he says. 'Don't

worry, they're at our place,' Mark says. 'They're always the first ones
to come and the last ones to go home. My old man's always bitching
about them.' Jack laughs nervously and dials the number. 'Tell her
we're coming over to protect her from getting raped,' Mark suggests,
and lights a cigarette. Jack grins, leaning casually against the door
jamb of the phone booth, chewing gum, one hand in his pocket. He's
really pretty uneasy, though. He has the feeling he's somehow
messing up a good thing.

o   o   o

Bitsy runs naked into the living-room, keeping a hassock between
herself and the babysitter. 'Bitsy ...!' the babysitter threatens. Arti-
ficial reds and greens and purples flicker over the child's wet body,
as hooves clatter, guns crackle, and stagecoach wheels thunder over
rutted terrain. 'Get outa the way, Bitsy!' the boy complains. 'I can't
see!' Bitsy streaks past and the babysitter chases, cornering the girl
in the back bedroom. Bitsy throws something that hits her softly in
the face: a pair of men's undershorts. She grabs the girl scampering
by, carries her to the bathroom, and with a smart crack on her glistening bottom pops her back into the tub. In spite, Bitsy peepees in
the bathwater.

o   o   o

Mr Tucker stirs a little water into his bourbon and kids with his
host and another man, just arrived, about their golf games. They set
up a match for the weekend, a threesome looking for a fourth. Holding his drink in his right hand, Mr Tucker swings his left through
the motion of a tee-shot. 'You'll have to give me a stroke a hole,' he
says. 'I'll give you a stroke!' says his host. 'Bend over!' Laughing,
the other man asks: 'Where's your boy Mark tonight?' 'I don't know,'
replies the host, gathering up a trayful of drinks. Then he adds in a
low growl: 'Out chasing tail probably.' They chuckle loosely at that,
then shrug in commiseration and return to the livingroom to join
their women.

o   o   o

Shades pulled. Door locked. Watching the TV. Under a blanket
maybe. Yes, that's right, under a blanket. Her eyes close when he
kisses her. Her breasts, under both their hands, are soft and yielding.

o   o   o

A hard blow to the belly. The face. The dark beardy one staggers. The lean-jawed sheriff moves in, but gets a spurred boot in his face. The dark one hurls himself forward, drives his shoulder into the sheriff's hard midriff, her own tummy tightens, withstands, as the sheriff smashes the dark man's nose, slams him up against a wall, slugs him again! and again! The dark man grunts rhythmically, backs off, then plunges suicidally forward — her own knees draw up protectively — the sheriff staggers! caught low! but instead of following through the other man steps back — a pistol! the dark one has a pistol! the sheriffs draws! shoots from the hip! explosions! she clutches her hands between her thighs — no! the sheriff spins! wounded! the dark man hesitates, aims, her legs stiffen towards the set, the sheriff rolls desperately in the straw, fires: dead! the dark man is dead! groans, crumples, his pistol drooping in his collapsing hand, dropping, he drops. The sheriff, spent, nicked, watches weakly from the floor where he lies. Oh, to be whole! to be good and strong and right! to embrace and be embraced by harmony and wholeness! The sheriff, drawing himself painfully up on one elbow, rubs his bruised mouth with the back of his other hand.

o   o   o

'Well, we just sorta thought we'd drop over,' he says, and winks broadly at Mark. 'Who's we?' 'Oh, me and Mark here.' 'Tell her, good thing like her, gotta pass it around,' whispers Mark, dragging on his smoke, then flicking the butt over under the pinball machine. 'What's that?' she asks. 'Oh, Mark and I were just saying, like two's company, three's an orgy,' Jack says, and winks again. She giggles. 'Oh, Jack!' Behind her, he can hear shouts and gunfire. 'Well, okay, for just a little while, if you'll both be good.' Way to go, man.

o   o   o

Probably some damn kid over there right now. Wrestling around on the couch in front of his TV. Maybe he should drop back to the house. Just to check. None of that stuff, she was there to do a job! Park the car a couple doors down, slip in the front door before she knows it. He sees the disarray of clothing, the young thighs exposed to the flickering television light, hears his baby crying. 'Hey, what's going on here! Get outa here, son, before I call the police!' Of course, they haven't really been doing anything. They probably don't even know how. He stares benignly down upon the girl, her skirt rumpled loosely around her thighs. Flushed, frightened, yet excited, she stares back at him. He smiles. His finger touches a knee, approaches the hem. Another couple arrives. Filling up here with people. He wouldn't be missed. Just slip out, stop back casually to pick up something or other he forgot, never mind what. He remembers that the other time they had this babysitter, she took a bath in their house. She had a date afterwards, and she'd just come from cheerleading practice or something. Aspirin maybe. Just drop quietly and casually into the bathroom to pick up some aspirin. 'Oh, excuse me, dear! I only . . . !' She gazes back at him, astonished, yet strangely moved. Her soft wet breasts rise and fall in the water, and her tummy looks pale and ripply. He recalls that her pubic hairs, left in the tub, were brown. Light brown.

o   o   o

She's no more than stepped into the tub for a quick bath, when Jimmy announces from outside the door that he has to go to the bathroom. She sighs: just an excuse, she knows. 'You'll have to wait.' The little nuisance. 'I can't wait.' 'Okay, then come ahead, but I'm taking a bath.' She supposes that will stop him, but it doesn't. In he comes. She slides down into the suds until she's eye-level with the edge of the tub. He hesitates. 'Go ahead, if you have to,' she says, a little awkwardly, 'but I'm not getting out.' 'Don't look,' he says. She: 'I will if I want to.'

o   o   o

She's crying. Mark is rubbing his jaw where he's just slugged him. A lamp lies shattered. 'Enough's enough, Mark! Now get outa here!' Her skirt is ripped to the waist, her bare hip bruised. Her panties lie on the floor like a broken balloon. Later, he'll wash her wounds, help her dress, he'll take care of her. Pity washes through him, giving him a sudden hard-on. Mark laughs at it, pointing. Jack crouches, waiting, ready for anything.

o   o   o

Laughing, they roll and tumble. Their little hands are all over her, digging and pinching. She struggles to her hands and knees, but Bitsy leaps astride her neck, bowing her head to the carpet. 'Spank her,

Jimmy!' His swats sting: is her skirt up? The phone rings. 'The cavalry to the rescue!' she laughs, and throws them off to go answer.

o   o   o

Kissing Mark, her eyes closed, her hips nudge towards Jack. He stares at the TV screen, unsure of himself, one hand slipping cautiously under her skirt. Her hand touches his arm as though to resist, then brushes on by to rub his leg. This blanket they're under was a good idea. 'Hi! This is Jack!'

o   o   o

Bitsy's out and the water's running. 'Come on, Jimmy, your turn!' Last time, he told her he took his own baths, but she came in anyway. 'I'm not gonna take a bath,' he announces, eyes glued on the set. He readies for the struggle. 'But I've already run your water. Come on, Jimmy, please!' He shakes his head. She can't make him, he's sure he's as strong as she is. She sighs. 'Well, it's up to you. I'll use the water myself then,' she says. He waits until he's pretty sure she's not going to change her mind, then sneaks in and peeks through the keyhole in the bathroom door: just in time to see her big bottom as she bends over to stir in the bubblebath. Then she disappears. Trying to see as far down as the keyhole will allow, he bumps his head on the knob. 'Jimmy, is that you?' 'I – I have to go to the bathroom!' he stammers.

o   o   o

Not actually in the tub, just getting in. One foot on the mat, the other in the water. Bent over slightly, buttocks flexed, teats swaying, holding on to the edge of the tub. 'Oh, excuse me! I only wanted . . . !' He passes over her astonishment, the awkward excuses, moves quickly to the part where he reaches out to— 'What on earth are you doing, Harry?' his wife asks, staring at his hand. His host, passing, laughs. 'He's practising his swing for Sunday, Dolly, but it's not going to do him a damn bit of good!' Mr Tucker laughs, sweeps his right hand on through the air as though lifting a seven-iron shot onto the green. He makes a *dok!* sound with his tongue. 'In there!'

o   o   o

'No, Jack, I don't think you'd better.' 'Well, we just called, we just, uh, thought we'd, you know, stop by for a minute, watch television for thirty minutes, or, or something.' 'Who's we?' 'Well, Mark's here, I'm with him, and he said he'd like to, you know, like if it's all right, just—' 'Well, it's *not* all right. The Tuckers said no.' 'Yeah, but if we only—' 'And they seemed awfully suspicious about last time.' 'Why? We didn't – I mean, I just thought—' 'No, Jack, and that's period.' She hangs up. She returns to the TV, but the commercial is on. Anyway, she's missed most of the show. She decides maybe she'll take a quick bath. Jack might come by anyway, it'd make her mad, that'd be the end as far as he was concerned, but if he should, she doesn't want to be all sweaty. And besides, she likes the big tub the Tuckers have.

o   o   o

He is self-conscious and stands with his back to her, his little neck flushed. It takes him forever to get started, and when it finally does come, it's just a tiny trickle. 'See, it was just an excuse,' she scolds, but she's giggling inwardly at the boy's embarrassment. 'You're just a nuisance, Jimmy.' At the door, his hand on the knob, he hesitates, staring timidly down on his shoes. 'Jimmy?' She peeks at him over the edge of the tub, trying to keep a straight face, as he sneaks a nervous glance back over his shoulder. 'As long as you bothered me,' she says, 'you might as well soap my back.'

o   o   o

'The aspirin . . .' They embrace. She huddles in his arms like a child. Lovingly, paternally, knowledgeably, he wraps her nakedness. How compact, how tight and small her body is! Kissing her ear, he stares down past her rump at the still clear water. 'I'll join you,' he whispers hoarsely.

o   o   o

She picks up the shorts Bitsy threw at her. Men's underwear. She holds them in front of her, looks at herself in the bedroom mirror. About twenty sizes too big for her, of course. She runs her hand inside the opening in front, pulls out her thumb. How funny it must feel!

o   o   o

'Well, man, I say we just go rape her,' Mark says flatly, and swings his weight against the pinball machine. 'Uff! Ahh! Get in there, you mother! Look at that! Hah! Man, I'm gonna turn this baby over!' Jack is embarrassed about the phone conversation. Mark just snorted in disgust when he hung up. He cracks down hard on his gum, angry that he's such a chicken. 'Well, I'm game if you are,' he says coldly.

o   o   o

8.30. 'Okay, come on, Jimmy, it's time.' He ignores her. The western gives way to a spy show. Bitsy, in pyjamas, pads into the livingroom. 'No, Bitsy, it's time to go to bed.' 'You said I could watch!' the girl whines, and starts to throw another tantrum. 'But you were too slow and it's late. Jimmy, you get in that bathroom, and right now!' Jimmy stares sullenly at the set, unmoving. The babysitter tries to catch the opening scene of the television programme so she can follow it later, since Jimmy gives himself his own baths. When the commercial interrupts, she turns off the sound, stands in front of the screen. 'Okay, into the tub, Jimmy Tucker, or I'll take you in there and give you your bath myself!' 'Just try it,' he says, 'and see what happens.'

o   o   o

They stand outside, in the dark, crouched in the bushes, peeking in. She's on the floor, playing with the kids. Too early. They seem to be tickling her. She gets to her hands and knees, but the little girl leaps on her head, pressing her face to the floor. There's an obvious target, and the little boy proceeds to beat on it. 'Hey, look at that kid go!' whispers Mark, laughing and snapping his fingers softly. Jack feels uneasy out here. Too many neighbours, too many cars going by, too many people in the world. That little boy in there is one up on him, though: he's never thought about tickling her as a starter.

o   o   o

His little hand, clutching the bar of soap, lathers shyly a narrow space between her shoulderblades. She is doubled forward against her knees, buried in rich suds, peeking at him over the edge of her shoulder. The soap slithers out of his grip and plunks into the water. 'I . . . I dropped the soap,' he whispers. She: 'Find it.'

o   o   o

'I dream of Jeannie with the light brown pubic hair!' 'Harry! Stop that! You're drunk!' But they're laughing, they're all laughing, damn! he's feeling pretty goddamn good at that, and now he just knows he needs that aspirin. Watching her there, her thighs spread for him, on the couch, in the tub, hell, on the kitchen table for that matter, he tees off on Number Nine, and – *whap* – swats his host's wife on the bottom. 'Hole in one!' he shouts. 'Harry!' Why can't his goddamn wife Dolly ever get happy-drunk instead of sour-drunk all the time? 'Gonna be tough Sunday, old buddy!' 'You're pretty tough right now, Harry,' says his host.

o   o   o

The babysitter lunges forward, grabs the boy by the arms and hauls him off the couch, pulling two cushions with him, and drags him towards the bathroom. He lashes out, knocking over an endtable full of magazines and ashtrays. 'You leave my brother alone!' Bitsy cries and grabs the sitter around the waist. Jimmy jumps on her and down they all go. On the silent screen, there's a fade-in to a dark passageway in an old apartment building in some foreign country. She kicks out and somebody falls between her legs. Somebody else is sitting on her face. 'Jimmy! Stop that!' the babysitter laughs, her voice muffled.

o   o   o

She's watching television. All alone. It seems like a good time to go in. Just remember: really, no matter what she says, she wants it. They're standing in the bushes, trying to get up the nerve. 'We'll tell her to be good,' Mark whispers, 'and if she's not good, we'll spank her.' Jack giggles softly, but his knees are weak. She stands. They freeze. She looks right at them. 'She can't see us,' Mark whispers tensely. 'Is she coming out?' 'No,' says Mark, 'she's going into – that must be the bathroom!' Jack takes a deep breath, his heart pounding. 'Hey, is there a window back there?' Mark asks.

o   o   o

The phone rings. She leaves the tub, wrapped in a towel. Bitsy gives a tug on the towel. 'Hey, Jimmy, get the towel!' she squeals. 'Now stop that, Bitsy!' the babysitter hisses, but too late: with one hand on the phone, the other isn't big enough to hang on to the towel. Her sudden nakedness awes them and it takes them a moment to remember about tickling her. By then, she's in the towel again. 'I hope you got a good look,' she says angrily. She feels chilled and oddly a little frightened. 'Hello?' No answer. She glances at the window – is somebody out there? Something, she saw something, and a rustling – footsteps?

o   o   o

'Okay, I don't care, Jimmy, don't take a bath,' she says irritably. Her blouse is pulled out and wrinkled, her hair is all mussed, and she feels sweaty. There's about a million things she'd rather be doing than babysitting with these two. Three: at least the baby's sleeping. She knocks on the overturned endtable for luck, rights it, replaces the magazines and ashtrays. The one thing that really makes her sick is a dirty nappy. 'Just go on to bed.' 'I don't have to go to bed until nine,' he reminds her. Really, she couldn't care less. She turns up the volume on the TV, settles down on the couch, poking her blouse back into her skirt, pushing her hair out of her eyes. Jimmy and Bitsy watch from the floor. Maybe, once they're in bed, she'll take a quick bath. She wishes Jack would come by. The man, no doubt the spy, is following a woman, but she doesn't know why. The woman passes another man. Something seems to happen, but it's not clear what. She's probably already missed too much. The phone rings.

o   o   o

Mark is kissing her. Jack is under the blanket, easing her panties down over her squirming hips. Her hand is in his pants, pulling it out, pulling it towards her, pulling it hard. She knew just where it was! Mark is stripping, too. God, it's really happening! he thinks with a kind of pious joy, and notices the open door. 'Hey! What's going on here?'

o   o   o

He soaps her back, smooth and slippery under his hand. She is doubled over, against her knees, between his legs. Her light brown hair, reaching to her gleaming shoulders, is wet at the edges. The soap slips, falls between his legs. He fishes for it, finds it, slips it behind him. 'Help me find it,' he whispers in her ear. 'Sure Harry,' says his host, going round behind him. 'What'd you lose?'

o   o   o

Soon be nine, time to pack the kids off to bed. She clears the table, dumps paper plates and leftover hamburgers into the garbage, puts glasses and silverware into the sink, and the mayonnaise, mustard, and ketchup in the refrigerator. Neither child has eaten much supper finally, mostly potato chips and ice-cream, but it's really not her problem. She glances at the books on the refrigerator. Not much chance she'll get to them, she's already pretty worn out. Maybe she'd feel better if she had a quick bath. She runs water into the tub, tosses in bubblebath salts, undresses. Before pushing down her panties, she stares for a moment at the smooth silken panel across her tummy, fingers the place where the opening would be if there were one. Then she steps quickly out of them, feeling somehow ashamed, unhooks her brassière. She weighs her breasts in the palms of her hands, watching herself in the bathroom mirror, where in the open window behind her, she sees a face. She screams.

o   o   o

She screams: 'Jimmy! Give me that!' 'What's the matter?' asks Jack on the other end. 'Jimmy! Give me my towel! Right now!' 'Hello? Hey, are you still there?' 'I'm sorry, Jack,' she says, panting. 'You caught me in the tub. I'm just wrapped in a towel and these silly kids grabbed it away!' 'Gee, I wish I'd been there!' 'Jack—!' 'To protect you, I mean.' 'Oh, sure,' she says, giggling. 'Well, what do you think, can I come over and watch TV with you?' 'Well, not right this minute,' she says. He laughs lightly. He feels very cool. 'Jack?' 'Yeah?' 'Jack, I . . . I think there's somebody outside the window!'

o   o   o

She carries him, fighting all the way, to the tub, Bitsy pummelling her in the back and kicking her ankles. She can't hang on to him and undress him at the same time. 'I'll throw you in, clothes and all, Jimmy Tucker!' she gasps. 'You better not!' he cries. She sits on the toilet seat, locks her legs around him, whips his shirt up over his head before he knows what's happening. The pants are easier. Like all little boys his age, he has almost no hips at all. He hangs on desperately to his underpants, but when she succeeds in snapping these down out of his grip, too, he gives up, starts to bawl, and beats her wildly in the face with his fists. She ducks her head, laughing hysterically, oddly entranced by the spectacle of that pale little thing down there, bobbing and bouncing rubberily about with the boy's helpless fury and anguish.

o   o   o

'Aspirin? Whaddaya want aspirin for, Harry? I'm sure they got aspirin here, if you—' 'Did I say aspirin? I meant, uh, my glasses. And, you know, I thought, well, I'd sorta check to see if everything was okay at home.' Why the hell is it his mouth feels like it's got about six sets of teeth packed in there, and a tongue the size of that liverwurst his host's wife is passing around? 'Whaddaya want your glasses for, Harry? I don't understand you at all!' 'Aw, well, honey, I was feeling kind of dizzy or something, and I thought—' 'Dizzy is right. If you want to check on the kids, why don't you just call on the phone?'

o   o   o

They can tell she's naked and about to get into the tub, but the bathroom window is frosted glass, and they can't see anything clearly. 'I got an idea,' Mark whispers. 'One of us goes and calls her on the phone, and the other watches when she comes out.' 'Okay, but who calls?' 'Both of us, we'll do it twice. Or more.'

o   o   o

Down forbidden alleys. Into secret passageways. Unlocking the world's terrible secrets. Sudden shocks: a trapdoor! a fall! or the stunning report of a rifle shot, the *whaaii-ii-iing!* of the bullet biting concrete by your ear! Careful! Then edge forward once more, avoiding the light, inch at a time, now a quick dash for an open doorway — *look out!* there's a knife! a struggle! no! the long blade glistens! jerks! thrusts! *stabbed!* No, no, it missed! The assailant's down, yes! the spy's on top, pinning him, a terrific thrashing about, the spy rips off the assailant's mask: *a woman!*

o   o   o

Fumbling behind her, she finds it, wraps her hand around it, tugs. 'Oh!' she gasps, pulling her hand back quickly, her ears turning crimson. 'I ... I thought it was the soap!' he squeezes her close between his thighs, pulls her back toward him, one hand sliding down her tummy between her legs. I Dream of Jeannie— 'I have to go to the bathroom!' says someone outside the door.

o   o   o

She's combing her hair in the bathroom when the phone rings. She hurries to answer it before it wakes the baby. 'Hello, Tuckers.' There's no answer. 'Hello?' A soft click. Strange. She feels suddenly alone in the big house, and goes in to watch TV with the children.

o   o   o

'Stop it!' she screams. 'Please, stop!' She's on her hands and knees, trying to get up, but they're too strong for her. Mark holds her head down. 'Now, baby, we're gonna teach you how to be a nice girl,' he says coldly, and nods at Jack. When she's doubled over like that, her skirt rides up her thighs to the leg bands of her panties. 'C'mon, man, go! This baby's cold! She needs your touch!'

o   o   o

Parks the car a couple blocks away. Slips up to the house, glances in his window. Just like he's expected. Her blouse is off and the kid's shirt is unbuttoned. He watches, while slowly, clumsily, childishly, they fumble with each other's clothes. My God, it takes them forever. 'Some party!' 'You said it!' When they're more or less naked, he walks in. 'Hey! What's going on here?' They go white as bleu cheese. Haw haw! 'What's the little thing you got sticking out there, boy?' 'Harry behave yourself!' No, he doesn't let the kid get dressed, he sends him home bareassed. 'Bareassed!' He drinks to that. 'Promises, promises,' says his host's wife. 'I'll mail you your clothes, son!' He gazes down on the naked little girl on his couch. 'Looks like you and me, we got a little secret to keep, honey,' he says coolly. 'Less you wanna go home the same way your boyfriend did!' He chuckles at his easy wit, leans down over her, and unbuckles his belt. 'Might as well make it two secrets, right?' 'What in God's name are you talking about, Harry?' He staggers out of there, drink in hand, and goes to look for his car.

o   o   o

'Hey! What's going on here?' They huddle half-naked under the blanket, caught utterly unawares. On television: the clickety-click of frightened running feet on foreign pavements. Jack is fumbling for his shorts, tangled somehow around his ankles. The blanket is snatched away. 'On your feet there!' Mr Tucker, Mrs Tucker, Mark's mom and dad, the police, the neighbours, everybody comes crowding in. Hopelessly, he has a terrific erection. So hard it hurts. Everybody stares down at it.

o   o   o

Bitsy's sleeping on the floor. The babysitter is taking a bath. For more than an hour now, he's had to use the bathroom. He doesn't know how much longer he can wait. Finally, he goes to knock on the bathroom door. 'I have to use the bathroom.' 'Well, come ahead, if you have to.' 'Not while you're in there.' She sighs loudly. 'Okay, okay, just a minute,' she says, 'but you're a real nuisance, Jimmy!' He's holding on, pinching it as tight as he can. *Hurry!* He holds his breath, squeezing shut his eyes. No. Too late. At last, she opens the door. 'Jimmy!' 'I *told* you to hurry!' he sobs. She drags him into the bathroom and pulls his pants down.

o   o   o

He arrives just in time to see her emerge from the bathroom, wrapped in a towel, to answer the phone. His two kids sneak up behind her and pull the towel away. She's trying to hang onto the phone and get the towel back at the same time. It's quite a picture. She's got a sweet ass. Standing there in the bushes, pawing himself with one hand, he lifts his glass with the other and toasts her sweet ass, which his son now swats. Haw, haw, maybe that boy's gonna shape up, after all.

o   o   o

They're in the bushes, arguing about their next move, when she comes out of the bathroom, wrapped in a towel. They can hear the baby crying. Then it stops. They see her running, naked, back to the bathroom like she's scared or something. 'I'm going in after her, man, whether you're with me or not!' Mark whispers and he starts out of the bushes. But just then, a light comes sweeping up through the yard, as a car swings in the drive. They hit the dirt, hearts pound-

ing. 'Is it the cops?' 'I don't know!' Do you think they saw us?'
'Sshh!' A man comes staggering up the walk from the drive, a drink
in his hand, stumbles on in the kitchen door and then straight into
the bathroom. 'It's Mr Tucker!' Mark whispers. A scream. 'Let's get
outa here, man!'

o   o   o

9.00. Having missed most of the spy show anyway and having little
else to do, the babysitter has washed the dishes and cleaned the
kitchen up a little. The books on the refrigerator remind her of her
better intentions, but she decides that first she'll see what's next on
TV. In the livingroom, she finds little Bitsy sound asleep on the floor.
She lifts her gently, carries her into her bed, and tucks her in. 'Okay,
Jimmy, it's nine o'clock, I've let you stay up, now be a good boy.'
Sullenly, his sleepy eyes glued still to the set, the boy backs out of the
room towards his bedroom. A drama comes on. She switches channels. A ballgame and a murder mystery. She switches back to the
drama. It's a love story of some kind. A man married to an ageing
invalid wife, but in love with a younger girl. 'Use the bathroom and
brush your teeth before going to bed, Jimmy!' she calls, but as
quickly regrets it, for she hears the baby stir in its crib.

o   o   o

Two of them are talking about mothers they've salted away in rest
homes. Oh boy, that's wonderful, this is one helluva party. She
leaves them to use the john, takes advantage of the retreat to ease
her girdle down awhile, get a few good deep breaths. She has this
picture of her three kids carting her off to a rest home. In a wheel-
barrow. That sure is something to look forward to, all right. When
she pulls her girdle back up, she can't seem to squeeze into it. The
host looks in. 'Hey, Dolly, are you all right?' 'Yeah, I just can't get
into my damn girdle, that's all.' 'Here, let me help.'

o   o   o

She pulls them on, over her own, standing in front of the bedroom
mirror, holding her skirt bundled up around the waist. About twenty
sizes too big for her, of course. She pulls them tight from behind,
runs her hand inside the opening in front, pulls out her thumb. 'And
what a good boy am I!' She giggles: how funny it must feel! Then,

in the mirror, she sees him: in the doorway behind her, sullenly watching. 'Jimmy! You're supposed to be in bed!' 'Those are my daddy's!' the boy says. 'I'm gonna tell!'

o   o   o

'Jimmy!' she drags him into the bathroom and pulls his pants down. 'Even your shoes are wet! Get them off!' She soaps up a warm washcloth she's had with her in the bathtub, scrubs him from the waist down with it. Bitsy stands in the doorway, staring. 'Get out! Get out!' the boy screams at his sister. 'Go back to bed, Bitsy. It's just an accident.' 'Get out!' The baby wakes and starts to howl.

o   o   o

The young lover feels sorry for her rival, the invalid wife; she believes the man has a duty towards the poor woman and insists she is willing to wait. But the man argues that he also has a duty towards himself: his life, too, is short, and he could not love his wife now even were she well. He embraces the young girl feverishly; she twists away in anguish. The door opens. They stand there grinning, looking devilish, but pretty silly at the same time. 'Jack! I thought I told you not to come!' She's angry, but she's also glad in a way: she was beginning to feel a little too alone in the big house with the children all sleeping. She should have taken that bath, after all. 'We just came by to see if you were being a good girl,' Jack says and blushes. The boys glance at each other nervously.

o   o   o

She's just sunk down into the tubful of warm fragrant suds, ready for a nice long soaking, when the phone rings. Wrapping a towel around her, she goes to answer: no one there. But now the baby's awake and bawling. She wonders if that's Jack bothering her all the time. If it is, brother, that's the end. Maybe it's the end anyway. She tries to calm the baby with the half-empty bottle, not wanting to change it until she's finished her bath. The bathroom's where the diapers go dirty, and they make it stink to high heaven. Shush, shush!' she whispers, rocking the crib. The towel slips away, leaving an airy empty tingle up and down her backside. Even before she stoops for the towel, even before she turns around, she knows there's somebody behind her.

o   o   o

'We just came by to see if you were being a good girl,' Jack says, grinning down at her. She's flushed and silent, her mouth half open. 'Lean over,' says Mark amiably. 'We'll soap your back, as long as we're here.' But she just huddles there, down in the suds, staring up at them with big eyes.

o   o   o

'Hey! What's going on here?' It's Mr Tucker, stumbling through the door with a drink in his hand. She looks up from the TV. 'What's the matter, Mr Tucker?' 'Oh, uh, I'm sorry, I got lost—no, I mean, I had to get some aspirin. Excuse me!' And he rushes past her into the bathroom, caroming off the livingroom door jamb on the way. The baby wakes.

o   o   o

'Okay, get off her, Mr Tucker!' 'Jack!' she cries, 'what are you doing here?' He stares hard at them a moment: so that's where it goes. Then, as Mr Tucker swings heavily off, he leans into the bastard with a hard right to the belly. Next thing he knows, though, he's got a face full of an old man's fist. He's not sure, as the lights go out, if that's his girlfriend screaming or the baby . . .

o   o   o

Her host pushes down on her fat fanny and tugs with all his might on her girdle, while she bawls on his shoulder: 'I don't *wanna* go to a rest home!' 'Now, now, take it easy, Dolly, nobody's gonna make you—' 'Ouch! Hey, you're hurting!' 'You should buy a bigger girdle, Dolly.' 'You're telling me!' Some other guy pokes his head in. 'Whatsamatter? Dolly fall in?' 'No, she fell out. Give me a hand.'

o   o   o

By the time she's chased Jack and Mark out of there, she's lost track of the programme she's been watching on television. There's another woman in the story now for some reason. That guy lives a very complicated life. Impatiently, she switches channels. She hates ball-games, so she settles for the murder mystery. She switches just in time, too: there's a dead man sprawled out on the floor of what looks like an office or a study or something. A heavyset detective

gazes up from his couch over the body: 'He's been strangled.'
Maybe she'll take that bath, after all.

o   o   o

She drags him into the bathroom and pulls his pants down. She
soaps up a warm washcloth she's had in the tub with her, but just as
she reaches between his legs, it starts to spurt, spraying her arms and
hands. 'Oh, Jimmy! I thought you were done!' she cries, pulling him
towards the toilet and aiming it into the bowl. How moist and rubbery it is! And you can turn it every which way. How funny it must
feel!

o   o   o

'Stop it!' she screams. 'Please stop!' She's on her hands and knees
and Jack is holding her head down. 'Now we're gonna teach you
how to be a nice girl,' Mark says and lifts her skirt. 'Well, I'll be
damned!' 'What's the matter?' asks Jack, his heart pounding. 'Look
at this big pair of men's underpants she's got on!' 'Those are my
daddy's!' says Jimmy, watching them from the doorway. 'I'm gonna
tell!'

o   o   o

People are shooting at each other in the murder mystery, but she's so
mixed up, she doesn't know which ones are the good guys. She
switches back to the love story. Something seems to have happened,
because now the man is kissing his invalid wife tenderly. Maybe
she's finally dying. The baby wakes, begins to scream. Let it. She
turns up the volume on the TV.

o   o   o

Leaning down over her, unbuckling his belt. It's all happening just
like he's known it would. Beautiful! The kid is gone, though his
pants, poor lad, remain. 'Looks like you and me, we got a secret to
keep, child!' But he's cramped on the couch and everything is too
slippery and small. 'Lift your legs up, honey. Put them around my
back.' But instead she screams. He rolls off, crashing to the floor.
There they all come, through the front door. On television, some-

body is saying: 'Am I a burden to you, darling?' 'Dolly! My God! Dolly, I can explain ...!'

o   o   o

The game of the night is Get Dolly Tucker Back in Her Girdle Again. They've got her down on her belly in the livingroom and the whole damn crowd is working on her. Several of them are stretching the girdle, while others try to jam the fat inside. 'I think we made a couple inches on this side! Roll her over!' Harry?

o   o   o

She's just stepped into the tub, when the phone rings, waking the baby. She sinks down in the suds, trying not to hear. But that baby doesn't cry, it screams. Angrily, she wraps a towel around herself, stamps peevishly into the baby's room, just letting the phone jangle. She tosses the baby down on its back, unpins its nappies hastily, and gets yellowish baby stool all over her hands. Her towel drops away. She turns to find Jimmy staring at her like a little idiot. She slaps him in the face with her dirty hand, while the baby screams, the phone rings, and nagging voices argue on the TV. There are better things she might be doing.

o   o   o

What's happening? Now there's a young guy in it. Is he after the young girl or the old invalid? To tell the truth, it looks like he's after the same man the women are. In disgust, she switches channels. 'The strangler again,' growls the fat detective, hands on hips, staring down at the body of a half-naked girl. She's considering either switching back to the love story or taking a quick bath, when a hand suddenly clutches her mouth.

o   o   o

'You're both chicken,' she says, staring up at them. 'But what if Mr Tucker comes home?' Mark asks nervously.

o   o   o

How did he get here? He's standing pissing in his own goddamn bathroom, his wife is still back at the party, the three of them are,

like good kids, sitting in there in the living-room watching TV. One
of them is his host's boy Mark. 'It's a good murder mystery, Mr
Tucker,' Mark said, when he came staggering in on them a minute
ago. 'Sit still!' he shouted, 'I'm just home for a moment!' Then
whump thump on into the bathroom. Long hike for a weewee,
Mister. But something keeps bothering him. Then it hits him: the
girl's panties, hanging like a broken balloon from the rabbit-ear
antennae on the TV! He barges back in there, giving his shoulder a
helluva crack on the livingroom door jamb on the way—but they're
not hanging there any more. Maybe he's only imagined it. 'Hey, Mr
Tucker,' Mark says flatly. 'Your fly's open.'

o   o   o

The baby's dirty. Stinks to high heaven. She hurries back to the living-
room, hearing sirens and gunshots. The detective is crouched outside
a house, peering in. Already, she's completely lost. The baby screams
at the top of its lungs. She turns up the volume. But it's all confused.
She hurries back in there, claps an angry hand to the baby's mouth.
'Shut up!' she cries. She throws the baby down on its back, starts to
unpin the nappy, as the baby tunes up again. The phone rings. She
answers it, one eye on the TV. 'What?' The baby cries so hard it
starts to choke. Let it. 'I said, hi, this is Jack!' Then it hits her: oh
no! the nappy pin!

o   o   o

'The aspirin ...' But she's already in the tub. Way down in the tub.
Staring at him through the water. Her tummy looks pale and ripply.
He hears sirens, people on the porch.

o   o   o

Jimmy gets up to go to the bathroom and gets his face slapped and
smeared with baby poop. Then she hauls him off to the bathroom,
yanks off his pyjamas, and throws him into the tub. That's okay, but
next she gets naked and acts like she's gonna get in the tub, too. The
baby's screaming and the phone's ringing like crazy and in walks his
dad. Saved! he thinks, but, no, his dad grabs him right back out of
the tub and whales the dickens out of him, no questions asked, while
she watches, then sends him – whack! – back to bed. So he's lying
there, wet and dirty and naked and sore, and he still has to go to

the bathroom, and outside his window he hears two older guys talking. 'Listen, you know where to do it if we get her pinned?' 'No! Don't you?'

o   o   o

'Yo ho heave ho! *Ugh!*' Dolly's on her back and they're working on the belly side. Somebody got the great idea of buttering her down first. Not to lose the ground they've gained, they've shot it inside with a basting syringe. But now suddenly there's this big tug-of-war under way between those who want to stuff her in and those who want to let her out. Something rips, but she feels better. The odour of hot butter makes her think of movie theatres and popcorn. 'Hey, has anybody seen Harry?' she asks. 'Where's Harry?'

o   o   o

Somebody's getting chased. She switches back to the love story, and now the man's back kissing the young lover again. What's going on? She gives it up, decides to take a quick bath. She's just stepping into the tub, one foot in, one foot out, when Mr Tucker walks in. 'Oh, excuse me! I only wanted some aspirin ...!' He embraces her savagely, his calloused old hands clutching roughly at her backside. 'Mr Tucker!' she cries, squirming. 'Your wife called—!' He's pushing something between her legs, hurting her. She slips, they both slip – something cold and hard slams her in the back, cracks her skull, she seems to be sinking into a sea ...

o   o   o

They've got her over the hassock, skirt up and pants down. 'Give her a lesson there, Jack baby!' The television lights flicker and flash over her glossy flesh. 1000 WHEN LIT. Whack! Slap! Bumper to bumper! He leans into her, feeling her come alive.

o   o   o

The phone rings, waking the baby. 'Jack, is that you? Now, you listen to me—!' 'No, dear, this is Mrs Tucker. Isn't the TV awfully loud?' 'Oh, I'm sorry, Mrs Tucker! I've been getting—' 'I tried to call you before, but I couldn't hang on. To the phone, I mean. I'm

sorry, dear.' 'Just a minute, Mrs Tucker, the baby's—' 'Honey, listen!
Is Harry there? Is Mr Tucker there, dear?'

o   o   o

'Stop it!' she screams and claps a hand over the baby's mouth. 'Stop
it! Stop it! *Stop it!*' Her other hand is full of baby stool and she's
afraid she's going to be sick. The phone rings. 'No!' she cries. She's
hanging on to the baby, leaning woozily away, listening to the phone
ring. 'Okay, okay,' she sighs, getting ahold of herself. But when she
lets go of the baby, it isn't screaming any more. She shakes it. Oh
no . . .

o   o   o

'Hello?' No answer. Strange. She hangs up and, wrapped only in a
towel, stares out the window at the cold face staring in – she
screams!

o   o   o

She screams, scaring the hell out of him. He leaps out of the tub,
glances up at the window she's gaping at just in time to see two faces
duck away, then slips on the bathroom tiles, and crashes to his ass,
whacking his head on the sink on the way down. She stares down at
him, trembling, a towel over her narrow shoulders. 'Mr Tucker! Mr
Tucker, are you all right . . . ?' Who's Sorry Now? Yessir, who's back
is breaking with each . . . He stares up at the little tufted locus of all
his woes, and passes out, dreaming of Jeannie . . .

o   o   o

The phone rings. 'Dolly! It's for you!' 'Hello?' 'Hello, Mrs Tucker?'
'Yes, speaking.' 'Mrs Tucker, this is the police calling . . .'

o   o   o

It's cramped and awkward and slippery, but he's pretty sure he got it
in her, once anyway. When he gets the suds out of his eyes, he sees
her staring up at them. Through the water. 'Hey, Mark! Let her up!'

o   o   o

Down in the suds. Feeling sleepy. The phone rings, startling her. Wrapped in a towel, she goes to answer. 'No, he's not here, Mrs Tucker.' Strange. Married people act pretty funny sometimes. The baby is awake and screaming. Dirty, a real mess. Oh boy, there's a lot of things she'd rather be doing than babysitting in this madhouse. She decides to wash the baby off in her own bathwater. She removes her towel, unplugs the tub, lowers the water level so the baby can sit. Glancing back over her shoulder, she sees Jimmy staring at her. 'Go back to bed, Jimmy.' 'I have to go to the bathroom.' 'Good grief, Jimmy! It looks like you already have!' The phone rings. She doesn't bother with the towel – what can Jimmy see he hasn't already seen? – and goes to answer. 'No, Jack, and that's final.' Sirens, on the TV, as the police move in. But wasn't that the channel with the love story? Ambulance maybe. Get this over with so she can at least catch the news. 'Get those wet pyjamas off, Jimmy, and I'll find clean ones. Maybe you better get in the tub, too.' 'I think something's wrong with the baby,' he says. 'It's down in the water and it's not swimming or anything.'

o   o   o

She's staring up at them from the rug. They slap her. Nothing happens. 'You just tilted her, man!' Mark says softly. 'We gotta get outa here!' Two little kids are standing wide-eyed in the doorway. Mark looks hard at Jack. 'No, Mark, they're just little kids ... !' 'We gotta, man, or we're dead.'

o   o   o

'Dolly! My God! Dolly, I can explain!' She glowers down at them, her ripped girdle around her ankles. 'What the four of you are doing in the bathtub with *my* babysitter?' she says sourly. 'I can hardly wait!'

o   o   o

Police sirens wail, lights flash. 'I heard the scream!' somebody shouts. 'There were two boys!' 'I saw a man!' 'She was running with the baby!' 'My God!' somebody screams, 'they're *all* dead!' Crowds come running. Spotlights probe the bushes.

o   o   o

'Harry, where the hell you been?' his wife whines, glaring blearily up at him from the carpet. 'I can explain,' he says. 'Hey, whatsa-matter, Harry?' his host asks, smeared with butter for some god-damn reason. 'You look like you just seen a ghost!' Where did he leave his drink? Everybody's laughing, everybody except Dolly, whose cheeks are streaked with tears. 'Hey, Harry, you won't let them take me to a rest home, will you, Harry?'

o   o   o

10.00. The dishes done, children to bed, her books read, she watches the news on television. Sleepy. The man's voice is gentle, soothing. She dozes – awakes with a start: a babysitter? Did the announcer say something about a babysitter?

o   o   o

'Just want to catch the weather,' the host says, switching on the TV. Most of the guests are leaving, but the Tuckers stay to watch the news. As it comes on, the announcer is saying something about a babysitter. The host switches channels. 'They got a better weather-man on four,' he explains. 'Wait!' says Mrs Tucker. 'There was some-thing about a babysitter ... !' The host switches back. 'Details have not yet been released by the police,' the announcer says. 'Harry, maybe we'd better go ...'

o   o   o

They stroll casually out of the drugstore, run into a buddy of theirs. 'Hey! Did you hear about the babysitter?' the guy asks. Mark grunts, glances at Jack. 'Got a smoke?' he asks the guy.

o   o   o

'I think I hear the baby screaming!' Mrs Tucker cries, running across the lawn from the drive.

o   o   o

She wakes, startled, to find Mr Tucker hovering over her. 'I must have dozed off!' she exclaims. 'Did you hear the news about the babysitter?' Mrs Tucker asks. 'Part of it,' she says, rising. 'Too bad,

wasn't it?' Mr Tucker is watching the report of the ball scores and
golf tournaments. 'I'll drive you home in just a minute, dear,' he says.
'Why, how nice!' Mrs Tucker exclaims from the kitchen. 'The dishes
are all done!'

o   o   o

'What can I say, Dolly?' the host says with a sigh, twisting the but-
tered strands of her ripped girdle between his fingers. 'Your children
are murdered, your husband gone, a corpse in your bathtub, and your
house is wrecked. I'm sorry. But what can I say?' On the TV, the news
is over, and they're selling aspirin. 'Hell, I don't know,' she says.
'Let's see what's on the late late movie.'

The Hat Act

In the middle of the stage: a plain table.

A man enters, dressed as a magician with black cape and black silk hat. Doffs hat in wide sweep to audience, bows elegantly.

Applause.

He displays inside of hat. It is empty. He thumps it. It is clearly empty. Places hat on table, brim up. Extends both hands over hat, tugs back sleeves exposing wrists, snaps fingers. Reaches in, extracts a rabbit.

Applause.

Pitches rabbit into wings. Snaps fingers over hat again, reaches in, extracts a dove.

Applause.

Pitches dove into wings. Snaps fingers over hat, reaches in, extracts another rabbit. No applause. Stuffs rabbit hurriedly back in hat, snaps fingers, reaches in, extracts another hat, precisely like the one from which it came.

Applause.

Places second hat alongside first one. Snaps fingers over new hat, withdraws a third hat, exactly like the first two.

Light applause.

Snaps fingers over third hat, withdraws a fourth hat, again identical. No applause. Does not snap fingers. Peers into fourth hat, extracts a fifth one. In fifth, he finds a sixth. Rabbit appears in third hat. Magician extracts seventh hat from sixth. Third hat rabbit withdraws a second rabbit from first hat. Magician withdraws eighth hat from seventh, ninth from eighth, as rabbits extract other rabbits from other hats. Rabbits and hats are everywhere. Stage is one mad turmoil of hats and rabbits.

Laughter and applause.

Frantically, magician gathers up hats and stuffs them into each other, bowing, smiling at audience, pitching rabbits three and four at a time into wings, smiling, bowing. It is a desperate struggle. At first, it is difficult to be sure he is stuffing hats and pitching rabbits faster than they are reappearing. Bows, stuffs, pitches, smiles, perspires.

Laughter mounts.

Slowly the confusion diminishes. Now there is one small pile of hats and rabbits. Now there are no rabbits. At last there are only two hats. Magician, perspiring from over-exertion, gasping for breath, staggers to table with two hats.

Light applause, laughter

Magician, mopping brow with silk handkerchief, stares in perplexity at two remaining hats. Pockets handkerchief. Peers into one hat, then into other. Attempts tentatively to stuff first into second, but in vain. Attempts to fit second into first, but also without success. Smiles weakly at audience. No applause. Drops first hat to floor, leaps on it until crushed. Wads crushed hat in fist, attempts once more to stuff it into second hat. Still, it will not fit.

Light booing, impatient applause.

Trembling with anxiety, magician presses out first hat, places it brim up on table, crushes second hat on floor. Wads second hat, tries desperately to jam it into first hat. No, it will not fit. Turns irritably to pitch second hat into wings.

Loud booing.

Freezes. Pales. Returns to table with both hats, first in fair condition brim up, second still in a crumpled wad. Faces hats in defeat. Bows head as though to weep silently.

Hissing and booing.

Smile suddenly lights magician's face. He smoothes out second hat and places it firmly on his head, leaving first hat bottomside-up on table. Crawls up on table and disappears feet first into hat.

Surprised applause.

Moments later, magician's feet poke up out of hat on table, then legs, then torso. Last part to emerge is magician's head, which, when lifted from table, brings first hat with it. Magician doffs first hat to audience, shows it is empty. Second hat has disappeared. Bows deeply.

Enthusiastic and prolonged applause, cheers.

Magician returns hat to head, thumps it, steps behind table. Without removing hat, reaches up, snaps fingers, extracts rabbit from top of hat.

Applause.

Pitches rabbit into wings. Snaps fingers, withdraws dove from top of hat.

Sprinkling of applause.

Pitches dove into wings. Snaps fingers, extracts lovely assistant from top of hat.

Astonished but enthusiastic applause and whistles.

Lovely assistant wears high feathery green hat, tight green halter, little green shorts, black net stockings, high green heels. Smiles coyly at whistles and applause, scampers bouncily offstage.

Whistling and shouting, applause.

Magician attempts to remove hat, but it appears to be stuck. Twists and writhes in struggle with stuck hat.

Mild laughter.

Struggle continues. Contortions. Grimaces.

Laughter.

Finally, magician requests two volunteers from audience. Two large brawny men enter stage from audience, smiling awkwardly.

Light applause and laughter.

One large man grasps hat, other clutches magician's legs. They pull cautiously. The hat does not come off. They pull harder. Still, it is stuck. They tug now with great effort, their heavy faces reddening, their thick neck muscles taut and throbbing. Magician's neck stretches, snaps in two: POP! Large men tumble apart, rolling to opposite sides of stage, one with body, other with hat containing magician's severed head.

Screams of terror.

Two large men stand, stare aghast at handiwork, clutch mouths.

Shrieks and screams.

Decapitated body stands.

Shrieks and screams.

Zipper in front of decapitated body opens, magician emerges. He is as before, wearing same black cape and same black silk hat. Pitches deflated decapitated body into wings. Pitches hat and head into wings. Two large men sigh with immense relief, shake heads as though completely baffled, smile faintly, return to audience. Magician doffs hat and bows.

Wild applause, shouts, cheers.

Lovely assistant, still in green costume, enters, carrying glass of water.

Applause and whistling.

Lovely assistant acknowledges whistling with coy smile, sets glass of water on table, stands dutifully by. Magician hands her his hat, orders her by gesture to eat it.

Whistling continues.

Lovely assistant smiles, bites into hat, chews slowly.

Laughter and much whistling.

She washes down each bite of hat with water from glass she has brought in. Hat at last is entirely consumed, except for narrow silk band left on table. Sighs, pats slender exposed tummy.

Laughter and applause, excited whistling.

Magician invites young country boy in audience to come to stage. Young country boy steps forward shyly, stumbling clumsily over own big feet. Appears confused and utterly abashed.

Loud laughter and catcalls.

Young country boy stands with one foot on top of other, staring down redfaced at his hands, twisting nervously in front of him.

Laughter and catcalls increase.

Lovely assistant sidles up to boy, embraces him in motherly fashion. Boy ducks head away, steps first on one foot, then on other, wrings hands.

More laughter and catcalls, whistles.

Lovely assistant winks broadly at audience, kisses young country boy on cheek. Boy jumps as though scalded, trips over own feet, and falls to floor.

Thundering laughter.

Lovely assistant helps boy to his feet, lifting him under armpits. Boy, ticklish, struggles and giggles helplessly.

Laughter (as before).

Magician raps table with knuckles. Lovely assistant releases hysterical country boy, returns smiling to table. Boy resumes awkward stance, wipes his runny nose with back of his hand, sniffles.

Mild laughter and applause.

Magician hands lovely assistant narrow silk band of hat she has eaten. She stuffs band into her mouth, chews thoughtfully, swallows with some difficulty, shudders. She drinks from glass. Laughter and shouting have fallen away to expectant hush. Magician grasps nape of lovely assistant's neck, forces her head with its feathered hat down between her stockinged knees. He releases grip and her head springs back to upright position. Magician repeats action slowly. Then repeats action rapidly four or five times. Looks inquiringly at lovely assistant. Her face is flushed from exertion. She meditates, then shakes head: no. Magician again forces her head to her knees, releases grip, allowing head to snap back to upright position. Repeats this two or three times. Looks inquiringly at lovely assistant. She smiles and nods. Magician drags abashed young country boy over behind lovely assistant and invites him to reach into lovely assistant's tight green shorts. Young country boy is flustered beyond belief.

Loud laughter and whistling resumes.

Young country boy, in desperation, tries to escape. Magician captures him and drags him once more behind lovely assistant.

Laughter etc. (as before).

Magician grasps country boy's arm and thrusts it forcibly into lovely assistant's shorts. Young country boy wets pants.

Hysterical laughter and catcalls.

Lovely assistant grimaces once. Magician, smiling, releases grip on agonizingly embarrassed country boy. Boy withdraws hand. In it, he finds he is holding magician's original black silk hat, entirely whole, narrow silk band and all.

Wild applause and footstamping, laughter and cheers.

Magician winks broadly at audience, silencing them momentarily, invites young country boy to don hat. Boy ducks head shyly. Magician insists. Timidly, grinning foolishly, country boy lifts hat to head. Water spills out, runs down over his head, and soaks young country boy.

Laughter, applause, wild catcalls.

Young country boy, utterly humiliated, drops hat and turns to run offstage, but lovely assistant is standing on his foot. He trips and falls to his face.

Laughter etc. (as before).

Country boy crawls abjectly offstage on his stomach. Magician, laughing heartily with audience, pitches lovely assistant into wings, picks up hat from floor. Brushes hat on sleeve, thumps it two or three times, returns it with elegant flourish to his head.

Appreciative applause.

Magician steps behind table. Carefully brushes off one space on table. Blows away dust. Reaches for hat. But again, it seems to be stuck. Struggles feverishly with hat.

Mild laughter.

Requests volunteers. Same two large men as before enter. One quickly grasps hat, other grasps magician's legs. They tug furiously, but in vain.

Laughter and applause.

First large man grabs magician's head under jaw. Magician appears to be protesting. Second large man wraps magician's legs around his waist. Both pull apart with terrific strain, their faces reddening, the veins in their temples throbbing. Magician's tongue protrudes, hands flutter hopelessly.

Laughter and applause.

Magician's neck stretches. But it does not snap. It is now several feet long. Two large men strain mightily.

Laughter and applause.

Magician's eyes pop like bubbles from their sockets.

Laughter and applause.

Neck snaps at last. Large men tumble head over heels with respective bloody burdens to opposite sides of stage. Expectant amused hush falls over audience. First large man scrambles to his feet, pitches head and hat into wings, rushes to assist second large man. Together they unzip decapitated body. Lovely assistant emerges.

Surprised laughter and enthusiastic applause, whistling.

Lovely assistant pitches deflated decapitated body into wings. Large men ogle her and make mildly obscene gestures for audience.

Mounting laughter and friendly catcalls.

Lovely assistant invites one of two large men to reach inside her tight green shorts.

Wild whistling.

Both large men jump forward eagerly, tripping over each other and tumbling to floor in angry heap. Lovely assistant winks broadly at audience.

Derisive catcalls.

Both men stand, face each other, furious. First large man spits at second. Second pushes first. First returns push, toppling second to floor. Second leaps to feet, smashes first in nose. First reels, wipes blood from nose, drives fist into second's abdomen.

Loud cheers.

Second weaves confusedly, crumples miserably to floor clutching abdomen. First kicks second brutally in face.

Cheers and mild laughter.

Second staggers blindly to feet, face a mutilated mess. First smashes second back against wall, knees him in groin. Second doubles over, blinded with pain. First clips second with heel of hand behind ear. Second crumples to floor, dead.

Prolonged cheering and applause.

First large man acknowledges applause with self-conscious bow. Flexes knuckles. Lovely assistant approaches first large man, embraces him in motherly fashion, winks broadly at audience.

Prolonged applause and whistling.

Large man grins and embraces lovely assistant in unmotherly fashion, as she makes faces of mock astonishment for audience.

Shouting and laughter, wild whistling.

Lovely assistant frees self from large man, turns plump hindquarters to him and bends over, her hands on her knees, her shapely legs straight. Large man grins at audience, pats lovely assistant's green-clad rear.

Wild shouting etc. (as before).

Large man reaches inside lovely assistant's tight green shorts, rolls his eyes, and grins obscenely. She grimaces and wiggles rear briefly.

Wild shouting etc. (as before).

Large man withdraws hand from inside lovely assistant's shorts, extracting magician in black cape and black silk hat.

Thunder of astonished applause.

Magician bows deeply, doffing hat to audience.

Prolonged enthusiastic applause, cheering.

Magician pitches lovely assistant and first large man into wings. Inspects second large man, lying dead on stage. Unzips him and young country boy emerges, flushed and embarrassed. Young country boy creeps abjectly offstage on stomach.

Laughter and catcalls, more applause.

Magician pitches deflated corpse of second large man into wings. Lovely assistant re-enters, smiling, dressed as before in high feathery hat, tight green halter, green shorts, net stockings, high heels.

Applause and whistling.

Magician displays inside of hat to audience as lovely assistant points to magician. He thumps hat two or three times. It is empty. Places hat on table, and invites lovely assistant to enter it. She does so.

Vigorous applause.

Once she has entirely disappeared, magician extends both hands over hat, tugs back sleeves exposing wrists, snaps fingers, Reaches in, extracts one green high-heeled shoe.

Applause.

Pitches shoe into wings. Snaps fingers over hat again. Reaches in, withdraws a second shoe.

Applause.

Pitches shoe into wings. Snaps finger over hat. Reaches in, withdraws one long net stocking.

Applause and scattered whistling.

Pitches stocking into wings. Snaps fingers over hat. Reaches in, extracts a second black net stocking.

Applause and scattered whistling.

Pitches stocking into wings. Snaps fingers over hat. Reaches in, pulls out high feathery hat.

Increased applause and whistling, rhythmic stamping of feet.

Pitches hat into wings. Snaps fingers over hat. Reaches in, fumbles briefly.

Light laughter.

Withdraws green halter, displays it with grand flourish.

Enthusiastic applause, shouting, whistling, stamping of feet.

Pitches halter into wings. Snaps fingers over hat. Reaches in, fumbles. Distant absorbed gaze.

Burst of laughter.

Withdraws green shorts, displays them with elegant flourish.

Tremendous crash of applause and cheering, whistling.

Pitches green shorts into wings. Snaps fingers over hat. Reaches in. Prolonged fumbling. Sound of a slap. Withdraws hand hastily, a look of astonished pain on his face. Peers inside.

Laughter.

Head of lovely assistant pops out of hat, pouting indignantly.

Laughter and applause.

With difficulty, she extracts one arm from hat, then other arm. Pressing hands down against hat brim, she wriggles and twists until one naked breast pops out of hat.

Applause and wild whistling.

The other breast: POP!

More applause and whistling.

She wriggles free to the waist. She grunts and struggles, but is unable to free her hips. She looks pathetically, but uncertainly at magician. He tugs and pulls but she seems firmly stuck.

Laughter.

He grasps lovely assistant under armpits and plants feet against hat brim. Strains. In vain.

Laughter.

Thrusts lovely assistant forcibly back into hat. Fumbles again. Loud slap.

Laughter increases.

Magician returns slap soundly.

Laughter ceases abruptly, some scattered booing.

Magician reaches into hat, withdraws one unstockinged leg. He reaches in again, pulls out one arm. He tugs on arm and leg, but for all his effort cannot extract the remainder.

Scattered booing, some whistling.

Magician glances uneasily at audience, stuffs arm and leg back into hat. He is perspiring. Fumbles inside hat. Withdraws nude hindquarters of lovely assistant.

Burst of cheers and wild whistling.

Smiles uncomfortably at audience. Tugs desperately on plump hindquarters, but rest will not follow.

Whistling diminishes, increased booing.

Jams hindquarters back into hat, mops brow with silk handkerchief.

Loud unfriendly booing.

Pockets handkerchief. Is becoming rather frantic. Grasps hat and thumps it vigorously, shakes it. Places it once more on table, brim up. Closes eyes as though in incantations, hands extended over hat. Snaps fingers several times, reaches in tenuously. Fumbles. Loud slap. Withdraws hand hastily in angry astonishment. Grasps hat. Gritting teeth, infuriated, hurls hat to floor, leaps on it with both feet. Something crunches. Hideous piercing shriek.

Screams and shouts.

Magician, aghast, picks up hat, stares into it. Pales.

Violent screaming and shouting.

Magician gingerly sets hat on floor, and kneels, utterly appalled and grief-stricken, in front of it. Weeps silently.

Weeping, moaning, shouting.

Magician huddles miserably over crushed hat, weeping convulsively. First large man and young country boy enter timidly, soberly, from wings. They are pale and frightened. They peer uneasily into hat. They start back in horror. They clutch their mouths, turn away, and vomit.

Weeping, shouting, vomiting, accusations of murder.

Large man and country boy tie up magician, drag him away.

Weeping, retching.

Large man and country boy return, lift crushed hat gingerly, and trembling uncontrollably, carry it at arm's length into wings.

Momentary increase of weeping, retching, moaning, then dying away of sound to silence.

Country boy creeps onto stage, alone, sets up placard against table and facing audience, then creeps abjectly away.

THIS ACT IS CONCLUDED
THE MANAGEMENT REGRETS THERE
WILL BE NO REFUND

A Selected List of Titles Available from Minerva

While every effort is made to keep prices low, it is sometimes necessary to increase prices at short notice. Mandarin Paperbacks reserves the right to show new retail prices on covers which may differ from those previously advertised in the text or elsewhere.

The prices shown below were correct at the time of going to press.

Fiction

☐	7493 9026 3	**I Pass Like Night**	Jonathan Ames	£3.99 BX
☐	7493 9006 9	**The Tidewater Tales**	John Bath	£4.99 BX
☐	7493 9004 2	**A Casual Brutality**	Neil Blessondath	£4.50 BX
☐	7493 9028 2	**Interior**	Justin Cartwright	£3.99 BC
☐	7493 9002 6	**No Telephone to Heaven**	Michelle Cliff	£3.99 BX
☐	7493 9028 X	**Not Not While the Giro**	James Kelman	£4.50 BX
☐	7493 9011 5	**Parable of the Blind**	Gert Hofmann	£3.99 BC
☐	7493 9010 7	**The Inventor**	Jakov Lind	£3.99 BC
☐	7493 9003 4	**Fall of the Imam**	Nawal El Saadewi	£3.99 BC

Non-Fiction

☐	7493 9012 3	**Days in the Life**	Jonathon Green	£4.99 BC
☐	7493 9019 0	**In Search of J D Salinger**	Ian Hamilton	£4.99 BX
☐	7493 9023 9	**Stealing from a Deep Place**	Brian Hall	£3.99 BX
☐	7493 9005 0	**The Orton Diaries**	John Lahr	£5.99 BC
☐	7493 9014 X	**Nora**	Brenda Maddox	£6.99 BC

All these books are available at your bookshop or newsagent, or can be ordered direct from the publisher. Just tick the titles you want and fill in the form below. Available in:
BX: British Commonwealth excluding Canada
BC: British Commonwealth including Canada

Mandarin Paperbacks, Cash Sales Department, PO Box 11, Falmouth, Cornwall TR10 9EN.

Please send cheque or postal order, no currency, for purchase price quoted and allow the following for postage and packing:

UK	80p for the first book, 20p for each additional book ordered to a maximum charge of £2.00.
BFPO	80p for the first book, 20p for each additional book.
Overseas including Eire	£1.50 for the first book, £1.00 for the second and 30p for each additional book thereafter.

NAME (Block letters) ....

ADDRESS ....

....

....